VOTE

BOOKISH AND THE BEAST

ALSO BY ASHLEY POSTON

THE ONCE UPON A CON SERIES

Geekerella

The Princess and the Fangirl

THE HEART OF IRON SERIES

Heart of Iron

Soul of Stars

BOOKISH AND THE BEAST

Once Upon a Con Series

By Ashley Poston

This is a work of fiction. All names, places, and characters are products of the author's imagination or are used fictitiously. Any resemblance to real people, places, or events is entirely coincidental.

Library of Congress Cataloging in Publication Data
Poston, Ashley, author.
Bookish and the beast : a novel / by Ashley Poston.
Summary: In this adaptation of the Beauty and the Beast fairy tale, the teenaged star of a popular science fiction movie franchise hides out in a small town, following a tabloid scandal, and meets the bookish Rosie Thorne who is still grieving over her mother's death.
CYAC: Celebrities--Fiction. | Grief--Fiction. | Love--Fiction.
LCC PZ7.1.P667 Bo 2020 DDC [Fic]--dc23

ISBN: 978-1-68369-193-8

Printed in the United States of America

Typeset in Sabon, Arkhip, and Univers

Cover illustration by Peter Greenwood
Cover design by Elissa Flanigan
Production management by John J. McGurk

Quirk Books
215 Church Street
Philadelphia, PA 19106
quirkbooks.com

10 9 8 7 6 5 4 3 2 1

To booksellers, librarians, and anyone
who feels bookish in their hearts

PART ONE

VILLAIN

He takes Amara roughly by the chin and whispers quietly, "I care about duty, princess." Their lips are so close, he feels the moment her breath hitches. She shudders as he runs his finger down the soft line of her cheek, the freckles that glow like constellations. "And you will not get in my way."

He leans in toward the princess, toward her lips, when he feels a sharp point at his chest, and glances down to the dagger.

Amara narrows her eyes. "I'm no fool, Ambrose Sond, and I will not let you jeopardize my mission, either. I know you're working for my father."

"I am working *with* him. There's a difference."

"I see none. You commit the same evil."

He leans closer to her, smelling the salty sweat on her skin and the lingering particles of gunpowder, even as the dagger presses more intently against his chest. One thrust, and it would pierce his heart, but he knows the princess better than she knows herself, he thinks.

"Then you aren't looking close enough," he murmurs, and then steps away, leaving her alone on the observation deck of the Skystalker.

ROSIE

Whenever you think your love life sucks, just remember that I fell in love with a boy whose name I didn't know.

Let's be clear: I didn't *mean* to fall in love. It just sort of happened, the way falling usually does. You trip on something you didn't see and, if you're me, you lose your heel and go stumbling into a stranger at the ExcelsiCon Ball who just so happened to be holding a glass of neon-yellow Galactic Twist punch that goes . . . absolutely everywhere.

And so now the front of your skirt is drenched with the sticky yellow Kool-Aid that looks more like, well, *pee* than Galactic Twist, and there isn't a bathroom in sight. With one glance, I could already tell my cosplay was ruined. So was the other person's cosplay, but he didn't seem to care as he stumbled on.

He *wasn't* who I fell in love with, by the way.

He's just the reason I met him.

If I didn't have my stupid mask on I probably would've seen the prop sword lying on the ground. Who puts a prop sword on the ground in the middle of the dance floor, anyway?

Apparently, with a quick look around, a person cosplaying as Cloud Strife did just before he broke down the Electric Slide.

I looped back for my heel, grabbed it off the ground before someone could kick it away, and left the dance floor to see if I could salvage my outfit. If I didn't love my friends so much, I would've just stayed in my hotel room and watched reruns of *The Great British Bake Off*. I was still contemplating the possibility, honestly.

Quinn and Annie had told me the ball would be good for me. They told me it would take my mind off what had happened this past summer. They told me . . . well, I guess it didn't really matter what lies those lying liars peddled to get me to come out of my hotel room. What mattered was the universal question:

How early was *too* early to leave a ball?

"You don't want to miss the magic, do you?" Annie had asked as she pulled me out of the room toward the elevators. "Last year we saw Jessica Stone—*the* Amara!—stand on a food truck to Romeo and Juliet her girlfriend. And the year before that, Darien—Darien *Freeman*! Carmindor *himself*!—proclaimed his undying love for Geekerella! What if this is your year?"

I'd never been to ExcelsiCon before—it always seemed too big and too loud—but I knew that Quinn and Annie were trying to get me to have as much fun as I could, because the last year has sucked.

It's sucked so terribly hard.

"Well, last I checked, Darien Freeman's taken," I had replied. "And so is Jess Stone."

"Yes, but look across this great expanse, Rosie." Quinn looped their arm into my free one, and they led me toward the hall balcony where, thirty floors below, the ExcelsiCon Ball began to come to life. "Do you smell that possibility?"

"All I smell is vom and con stink," I replied.

Yet I caved, because *wouldn't* it have been wonderful to find Prince Charming at the ball? They knew I was a romantic at heart—my mom fed me a healthy dose of fairy tales and romance novels when I was little—and they knew I was a sucker for every rom-com known to humankind, and so they tempted me with lies of Happily Ever After.

After all, if anyone was to find love somewhere romantic, why couldn't it be me? Why not this year? Why not make something memorable to lessen the pain in my chest?

Still, though, I should've listened to my gut telling me to just *stay in the hotel room*. Because not five minutes after Quinn and Annie dragged me down to the ExcelsiCon Ball, I had lost them in the masses of people.

There were just so *many*.

I tried looking for them—they were hard to miss, dressed as floating glowing neon goldfish ("We're the snacks that smile back!" Quinn had said with a wink). I had put together a closet cosplay that I found in my, well, closet—an unassuming black crop top and a white skirt, and an empty shot glass around my neck.

. . . A shot in the dark, get it?

No one ever does.

It only took another few minutes for me to become absolutely overwhelmed, run into a Nox King who spilled his Galactic Twist all over my cosplay, and bail from the ball. I returned to the elevators and squeezed into the first one available, damned which floor. To my utter chagrin, it only took me up to the tenth floor, and I let myself out to escape the smell of sweat and hairspray clogging the elevator.

The tenth floor was mostly a lobby overlooking the chaos below. It was quiet here, at least. Much quieter than I expected, given the thumping bass down below. There wasn't a chance I was getting back into those elevators anytime soon—it looked like the one I just came out of broke on the fifteenth floor, and the other two were . . . well, to put it politely, not in the best shape.

Great, I guess I wasn't going back to my room after all. And I was stuck in a damp skirt.

There was a door that opened to a small outside area, and I let myself out. The night air was crisp, and warm. I sucked in a lungful of fresh air to calm my nerves. There were only a few people on the garden balcony—a couple dressed as Pokémon making out in the corner, and a guy leaning against the balcony rail.

Oh, I thought as I walked up beside him to enjoy the view, *he's got a nice butt.*

Not that it really mattered. I leaned against the railing and tried to see the damage to my outfit in the low rooftop light, patting down the stains with the wad of napkins I stole from the drinks kiosk on the way here. For once, I was happy that everyone was downstairs dancing the night away to a dubstep version of "The Imperial March," because here it was so nice and quiet—so quiet my ears rang.

My skirt was ruined, that much I could guess. I just wanted to go back to the hotel room and get out of these heels and take a hot shower to get all of the con grime off me. There was a book in my suitcase just calling my name—the new *Starfield: Resonance* companion novel.

I'd rather be saving the galaxy with the insufferably kind Carmindor than be on this balcony praying for the night to end already.

"A shot in the dark, right?"

The voice startled me.

I glanced up to the guy, because it certainly wasn't the couple playing tongue hockey who asked me. He was unnervingly tall, but then again I was known for two things—being stubborn, and being short. "What?" I asked.

He motioned to my costume. He wore a very well-put-together General Sond costume, complete with beautiful long white-blond hair and a crooked smile, and a mask that covered just enough of his face to make him look alluring and absolutely unidentifiable. "Your cosplay," he followed up. He had a strange accent. I couldn't place it—but it sort of sounded like those fake American accents you sometimes hear on TV from actors who are very clearly not American. It was too hometown, too clean. "A shot in the dark?"

I glanced down at my costume. "*Technically* I'm cosplaying the title of the thirty-seventh book in the extended-universe saga of *Starfield, A Shot in the Dark* by Almira Ender."

His eyebrows jerked up over his mask. "Oh, well, I stand corrected."

"It's a really deep cut, though," I quickly added.

"Oh, I do see it," he replied, cocking his head. He pointed down to the hem of my skirt. "The little *Starfield* logo trim at the bottom. That's a very nice touch."

"You think?"

"Of course. There's thought to it."

"I just didn't have the money for a nice costume," I replied, motioning to his very, *very* nice costume, and then realized my mistake. "Oh God, that sounded like an insult! I didn't mean it that way, I promise. I'm just, you know, saving up for college and all, and—" I forced myself to stop talking, I babbled when I got nervous.

"No, no, I didn't take it that way at all!" he said, though his voice was full of thinly disguised laughter. He leaned closer to me—just a little—enough to whisper, "You want to know a secret? This costume isn't mine. It's for my job, so they let me borrow it for the night."

"Just tonight?"

"Well, this weekend."

"That must be quite a cool job, then, if you have to dress as Sond for it."

He smiled again. "Yeah. So, did you come out to escape the socializing, too?"

"I know I'm going to sound boring, but I'm not really big on parties," I said.

"That *does* sound boring."

"Hey!"

"I was agreeing with you!" He laughed. "I've never known anything else. Parties, socializing, loud music, and lots of people. It's a place I can get lost in."

"Yeah, I hate that feeling."

"I love it," he replied, closing his eyes. "It's like being invisible."

I didn't know what to say, but I wanted to reach out and touch his shoulder. We barely knew each other, but it felt like he had just admitted something to me that he'd never told anyone else before. Maybe he realized that, too, because his shoulders went rigid. I stilled my hand to keep it by my side.

"What's home for you?" he asked.

I gave a one-shouldered shrug. Home, to me? If I was going to scare him away, I might as well start with the most boring part of me. "A small town and a quiet library, where sunlight slants through the window just right, making everything golden and soft and . . ." I trailed off, because I hadn't thought about that in a long time. Not since the funeral. "My mom used to call them golden afternoons."

"That sounds magical."

"It is. You should visit. Maybe I can tempt you to the dark side with hot chocolate and a good book."

He smiled, and there was a delicious dare tucked into the edges. "That sounds like a challenge."

"Oh no," I replied, returning that devil-may-care smile, imagining what he would look like in a certain slant of golden light, curled into a wingback chair with my favorite book. "It's a promise."

"I can't wait, then," he said earnestly. Then something caught his eyes behind me, and I began to look over my shoulder when he said, "This might sound a little forward, but would you want to go for a walk? With me?" He outstretched his hand.

I thought about Quinn and Annie dancing the night away, and about the book waiting for me back in my hotel room, and how improbable this was, and for the first time in my life—

I pushed those thoughts aside.

I took his hand, because this moment felt like a dandelion fluff on the wind—there one moment, walking the streets of Atlanta and eating Waffle House, and talking on the rooftop of one of the hotels until the sun rose and all of the cosplayers down below were stumbling their way home, the memory so visceral I can still smell the strange scent of his cologne, lavender mixed with oak, and then, well—

Gone.

BUT EVEN THOUGH HE'S GONE, I can't get him out of my head a month later when I should totally be over it by now, as I scan my math teacher's box of jumbo condoms at the Food Lion where I work. I try not to make eye contact as I read off the total and he pays, also avoiding eye contact. He leaves the grocery store as quick as the clip of his shined loafers will let him.

I massage the bridge of my nose. Minimum wage will never pay for the years of therapy I'll need after this.

Maybe I can put some of this—any of this—into the college essay I've been failing to write for the last week, but what college admissions officer would want to read about some lovesick fool ringing up condoms for her calculus teacher? Right, like *that'll* win over admissions.

Suddenly, from the other side of the cashier kiosks, Annie cries, "It's here! It's *here*!" as she vaults over her checkout counter and comes sliding toward mine.

Already?

Every rumor on every message board said that it would drop at six—I check the time on my cashier screen. Oh, it is six. I quickly key out of my register so the manager won't yell at me for goofing off on the job—technically I'm on break!—and turn off my cashier light even though there are two people in line.

"Hey!" one of the customers shouts.

"Three minutes!" I reply.

"This is *life-changing*!" Annie adds, holding up her phone screen for us. The glare of the halogens above us catches on the edges of the screen protector as she sticks one earbud into her ear and hands me the other.

The trailer begins to play.

Darkness. Then, a sound—the beat of something striking the ground. Sharp, high-pitched, steady.

Coming this December . . .

It's only September, and December feels like a lifetime away. We've been waiting a year and a half for the sequel—a *year*! *And! A half!*—and my twisting stomach can barely stand it.

There is a soft, steady beat that echoes over the sweet, low horn of the *Starfield* theme.

The text fades and there is Carmindor kneeling in front of the Noxian Court. His lip is bloodied, and there is a gash across his eyebrow. He looks to have been tortured, his arms bound tightly behind his back. His eyes are shadowed by his disheveled hair.

"Prince Carmindor, we find you guilty," says a soft, deep voice.

The other members of the court, of the different regions in the Empire, some emissaries from far-reaching colonies, representatives from the Federation, all dressed in their pale official colors. Their faces are grim. At the head of the court is a throne, where the ruler of the Nox Empire should sit, but it is empty.

"Guilty of conspiring against the Empire," the same voice says. "Of treason."

There are flashes of the first movie—Carmindor at the helm of the *Prospero*, the defiant faces of Euci and Zorine beside him, the fight between the Nox King and Carmindor on Ziondur, the moment Amara says goodbye to Carmindor and locks him on the bridge—

"But most of all," the voice purrs, and the blurry image of a man in gold and white, hair long and flowing, looking like a deity of the sun, slowly comes into focus. Bright blue eyes, white-blond hair, a sharp face and a pointed nose, the hem of his uniform glowing like burning embers. A chill curls down my spine. "We find you guilty of the murder of our princess, our light—our Amara."

Amara's ship swirls into the Black Nebula, her smile, her lips saying words without any sound that mysteriously look like "*ah'blen*"—

A hand grabs Carmindor's hair and forces his head back. Lips press against his ear, and the prophetic voice of General Sond whispers, "No one is coming for you, princeling."

Annie gasps, pressing her hand to her mouth. Because Carmindor's eyes—his eyes are the pale, pale white of the conscripted. The beat—the clipping sound—gets louder. It sounds like the drum of a funeral march, like the coming of a predator, like a countdown to the end of the world.

The screen fades to black again, and then on the next beat—two pristine black boots, heels striking against the ground. The flutter of a long uniform jacket the perfect shade of blue. The errant flash of bright red hair—as red as a supernova. The glimmer of a golden tiara.

Annie grabs my wrist tightly, and squeezes. I know—I *know*.

It's her.

The camera pans with her as she makes her way toward the throne, from her fluttering Federation coat to the golden stars on her shoulders, to her face. You can tell she's different. That she isn't the same princess who sacrificed herself to the Black Nebula. She's new, and unpredictable, and impossible.

My heart kicks in my chest, seeing her again, returned from some improbable universe, and my eyes well with tears.

Because for once death isn't final.

For once, for once, love is enough.

And the left side of Amara's mouth twitches up.

The screen snaps to black—and then the triumphant orchestra of the *Starfield* theme swells into our ears, and the title appears:

STARFIELD: RESONANCE

And then it ends.

We stare at the blank screen for a moment longer. My heart hammers in my chest. It's real. It's happening. And Amara is back—*our* Amara.

Finally, Annie whispers. "I . . . I think I just popped a lady-boner—"

"A-*hem*."

Annie and I whirl around toward the sound of our manager, Mr. Jason. He's red-faced and standing with his arms crossed over his chest in the middle of our respective cash registers. She quickly yanks the earbud out of my ear, rolls up the wires, and shoves the cell phone into her apron.

"If I see you two with cell phones out one more time tonight . . ." he warns, wagging his finger at us, "then I'll—I'll . . ."

Uh-oh, he's so flustered he doesn't have words.

"We won't, sorry, sir," Annie says, and Mr. Jason nods, not quite believing her, and turns on his heel back to his office.

I let out a sigh of relief.

Annie mouths, *Yikes*.

I agree. He's really not in the best mood tonight. We shouldn't push our luck. Mr. Jason is known to have two modes: absent and dickweed. At the moment, he's in full dickweed mode.

After I ring up the waiting customers, I straighten my aisle and leave to wrangle the shopping carts from the parking lot. There's a toy dispenser outside that is calling my name, and I've got just the quarter that feels lucky enough for me to test it.

"Going to go try it again?" Annie calls to me as I wander toward the automatic doors.

"After that trailer, I'm feeling lucky," I reply, flipping the quarter with my thumb, and step outside in the warm September evening.

There is a *Starfield* toy dispenser by the grocery cart lane, featuring the old characters from the TV series, though the Amara really looks nothing like Natalia Ford. She's in this skimpy bodysuit with a pistol, and honestly Princess Amara would burn the entire dispenser if she saw that. Carmindor and the other six collectibles look somewhat like themselves, at least, though I've gotten so many Carmindors I could melt them all down and make a life-sized Carmindor to use for target practice whenever I decide to take up axe-throwing.

Maybe today, though, I'll finally snag a Sond.

I pop the quarter into the *Starfield* toy machine. A toy rolls out, and I fish it out of the metal mouth and shake it. It doesn't *sound* like another Carmindor. Maybe Amara? Euci?

Ugh, I have enough Eucis, too.

The outside of the shell reads, *LOOK TO THE STARS AND CHASE YOUR DESTINY*!

Dare I disturb the universe, crack open the egg, and find out what my future holds?

I'm about to twist the sucker open when someone calls my name. Like, not just calls from across the parking or anything, but like . . . megaphone calls my name.

I glance up.

And pale.

Oh, *no*.

Garrett Taylor is standing in the bed of his Ford truck with a karaoke machine. On the window of his muddy black truck, he dramatically unfurls a banner that says, *HOMECOMING?*

What the . . .

Oh.

Oh Jesus Mother Mary Aziraphale Crowley.

The realization of what's happening hits me like the *Prospero* fresh out of hyperdrive. And I don't have time to escape.

"Rosie Thorne," Garrett begins valiantly, turning his snap-back around. Tufts of his chocolate-brown hair stick out the hole in the back of his cap, shaggy around his ears. A silver stud glints in his left ear. "You and I are a tale as old as time," he says into the microphone, trying to be smart and funny.

He's none of the above, and this is one hundred and ten percent *mortifying.*

Forget the carts in the parking lot. I try to make it back into the store before he can do something I will regret.

"Rosie!" he calls after me, vaulting off the flatbed, and races to cut me off. He succeeds. Barely. "What do you think?" he asks, motioning to the large *HOMECOMING?* banner. His posse follows him with their expensive GoPros, and I can feel their tiny bulbous camera eyes slowly leeching my soul.

Ever since he went viral on YouTube, I can't *stand* him. He was fine before, but now he's just insufferable. Everything has to be video'd and monetized.

"Garrett," I say, putting my hand up so the GoPros can't capture my face, "I'm flattered, but—"

He grabs me by the hand I was using to block the cameras and squeezes it tightly. "Don't say it! Just think on it, okay?"

"I *did* think—"

"Rosie, you know as well as I do that we're a team! Remember back in elementary school? We were the best Red Rover pair."

"We have similar last names so we had to stand by each other—"

"And then in middle school, we made the best English projects together."

I try to yank my hand out of his. "I did all of the work!"

"And I'm sorry high school hasn't been very kind to you. Not since your mom died, and you had to move into a bad apartment after you had to pay for the medical bills—"

All things that make my skin crawl when he brings them up. Things that he has no right to say—period. Especially not on camera.

"—but I want to make your last Homecoming the most magical it can be. Yeah? Remember back on the playground? I promised you I'd look after you."

"I'm not a charity case, Garrett," I snap, finally able to pull my hand free. "Is that what you're doing? 'Oh, poor Rosie, she's had a tough time—'"

"You're also really pretty, if that helps," he adds, and his two henchmen wince. He realizes a moment too late his folly, because I'm already halfway back into the grocery store. "Wait! That's not what I meant!"

"You're just too kind, Garrett," I tell him over my shoulder in the most sickeningly sweet voice I can muster. "I don't deserve you."

I return into the grocery store, and as soon as I'm out of direct eyesight from Garrett, I duck down behind a line of shopping carts and watch as he returns to his truck with his two goons, waving at them to quit recording. Then they hop into his truck and they drive away, the *HOMECOMING?* banner flapping in the wind like a strip of toilet paper on the bottom of a shoe.

I pull out my phone to text Quinn.

ROSIE (6:16PM)

*—YOU. WOULDN'T. BELIEVE.
WHAT. JUST. HAPPENED.*

QUINN (6:16PM)

*—Oh no did Annie just throw down an
entire bottle of kombucha again?*

ROSIE (6:17PM)

—No but

"*Rosie!*" I hear Annie hiss, and when I look up she's at the register, making a motion to hang up the phone. But I'm not even on the—

The intercom squeaks and the tired voice of my manager says, "Rosie Thorne, please report to the office. *Immediately*."

Shit.

Annie sighs to the heavens.

Well, time to grovel, I guess. Dejectedly, I stand and brush off my work slacks—someone really needs to clean the floors—and make my way toward the back of the store. The manager's office is situated in the far left corner, shoved between the frozen produce and the meat counter, so it always smells like frozen chickens and artichokes. I knock on the metal door before I poke my head into his office. Mr. Jason is sitting behind a crappy desk, vigorously pumping a smiley-face stress ball. He motions me inside, and I close the door gently behind me.

"Just let me explain," I begin, but he holds up a hand and I quickly fall silent.

He doesn't say anything for a long moment. Mr. Jason is one of those guys who hangs his screenwriting degree behind his desk to remind himself of all of the mistakes he's made in his lifetime, now a lowly grocery store manager in the middle of nowhere rather than some award-winning screenwriter in LA. Maybe once he had a head full of black hair, but he opted to buzz it short when he started going bald. I only wish he'd shaved off his porn-stache too, but we can't always get what we want.

"What did I tell you," he says quietly, "about your phone?"

"You see, out in the parking lot—"

"This is your third write-up, Rosie," he interrupts.

I stare at him, uncomprehending. "Third? That can't be right."

He flips open a folder on his desk—a folder I hadn't noticed before—and begins reading from a detailed write-up form. "First write-up happened last summer, when you told Travis Richardson—and I quote—'sit and rotate' while presenting him the middle finger."

"I turned him down, so he told me I'd die alone with seven cats!"

He went on, "And the second write-up was this past spring, when you filmed a TikTok in the middle of the frozen meats section to the song—"

"'If I Can't Love Her' from the ending credits of *Starfield*, yeah I remember that one," I mutter to myself. "But it went viral! I mean, sure I did a few bad things, but I'm a good employee! I was an employee of the month!" I add, flinging my hand back to the wall of photos behind me.

Mr. Jason closes the file and gives me a weary look. "Listen, Rosie. I understand that life without your mother must be difficult."

The words are like a sword through my middle. My hands involuntarily fist.

"It must be tough," he goes on, as if he understands what I went through, as if he knows what it's like to have part of your heart ripped out, "and I've read in plenty of coping books that acting out is a part of healing, but—"

"I'm not acting out!" I interrupt, shoving myself to my feet, but he just stares at me with this sorry sort of look in his eyes. It's the same look I've seen in the eyes of teachers, and neighbors, and classmates, and strangers alike.

And something in me breaks. It snaps. Right in two.

I claw at my name badge, unhook it, and slam it onto the desk. "I quit."

"Rosie!" He gives a start, rising to his feet. "We can talk about this—"

I force myself to my feet and leave the office, anger pulsing through me like white-hot fire. I grab my bookbag from the lockers and I don't look back.

Annie looks up from her phone, which she has, unlike me, artfully hidden under the counter, as I pass her toward the front doors. ". . . Rosie?"

I don't stop for her. My eyes are burning with tears, because he had the nerve to look at me like that. My mom died. Yeah, that happened. Yeah, it sucked. Yeah, there's a hole in my chest where she should be but it's empty because she no longer exists.

I get it.

I just hate the look people give me. The pitying one. The one that, behind the sadness in their eyes, they're thinking *I'm glad it was her and not me.*

"Rosie," Annie calls, but I'm already halfway out of the store.

"I'll see you at school tomorrow," I say before the automatic doors close on me. I'm so angry I don't slow down until I wrench open the door to my antique mustard-yellow hatchback and buckle myself in.

It's finally quiet.

My hands are still shaking as I curl them around the steering wheel and breathe out a long breath. The kind of breath my therapist told me to breathe out whenever I felt the world spinning out of control. I'm okay. Everything's fine.

Everything *will* be fine.

That's when I remember the toy egg I crammed into my pocket before the whole fiasco started. I take it out, and shake it one more time.

Please, please let it be Sond.

I crack it open.

A small plastic figurine falls out. White-blond hair and a purple uniform. I smirk a little to myself and curl my fingers around the tiny General Sond, remembering the boy on the balcony. He didn't look at me like I was broken, something that couldn't be fixed. I wish I'd gotten his name. I wish I had pressed more ardently, even though I asked, again and again—

And each time he'd just smile at me and say, "You should guess."

"That's no fair, you won't give me any clues! Fine, I won't tell you mine, either. You'll have to guess."

He chuckled. "How many guesses do I get?"

"Until morning," I decided.

"Until morning," he agreed.

I wish I could go back and live in that night forever. But . . . it doesn't matter what I wish, because that night is over, like the boy himself, one moment there—then by morning, gone.

VANCE

"Can you turn that down? I have a beastly migraine," I murmur, passing the living room where Elias is watching some lip-syncing contest. I grab a bottle of water out of the refrigerator, crack open the cap, and drain half. I press the cool plastic against my forehead, but it does very little to alleviate my headache. "Do we have any medicine?"

Elias leans his head back to look into the kitchen. "Try left cabinet, bottom shelf."

I find some generic shite that will work better than nothing. I swallow it down with a gulp of water and grab a biscuit from the pack above the refrigerator.

"Ooh, come here. I think Darien is about to go on," Elias calls.

The *last* thing I want is to see my costar, but then I hear David Bowie purr through the TV speakers, and I slowly ease my way into the living room.

"Bloody hell," I mutter through a mouthful of biscuit as Darien Freeman lip-syncs to "Do You Know the Babe" on live television.

In any other circumstance, I would rightly be laughing my ass off as he humiliates himself in front of millions of viewers, but I almost choke on my biscuit as he breaks into a tap-dancing number.

"Just think, that could've been you," Elias comments, nonplussed by the situation at hand, while the sight of Darien Freeman dressed as a sexy Halloween version of the Goblin King from *Labyrinth*—a sparkly leotard and fishnets, with an exciting blond wig—will haunt me for the rest of my life.

It is very akin to watching a train wreck in slow motion. The lights flare on and he pulls out a riding crop and slaps his thigh.

The crowd, at least, goes wild. They wave around posters that say *WANNA WABBA WABBA WITH ME?* and *YOU SAVED AMARA!* and *I'M SINGLE* and *I LOVE YOU DARE-BEAR!* And a lot of other signs that should honestly be blurred out. He does a full-on split as the song ends and the entire audience erupts into chaos.

Well, *that* performance will certainly give Tom Holland a go.

"I'm going to bed," I announce, because my migraine is only getting worse watching this, but even as I say that I find myself pulling my leg over the couch and sinking down into the cushions beside Elias. He's curled up in the corner of the L-shaped couch in his comfortable blue robe, his wet dark hair gently curling against his neck. He's my stepdad's uncle, and my current guardian—for a multitude of reasons.

Sansa, my German shepherd, is stretched out on the other side of him. She barks at something only she can hear.

"Shh, Sansa, we're watching an idiot in his natural habitat," I tell her, earning a snort from Elias.

On the screen, the two judges rush over to Darien as he stands, that big dumb smile on his face, taking off his wig and flicking his sweaty black hair out into the crowd. They howl. He winks at them.

Jessica Stone, who is also my costar and who plays Princess Amara of the *Starfield* kingdom, lounges on the spectator couch in a bedazzled golden dress. She stares at Darien, openmouthed, and I can't tell if she's actually surprised Darien did that split, or pretending.

"What a performance!" the female announcer cries.

The male announcer agrees. "And that was Darien Freeman as the sexy Goblin King! How do you feel after that performance?"

"I feel like I'm going to win this," Darien says to the audience, grinning, and then turns to Jess to add, "Sorry, *ah'blena*," with a wink. She sticks out her tongue at him. The teen girls in the front row squeal as he says *ah'blena* like he just hit the sweet spot of their souls. "I couldn't ask for a better opponent."

"Or a better costar," she adds.

"*Or* a better costar."

"Speaking of costars, now I've got to know," the announcer says, leaning toward Darien a little, and I can feel a chill curl up my spine. "Do you think you could ever get Vance Reigns on the show?"

"Never," I reply, putting my feet on the coffee table. I steal a piece of popcorn from Elias, and one for Sansa, before Elias bats my feet off the table with a glare because it's not our house.

It doesn't matter—if I ruin something, I'll just buy the owner a new one.

"I mean, after he returns from his break, of course," the female announcer agrees with a smile.

"My *break*?" I mutter. "More like exile."

"That's a little dramatic, don't you think?" Elias says.

Darien laughs. "I'll see what I can do. No promises. But! I can give you one thing that I know you've been waiting for."

Jess nods from the sofa. "The first-ever look at *Starfield: Resonance*!"

I finish off the last few kernels of popcorn and roll off the couch. "All right, I'm heading to bed—"

"Let Sansa out first," Elias reminds me.

"How could I forget my good girl? My best girl!" I scrub Sansa behind the ears. Her pink tongue lolls out happily, and she slides off the couch and follows me to the back door. Sometimes it feels like Sansa's the only girl who doesn't care that I'm Vance Reigns. It's because she doesn't understand the concept of an A-list film star with a track record for bad ideas, but I'd like to think it's because I give her extra treaties when Elias isn't looking. I slide the door open, and she trots out as I find the floodlights and flip them on. Sansa's ears whirl around, and she darts out into the darkness beyond the pool and the shed and into the backyard.

I shove my hands into my pockets and kick a rock into the pool, and watch it sink to the bottom.

Everyone keeps calling this a *break*, but it's not.

I didn't choose this.

My stepfather did. "If you can't grow up, then you're going to learn the hard way," he'd said.

He thought that by taking away all of my toys, my cars, my friends, he could somehow punish me for—for what? Having a little fun? As if he could throw me into some nowhere town to teach me a lesson.

Well, joke's on him.

The only lesson I'm learning is how to absolutely ignore him the second I turn eighteen on October 11. As soon I do, I'm out of here. Just a month more.

I can endure this for a month.

THE MOMENT MY FLIGHT FROM LA ARRIVED, I hated this place. Four hours in an airplane, and it seems like I landed on another world. Into the tiniest airport imaginable. One terminal, twelve gates. Outside, it wasn't much better. Too many trees, all still somehow green even though it was September. A hired driver in an old tweed suit drove me to the middle of nowhere and deposited me in front of a house that looked like a castle, though, complete with a drawbridge and two turrets and a mazelike rose garden in the back, built of gray stones and some recluse's pipe dream. I came with my suitcase and nothing else. My driver pulled away without even a second glance. He left me to be murdered by goats or cows or whatever the hell is in the middle of farmland.

I slung my duffel bag over my shoulder and squinted up at the place where I'd be living for the next few months.

"You can't keep doing this, Vance," my stepfather had said when he sentenced me here. "Maybe some time away will help you see things differently."

And it just so happened that the director of *Starfield: Resonance*—my stepfather's best friend—had a house she wasn't using.

The front door was unlocked, so I let myself in and took my Lacostes off in the foyer. I was expecting swords on the walls and skeletons hanging, mouths agape, but the inside of the castle looked right good, really. The floors were a dark wood and while the walls were bare stone, they were decorated with paintings from IKEA and *Better Homes and Gardens*.

It would have to do.

"Elias, I'm here," I called as I dumped my duffel bag in the hallway and made my way into the living room. It was wide and open, with two long couches and a TV, and in the corner there was a baby grand piano. The back wall was nothing but glass windows that looked out onto the hedge maze and a pool. I found the drawstring to the curtains and drew them closed.

The refrigerator was stocked, so Elias had to be *somewhere*. I grabbed an apple from the fruit bowl and bit into it as I wandered through the rest of the house. Bathroom, laundry room, abandoned study—

The last door on the first level was ajar, so I eased it open.

Shelves and shelves of novels lined the walls, those cheap dime-store extended-universe sci-fi books you used to be able to find at petrol stations and grocery stores. There must've be hundreds of them—*Star Wars*, *Star Trek*, *Starfield*, at a cursory glance.

A library.

Such a pity books were a waste of time.

Footsteps came from the hallway, and Elias, my guardian, popped his head into the library, brown-gray hair and a cheerful face. He threw his hands up when he found me. "There you are! I heard someone come in, but I thought for a moment it was a nosy neighbor or something—Sansa! *No!*"

Suddenly, a brown and black blur zipped past his legs. The dog leapt at me, pink tongue slobbering over my face. "Ooh, you missed me? You missed me, good girl?"

"She has *not* been good," Elias pointedly replied. "She tore up three rosebushes already. *Three!*"

I scrubbed her behind the ears. "Why don't we make it four, good girl? Huh?"

"Vance."

"You know I'm having a laugh," I told him, and then whispered to my sweetest thing, "Destroy them all."

Elias rolled his eyes. "How was the flight?"

I shrugged. "Fine."

Sansa went off to sniff around a box of even more books and snorted, as though it wasn't anything of interest.

Elias folded his arms over his chest. "*Fine*, huh."

"Oi, yeah, *fine*," I replied, and pulled my hood up over my head as I left the library. "The bedrooms upstairs?"

"All three of them—Vance, it went viral."

I paused. Debated my words carefully. ". . . What?"

"You flipped off every single journalist at the airport."

"Oh, *that*." I spun back to Elias and spread my arms wide. "Just appeasing my fans. And they were hardly journalists. All paparazzi from what I can tell."

Elias massaged the bridge of his nose. "You can't keep doing this—"

"Or what?" I laughed. "I'll be banished to hell? News flash, I think we're already there."

"This isn't hell." He sighed. "It's a charming little town, really, if you'd give it the chance—"

"I'm tired," I interrupted, turning out of the library. I gave him a wave. "Nice chat," I added as I left for the stairs. The flight had been long, and the car ride to my prison had been a good deal longer, and I was tired and hungry and I just wanted to close myself into a room and sit in silence.

My head was pounding.

IT STILL IS A WEEK LATER.

As Sansa finishes up her business near the rosebushes, my phone vibrates. I fish it out of my pajama pocket. It's a headline from one of the gossip magazines I follow. Though they usually publish shite, sometimes it's good to have a leg up on the rumors circulating around.

HOLLYWOOD'S FAVORITE COUPLE ON THE ROCKS?! it reads, showing a picture of Darien and Elle from the set of *Starfield: Resonance*. It was a candid shot, taken as Darien's girl plants a kiss on his cheek. Photoshopped question marks flutter around them like bats.

Well, at least the tabloids have stopped pestering me for the moment.

The less the press talks about me, the sooner I can get out of this damn town.

Sansa comes back with a stick and sits at my feet. I pocket my phone again and scrub her behind the ears. I take the slobbery stick from her mouth.

"The car wreck wasn't my fault," I tell Sansa, but she only wags her tail, looking from the stick, to me, and back to the stick. She doesn't care.

Neither did anyone else.

In anger, I throw the stick—hard. It arcs high into the darkness and disappears somewhere beyond. Sansa takes off running, vaulting over those stupid rosebushes.

I wait for a moment. Then another.

"Sansa?" I call.

But she doesn't come back.

ROSIE

"AND WE REACH THE STARS, THE STARS, FOREVER IN THE STARS, THE STARS," I howl with the music, sobbing as I clutch my Sond figurine to my chest, trying to figure out what the hell I'm going to tell my dad so that I'm not the glaring disappointment that I most certainly am. I had one job—one!—to keep my job at the grocery store to save for college. And yet here I am driving through the back streets of Haven's Hollow, North Carolina, so I can avoid going home and telling my dad that yes, his daughter *did* get fired and therefore will never be able to earn enough money for room and board, not to mention tuition.

I am an utter failure. But at least I finally got Sond.

And so, I sing.

"REACH INTO THE STAAARS WITH ME, FLYYYY WITH ME, FOREVERRRR—"

A bear of a dog darts out in front of my car.

"—OH *SHIT*."

I slam on the brakes. My poor hatchback squeals to a stop, and by the time it does, the dog's gone. I couldn't have imagined it, could I? No, there was definitely a dog, but there aren't many houses around here. The poor thing's probably lost.

I pull over to the side of the road and pop on my hazards before I get out of the car, my keys between my knuckles like my dad taught me. Not to defend against a dog, obviously, but from everything else.

Always be prepared for zombies and murderers.

Perhaps not in that order.

I wipe my eyes dry and look about the road. The evening is humid—on par for September—and fireflies spark to life as night descends. It's the kind of evening that's ripe for a murder.

I can see the headlines now—*LIBRARIAN'S DAUGHTER KILLED WHILE TRYING TO RESCUE GHOST DOGGO.*

How mortifying.

Gravel crunches behind me, and I whirl around—

There, standing at the edge of my car by the rear bumper, is the same large brown-and-black dog. Her tongue flops out as she wags her tail.

"Oh, hey there, girl," I croon, clicking my tongue to the roof of my mouth to get her to come closer.

It's super effective!

The dog bounces up to me and begins to give me kisses on the face. I laugh, about to tip over from the very force of her, and scratch her behind the ears. "What're you doing around here? Are you lost? Where's your owner?"

The dog doesn't answer, and there's no one on this road. She must've escaped from someone's backyard, because she has a pretty pink collar with a dog tag. But when I try to get a closer look at it, the dog shies backward. I can't grab hold of her quickly enough before she darts across the street and down a dirt road.

"Hey—no, wait!" I cry, and follow her, aiming my key behind me to lock my car. The horn beeps, lights flash, and I tell myself that this is *not* how I'm going to die, being led down a dirt road after a runaway canine. Besides, most terrible horror movies don't have nice dogs that lead you out into the middle of nowhere—but that would be a good beginning to one of those *Saw* movies.

. . . Don't think about that.

"Hey—slow down! I'm not going to hurt you!"

The dog doesn't seem to care. She darts across the street and into the lawn of . . .

I come to a stop at the edge of the driveway.

Oh.

It's the old abandoned castle-house. It's not *really* a castle—it's too small—but whoever built it made it look like one. It's kinda notorious in our town; the castle-house is tall, at least three stories—maybe four with an attic—with two turrets that may or may not be just for show and stained glass around the large wooden front door. There's a moat that cuts in front of the house, fed from a small stream in the woods, and a drawbridge to the front steps. The house is a weird blend of medieval and modern. There are even lions on the cement posts at the end of the driveway.

When I was little, Mom used to tell me that the house was built by fairies for a very special prince. His parents sent him to live there, hoping to hide him away from the rest of the world and protect him.

"But doesn't he get lonely?" I had asked her when she first told me the story. "In that house all alone? Why would his parents send him there?"

She wrapped me in her arms and said, "Because the world

is big and terrible sometimes, and parents want to protect their children."

"Then I'd visit the prince! I'd make sure he wasn't lonely!"

My mom laughed. It was a silly, stupid story, but somehow it stuck with me. Even though there are no such thing as princes.

And fairy tales are a bunch of bullshit.

If they weren't, then my Dead Mom plot twist would've given me the ability to speak with animals. Or something else suitably Disney-esque.

The truth is, the house was built by some eccentric millionaire back in the mid-'90s, who moved away because they probably realized nothing changed in this small town, with one road in and one road out. They probably got sick of being in the middle of nowhere and left to have grand adventures in the great wide somewhere.

It's been rented out over the years, but I've never met anyone who lived there, and as far as I know, it's vacant now, too.

"Dog!" I hiss, quickly following the shadow of the mutt down the driveway, but then I lose her in the dark of the house. Cursing, I quietly make my way up to the front door. It's ajar, so I push it the rest of the way open and sneak in.

Strange. Why is the door unlocked if the house is empty?

I should leave. My common sense is telling me not only to leave, but to hurry back to my car and go home and just break the news to my dad. At least then I won't be murdered.

But . . . for some reason I can't get Mom's story out of my head. About the prince alone in the castle. It's not real—he's not real.

But . . .

I've never been in this house before. And it doesn't look like there's anyone home.

As a precaution, I pull out my phone, turn the flashlight on because the sun is beginning to set, lengthening the shadows in the house, and press record. If I die here, at least there might be physical evidence.

"Dog?" I call again, and my voice echoes through the house.

There are dozens of cardboard boxes piled everywhere. It looks like one of those houses perpetually between one renter and another, constantly changing, never quite a home for anyone. I know that kind of look. Since Mom died, Dad and I moved from one place to another, hopping to where rent was cheapest.

Dad always reminded me that it was never the house that mattered, because home is never really a physical place.

But jeez, someone could at *least* move into this place and gussy it up a little. The interior is beautiful, with exposed stonework and steepled wooden roof beams. I don't know half of the architectural jargon, but it's pretty, and at least—unlike most of the houses around here—it *doesn't* use antlers in all of the decorating.

I step into the foyer and ease the door shut behind me.

"Dog!" I whisper a little more urgently.

Something clatters to my left, and I whirl toward the kitchen and an open hallway that leads, probably, down to the garage. But there's a door to the left, just across from the kitchen, that's slightly open. Maybe the dog went that way.

Quietly, I creep toward the door and slowly push it open.

There are shelves of worn paperbacks and dime-store novels and gilded hardbacks, and boxes stacked high with even more books in them. The last bits of sunlight spills in from the two room-height windows, illuminating the books, catching the gentle sparkle of dust.

My breath catches in my throat.

I can recognize these books from anywhere—even ten, fifteen

feet away. I know their spines. I know their titles. I know their thirty-year-old smell. In a few quick strides, I am at those books, my fingers running down their broken, well-loved spines, lingering on the *Starfield* insignia on each one.

The Star Brigade.

In The Night Abyss.

The Last Carmindor.

Starfield Forever.

My heart thrums in my throat. I know the names, I know the plots, I know the orders—all of the books in the extended universe of *Starfield*. And on the shelf next to them, *Star Wars*, and *Star Trek*, and more obscure alternate-universe series, but the biggest collection is *Starfield*. Although the show only ran for fifty-four episodes, the extended universe of books lasted decades. My childhood was filled with these old illustrated covers; my fondest memories sit between these pages.

Because, you see, my mom loved books and Dad still loves books, and so I do, too.

But there is so much *more* in those words than just loving books. I love the smell of them. I love the way their bindings look pressed together on a shelf. I love the feel of pages buzzing through my fingers. I love big books and small books. I love words and how they're strung together, and most of all, I love the stories. I love how books are not really just books at all, but doorways.

They are portals into places I've never been and people I'll never be, and in them I have lived a thousand lives and seen a thousand different worlds. In them I can be a princess or a knight of valor or a villain—I can be coveted, I can conquer on evils, I can defeat Dark Lords and destroy the One Ring and unite a Federation on the brink of collapse. In them I'm not simple, going-nowhere, unable-to-write-a-stupid-college-essay Rosie Thorne.

And I love, deep down, that the best memories I have of my mother are those of her reading to me, her voice soft and sweet. The memory is like a bright flare that I never want to go out, and I'm afraid if I stop reading, her voice will fade. I refuse to love anything more than books and stories and *Starfield*.

I refuse to let my mom go.

And here—here in this strange, dark library . . .

I pull the closest volume down off the shelf.

It's well-worn, the binding cracked and the pages yellowed and dog-eared, loved almost beyond recognition. There's a coffee stain on the top left corner, and as I slowly flip through the pages, they smell like old enchanted libraries and summer reads.

STARFIELD, the title reads in big, blocky letters, and then underneath, *The Starless Throne*.

The cover is one of those old early '90s covers—reminiscent of illustrated paperback fantasies. General Sond's long blond hair is tossed in the wind as he looks out onto an exploding daystar, Carmindor on the other side, gazing back with this tragic look in his eyes. It was the first book that detailed the history of the general and the prince. It was the story behind those three brief episodes in the TV series. It gave flesh to an otherwise forgotten character in the great wide cosmos of *Starfield*.

My fingers shake as I trace over the author's name—*Sophie Jenkins*.

And I smile, because this was the book my mom loved the best. It even looks like her copy, the spine broken and the pages read, but it can't be hers. Hers is gone.

Without thinking, I press the book tightly to my chest.

I want to dive into the stories, I want to memorize their plots, I want to venture into the abyss of their pages and get lost in the

Federation of stars. I want to spend all night reading it, studying her words, trying to find my mother in each vowel and syllable, memorizing the legacy she left behind.

I want to—

The ceiling creaks.

I freeze.

It sounds like . . . *footsteps*.

There's someone in the house.

Oh—oh *no*. This does not end well for most—if not all—unsuspecting victims that venture into an abandoned building. I need to get out of here as fast and quietly as possible. Maybe Freddy Krueger doesn't know I'm here yet.

One can only hope.

I slide one foot back along the wooden floor, and then another, quietly making my retreat out of the library. The footsteps leave to the right, out of whatever room is above me. I let out a breath of relief—until I realize, with a bolt of horror, the footsteps seemed to disappear toward the *stairs*.

Oh, Noxballs.

I'm dead.

All I wanted to do was catch a dog, and I ended up in a murder-house about to get murdered by a murderer.

There is a shadow at the base of the stairs, tall and broad and man-shaped. I feel my knees begin to give with fright. My heart slams into my chest. I'm going to die, I'm going to die, I'm going to—

Get a grip.

But even in the dark, his eyes catch the light of the moon that reflects off the pool in the backyard.

"What are you doing here?" the shadow's voice rumbles, soft and angry.

I swallow the bile rising in my throat.

What do we say to the god of death?

Not today, sucker.

I spin on my heel toward a glass door that's ajar and make a run for it. The dog, wherever the dog is, can fend for herself. I scramble out into the backyard to where the pool and some sort of garden is.

"Wait—*stop*!"

A hand fastens around my arm. My reflexes kick in. I spin around, bringing my elbow up, and nail the murderer straight in the face. As I do, the floodlights pop on. And that's when I see him—really see him. Blond hair, blue eyes, a chiseled jaw, and a scar on the bottom left side of his lip. He stumbles back with a cry of pain.

Oh my God—oh my God, it's Vance—it's Vance Reigns! It's—he is—oh my *Go*—

My heels teeter off the edge of the pool. I pinwheel my arms back, and finally realize *oh, I still have the book* before I fall backward into the water, taking the priceless edition of *STAR-FIELD* with me.

SHE *ALMOST* BROKE MY BLOODY NOSE!

The girl bursts through the surface of the water with a gasp, swiping the chlorine from her eyes, before she settles her attention on me again. Because yes, yes, she did bloody well recognize me. "Y-y-you . . ."

A book floats up beside her, and I massage the bridge of my nose, trying to keep my feelings under control. My stupid, sodding, fecking luck. I can't even hide in the middle of nowhere.

I grind out, for the umpteenth time, "*What* are you doing here?"

She scrambles toward the edge of the pool and grabs onto it, staring at me from between bangs plastered to her forehead, eye makeup melting around her eyes like candle wax. Her teeth chatter loudly. "I—I w-w-was—"

"Come to stare? Take a picture? Tweet it to your mates? Oh, you found the elusive Vance Reigns! Congrats!"

Her eyes widen. "What? N-n-no—"

"Gonna go sell some photos to TMZ, are you? Try to get rich

off my agony?"

"I w-was looking fo-for—"

"Sod *off*—"

"—a *dog*," she finishes.

From the other side of the pool, there is a woof. Sansa sits at the edge and wags her tail happily. I purse my lips, trying not to look too grateful that she returned. I'll give her a good belly scritch later.

And I will *never* let her off her lead again.

The girl begins to say something more when the back door opens to Elias, sweating profusely through his button-down shirt. He went out to try to find Sansa when she escaped, while I waited behind to see if she'd come back. He begins to say something when his gaze drifts to our intruder. "Why is . . . there a young woman in our pool?"

The girl waves, her teeth chattering and her lips beginning to turn blue. "H-h-hey."

"DON'T FRET, I'm sure the book wasn't *that* important," Elias says as he brings the girl a hot cup of tea. She's sitting on the edge of the couch with a towel thrown over her shoulders, dripping all over the expensive beige rug. Elias made her call her father, who is sitting quite stiffly beside her, a silver-haired man who can't be any older than Elias himself. He came straight from his job, apparently, though I'm not certain what kind of job lets a bloke wear a rainbow bow tie and red suspenders.

Every now and again, when the girl thinks I'm not looking, she'll cut her eyes back at me sitting on the piano bench in the corner of the room. My arms are folded over my chest, finger tapping on my biceps.

I don't believe for a second she came into this house searching after a random stranger's dog. What kind of person does that?

None that I know.

Well, except Darien. Probably. If the dog wore a *Starfield* costume or something.

The girl accepts the cup of tea gratefully as her father says, "Really, I'm sure we can pay for the book—"

Elias begins to wave him off when his phone rings. He excuses himself for a moment as he fishes it out of his back pocket, and answers. "Ah! Thank you for calling on such late notice. We've had—an incident," he says as he quickly moves into the library and closes the door behind him.

She wilts a little beside her father. He drums his fingers on his knees nervously, and then he stands and says, "May I use your bathroom?"

"Second door to the left," I say, pointing down the hall toward the foyer, and he leaves.

When we're alone, the girl takes a tentative sip of tea and wrinkles her nose. Elias makes terrible tea, which she seems to realize because she sets it down gently on the coffee table and pulls the towel tighter around her shoulders. There's a birthmark on the side of her neck, but I can barely see it between the strands of her mousy brown hair. If she had a wire on her to record our conversations, it would've been ruined in the pool, but a video camera could easily take a swim. She could be hiding it anywhere on her person—in her jeans pocket, her shoe, her . . .

I glance at her chest, and quickly look away.

She doesn't strike me as the type.

"I'm sorry if this sounds weird," she says then, startling me from my thoughts, "but have we met before?"

Oh, that's *charming*.

"You've probably seen me before," I reply tightly.

"No, I mean—"

"Why'd you come in here?" I interrupt. "You saw the door was open, boxes in the foyer, surely you could guess the situation."

"I . . . just did," she replies, which isn't a good reply at all. "I was looking for your dog. She came barreling into the road, so I stopped to try to get her. I thought she was lost or something."

"And when she went into this house?"

She opens her mouth. Closes it. Opens it again. She hesitantly glances down the hallway toward the bathroom, and finally settles on ". . . I don't know."

I run my fingers through my hair aggravatedly. "I don't see what you people bloody *want* from me."

"Nothing," she says, surprised. "In fact, I really like—"

The door to the library opens and Elias steps out again, thumping his cell phone against his chest. He has a drawn look across his face that is never a good tell. About the same time, her father comes back from the bathroom saying, "That is a *beautiful* painting. Where did you get . . ." He trails off, though, when he sees the grim look on Elias's face.

Elias presses his lips together and says, as if he's delivering fatal news, "So, that book. It turns out it was, well . . ."

"A first-edition *Starfield* original," the girl fills in glumly. "I know."

Her father balks. "You must be joking. The only book in the *Starfield*-verse that has that kind of collector's tag is . . ." But then he trails off and, peculiarly, he and his daughter exchange the same look.

They know something. About the book. Something secret between them.

Coming in here to look for my dog, my ass.

Elias hesitates and glances to me, as if I can somehow possibly get him out of whatever he's about to say. I don't know books. I have no idea what any of that means. I wrap my arms tighter over my chest and stand from the piano bench. Whatever, I'm going back to my room.

As I start toward the stairs, he says, "The worst part is, the owner of the house—which is neither of us—might want to press charges for the damages."

I freeze at the bottom of the steps and glance over to them on the couch. The girl curls her fingers into the edges of the towel tighter, knuckles turning white.

Her father clears his throat. "How much are we talking here exactly?"

"Fifteen hundred," Elias replies.

"Oh, dear," he mumbles.

His daughter has gone pale, which is already quite a feat seeing as how she looks one shade off from a ghost already. "We . . . don't have that."

Her father, on the other hand, is already reaching into his tweed jacket. He pulls out a checkbook. "Fifteen hundred?" he asks to clarify. "Does anyone have a pen?"

"Dad!" the girl hisses.

He mumbles something to her, and she growls something back, and they stare at each other in a standoff until, finally, he closes his checkbook and she turns back to Elias. Her mouth works as she searches for something to say. And then, unexpectedly, she finds the words. "This is my mistake, not his."

"Well, then that leaves us in a conundrum," Elias replies patiently.

She agrees. "I'll work off the debt, then? I'll do whatever you want—cook, clean, garden. Until I pay you back."

"Rosebud, you barely clean your own room," her own father says, ratting her out.

She wilts. "I can try?"

I resist the urge to snort—not because she couldn't do those things, because obviously I'm not any better—but because she would even *offer* to do things she quite possibly sucks at. "We don't need any of those things," I say instead.

She wilts so much she almost fades into the couch. "Well, I . . ."

"Do you like books?" Elias asks. When I shoot him a look, he refuses to meet my gaze. *Don't* encourage *her*, I want to scream, until I notice that she is no longer wilting.

In fact, she is positively radiating.

"More than Carmindor loves the view from the observation deck," she replies. "More than Picard loves his model starships. More than Darth Vader loves the Dark Side. More than Sond—"

"We get it," I interrupt.

"Well . . ." Elias tilts his head thoughtfully, glancing from her father back to her again. "We do have that *entire* library, and it would be nice to fix it up for Na—the owner of the house. I was going to have it be your job, Vance, but because of this recent occurrence it might be nice for you to have some help. In exchange, perhaps we could cover the cost of the book."

I stare at Elias, for he has betrayed me far more than I could have predicted. "You're joking."

Because first, I wasn't going to organize a *library*. What did he take me for, a maid?

And second, I certainly wasn't going to do it with her.

But she, on the other hand, seems absolutely ecstatic about

this turn of events.

"*Really?*" She sits up, her eyes wide.

Her father shakes his head. "You have work after school, Rosie."

She winces at that and turns to him. "Well, um, actually . . ."

"Never mind." He sighs and massages the bridge of his nose. "All right. All right—but I do have a few questions and some concerns," he adds, and his eyes flicker back to me.

My back stiffens at the insinuation. Honestly, I'm too busy ruining my own life to ruin someone else's. Elias agrees and asks the girl's father to walk with him while they discuss the details, probably with the owner of the house. He disappears into the library again with Elias, leaving the girl and me in the living room alone.

She sits quietly, twirling a lock of wet hair around her finger. What kind of game is she playing? Her father was clearly ready to write a check, so why didn't she let him? And why does Elias think that her helping me with that stupid library will cover the cost of that book?

I'm not so self-absorbed as to think that she's staying because she wants to get close to me—I'm not stupid. The tabloids have been the opposite of kind, having all but set my career on fire. And anyone who comes near me gets the same treatment. My manager said that I should lay low for a while, advised my stepfather to put me somewhere where I can't get into trouble. Let the rumors die down before the release of *Starfield: Resonance*—or else my reputation might bleed into the movie.

And my stepfather's business.

But I can't think of another reason why she would agree to sacrifice her afternoons to come to a library of all places. I clench my teeth and feel a muscle twitch in my jaw.

I don't like her.

After a moment she turns to me and says, "My name is . . ." but I'm already halfway up the stairs, and gone. I don't need to know her name. I don't need to get to know her.

It's best if I don't.

ROSIE

When Dad and I finally make it back to the apartment, he tugs his tie loose and heads to the liquor cabinet and the bottle of bourbon at the top. "Well, that was an interesting evening," he says with a sigh. "And interesting people. Isn't that boy—?"

"Vance Reigns," I reply, dumping my bookbag down at the kitchen table. Even though I finished my calculus homework during lunch today, I still need to start on that essay for my college application, and that English report due next week—my life feels like a never-ending stream of to-do lists.

"Vance Reigns, Vance Reigns . . ." Dad mutters, pouring himself a drink. "Doesn't he play Sond?"

"Bingo."

Though he did seem familiar for moment before I took a splash in the pool, but it's probably my imagination. He has been trending a lot on social media recently, after all—and never for anything good.

"Well, it seems you'll be getting to know him rather well these next few weeks," Dad says as he grabs the plethora of menus from the counter and slides into a chair opposite of me at the table. "Mr. Rodriguez and I talked it out, and as long as you sign an NDA and don't, you know, write about your experiences on a very public forum, it should be quite the experience. Since you got fired from the grocery store," he adds in a deadpan voice.

I give a start. "How did you . . . ?"

"Annie called me at work," he replies. "Told me that you got fired."

"I quit, actually," I reply nobly.

He sighs and waves the menus at me, deciding to drop the argument. Which means he isn't that upset with me. "What do you want to eat?"

"I'm not really hungry," I mumble in reply, taking out my laptop from my bag, and I open it up to the Word document, and the title, *WHY I SHOULD BE CONSIDERED FOR NYU*. The rest is still, unsurprisingly, blank.

Because honestly? I am not all that remarkable. I'm just known as the girl whose mom died last year, and I don't want to write about *that*. I don't want to remember how the hospital smelled so sterile, and how Mom's hand was so cold, and her breath so shallow. I don't want to remember the last words she said to me ("Be good, Rosebud"), and I don't want to remember that I had to leave the room. I don't want to remember walking to the soda machine at the end of the hallway and getting an Orange Crush when I asked for a Diet Coke.

I don't want to remember the slow walk back to her room. Dad standing at the door. Tears dripping down his face. The Orange Crush forgotten on the ground. The swell of grief that seemed to root all the way down into my toes.

No, no, no.

The moment that changed my life was the moment that ruined it, and I'm sure no college wants to read about that.

I wave my hand at the menus. "You pick."

He sighs, raking his hands through his gelled hair to dishevel it. It's somewhere in the range of silver, the sides darker to fit his natural color. When he started going gray a few years ago, his barber convinced him to just go full silver, so he now dyes it. He hasn't gone back since. He says it makes him feel cool, and honestly the silver hair makes it easier to spot him in a crowd. Dad used to be in a punk band in the '90s. There are a few pictures floating around of him on the dark web, but the less people who know that my dad used to tour with the likes of Green Day, the better.

He scrunches his nose and says, "How about sushi? From Inakaya?"

"Whatever you'd like," I reply with a wave.

"Two Californias and a salmon?"

"And a few spring rolls?"

"Spring rolls it is." He pulls his cell phone out of his back pocket and calls in the order. The restaurant knows us by name, we order out so often. It's also the only sushi place in town that has remotely fresh fish. When you're in backwater nowhere, it's hard to find anything that isn't flash-frozen fast food.

Then he downs the rest of his drink, and as he sets his empty glass on the table he asks, "So what was it like?"

I glance up from the mesmerizing blinking cursor. "What was what like?"

"The book. You know, before it took a dive."

The book.

The *Starfield* extended-universe books have been out of print for a number of years, but you can still find one floating around at a used bookshop, dog-eared and spine-broken. Mom had a whole collection of them. They were her pride and joy.

I smiled softly. "It smelled like old pages."

He gave a wistful sigh. "They all do."

As he says this, a thought occurs to me, and I sit up a little straighter. "Wait a minute, do you think Mom's books are in that library?"

"Oh, no," he replies, rocking his glass of bourbon from side to side. "Remember, we sold all of hers to some collector in LA. I doubt those are hers. But it was a good thought."

My heart sinks down into the pit of my stomach. "Yeah. That would've been impossible, I guess."

"The world's filled with impossible things, Rosebud," he replies after a moment, and gives a shrug. "Maybe I'm wrong."

But we both highly doubt that.

As I try to find something to write about—the only moment that changed my life is the one moment I don't want to ever think about again—Dad goes to change out of his work clothes. He's been trying to get the director of the library to make their work attire more flexible for years, but alas his campaigning has been for naught so far, so he stands at the circulation desk every day in pressed trousers, a button-down, and a bright neon tie, and tries not to look too grim-lovely. (The director also tried to get him to take the gauges out of his ears, but while you can take the punk out of the band, you can't take the punk out of the punk.)

I'm just about done with my homework when the delivery guy knocks on our door and Dad answers it in his neon-orange gym shorts and a *MOTION CITY SOUNDTRACK* T-shirt. Dad fist-bumps the delivery guy, Wes, and they talk for a moment about his first semester at the local tech college, before Wes heads on his way. Dad takes the bag of sushi and tips him. "Thanks, man. Safe driving!"

Then he closes the door, and sometimes I have to wonder how he's so friendly to literally everyone he meets. It's second nature to him, as easy as breathing. I can barely talk to one person without slipping up and blurting out things I'll later send myself into a panic spiral over.

Dad holds up his bounty as he parades it into the kitchen. "Dinner has arrived! It makes miso happy."

I stare at him. "Dad."

"I know, I know," he replies dramatically, and he sits down opposite me again. I close my laptop—it's wishful thinking that I'll be able to write that essay tonight—and shove it to the far side of the table. He begins to unpack the food from the bag. "I'm soy awesome you can't stand it."

"DAD."

"I'm on a roll."

I begin to melt under the table.

He smiles and hands me a pair of chopsticks. "Okay, okay. But you gotta let me have a little fun sometimes. Some people would kill for my pun skills."

"Yeah, they're to die for."

He jabs a chopstick at me. "A-ha! *See!* Aren't they fun?"

"Whatever." I tear open a packet of soy sauce and pool it in a corner of the plastic sushi tray. Dad takes out the spring rolls, putting one on his plate and giving another to me.

He slides the last one to the third seat at the table, and there is a quiet moment.

"Hey, Dad?"

"Yeah?" He pulls out a pair of cheap chopsticks.

"I love you."

He smiles. "I love you too . . . and dim sum."

"Ugh." I roll my eyes and throw a chopstick at him. It clatters across the table, but he catches it before it rolls off and hands it back to me in a truce.

VANCE

THE ROOM IS TOO BRIGHT because for some godforsaken reason all of the curtains have been pushed back, and it makes my headache sharper. Who in the bloody *hell* opened them? The culprit soon becomes clear. Elias stands to the side of my bed, waiting patiently. I snarl against the light and press the palms of my hands against my eye sockets.

"For the love of God, please close the curtains." I groan.

He shakes his head defiantly, hands on his hips. "It's a beautiful morning and you *will* leave your room today."

"Whatever for?"

He opens his mouth, and then closes it again. "Because . . . it's a beautiful day?"

I grab the covers and pull them over my head. "Good night. Close the curtains as you leave—"

"*Vance*." He tries to stop me.

"*Elias, what?* I'm here, okay? I am here, in the middle of nowhere, wasting away. I don't exist. So let me bloody well not exist." I grab my pillow and pull it onto my head.

He sits at the edge of my bed, and he says softly, "Your mother called."

Of course she did.

"She wants to speak with you."

Oh, she wants to speak with me *now*, but she had nothing to say when my stepfather banished me here?

That's rich.

She tried to confront me before I left last week, and we ended up having a row. She said some nasty things. I said some things back. That was when it was decided that my stepfather's best friend, Elias Rodriguez—my godfather, essentially—would look after me in the interim. My stepfather certainly wouldn't. He paid more attention to the movies he produced than to his own son.

Tragic, I know.

It's just so *hard* being Vance Reigns, heir to Kolossal Pictures, prince of Hollywood, et cetera, et cetera.

Whatever.

I figure if I ignore Elias long enough, he'll leave, and finally he does and closes the door behind him. If I never talk to my mother again, it will be too soon. She can leave voice mails all she wants.

I don't care whether it's a beautiful day. I don't care what I'll be missing. I don't very well care about any of it. I just want to exist here, do my time out of the media, and leave. It's not as though I wanted any of this to begin with.

Yes, I like a little bit of chaos. And yes, I might have gotten into some easily preventable trouble more often than not. I mean, wouldn't you want to shake things up now and again if everything you ever did was watched over, quite meticulously, by not only your overbearing mother but also hundreds of thousands of fans?

I suppose I could have called a taxi for Elle after the *Starfield: Resonance* wrap party. I could have just ignored the paparazzi.

I could have not lost control and careened my Tesla into a small reservoir half a mile from where Elle wanted to be dropped off.

But I'd be out of my mind to think that was the tipping point. It was an amalgamation of all of it—the late-night parties at the flat, the clubbing, the revolving door of men and women throughout my dating life. The stunt with Jessica Stone last year at ExcelsiCon didn't help matters, either.

Everyone loves the allure of a bad boy. They love him right up until he crosses that invisible threshold. They cheer him on, they fall in love, they protect him—

Until, suddenly, they don't.

And then they become the villain. The cautionary tale.

In other words: me.

ROSIE

ANNIE AND QUINN ARE WAITING FOR ME outside Quinn's house at the end of a beautiful tree-lined street. We've all been together for as long as I can remember. One day we all sat on the same tire swing in kindergarten, the one under the big oak tree in the corner of the yard, and—well—that was it. History was made and the bonds of friendship forged, and we didn't even have to go to the summit of Mount Doom to do it.

I can't imagine a single day of my life without either of them.

My best friends wait at the edge of the driveway as I pull up. "Hurry, hurry, hurry!" I say as Quinn and Annie climb into the back seat. I lift the drink carrier with two coffees over the passenger seat and hand it to them. "Java Hutt took way longer this morning."

Annie pulls her springy red hair back into a scrunchie and buckles up. "Can we blame Java if we miss homeroom?"

"I'd rather miss first period," Quinn says, taking the two coffees. They hand one to Annie. Quinn is one of the best-dressed people I've ever met. They're stylish and cool, the kind of person you *wish* you could dress like. For instance, today they're rocking plaid straight-legged pants, suspenders, and a *Starfield* T-shirt. They pull a lock of their short teal bob behind their ear. "I didn't do the reading for Gunther's class."

"Oh, the one on microorganisms?" Annie asks. "I can give you my notes."

I scoff, pulling out of the driveway. "There are more doodles on your notes than actual notes."

"I get bored!" Annie shrugs, then leans up behind the driver's seat. "And don't think you can just get away with not telling us what happened last night. I tried calling you for *hours* and it went straight to voice mail! We thought you'd died."

"I was already writing the eulogy," Quinn agrees. "What happened to you? Annie said you got fired."

"I did. And it's . . . *complicated*."

I watch my two best friends exchange a look in the rearview mirror, and both of them lean forward between the seats, prodding me to go on.

"You wouldn't believe me even if I told you."

Quinn takes a long drink of their iced Americano before they say, "Try me."

Last night, as Dad and I were leaving, Mr. Rodriguez *did* ask us to keep this arrangement to ourselves. Which, I mean, we *will*. Annie and Quinn are basically an extension of myself, aren't they? Best friends always are.

I trust them with my life.

"You have to promise not to tell anyone," I said gravely, and my two best friends exchange another look.

Annie says, "I think we're going to be late to homeroom."

To which Quinn says to me, "Go on."

I start with Vance's dog, Sansa, running out in front of my car, and how I followed her into the castle-house. How I found the library, and the book, and how I ended up in the pool and having to owe over a thousand dollars because of my sticky fingers. And then I told them about Vance, and Mr. Rodriguez, and our agreement. I go the speed limit as I tell them, knowing the exact ten-minute drive to my paid parking spot.

The high school is smack in the middle of town. Down the road is the middle school, and the elementary school sits at the end of Main Street like a hundred-year-old spooky remnant of ye olden days. I mean, the high school looks just as ancient, but at least it was built in the '50s and has central AC. The elementary school still has *window units*. I shiver, remembering this past summer.

Barbaric, putting snot-nosed kids through the armpit of hell.

As I recount last night, I honestly can't believe it happened myself. It sounds like something out of a rom-com—and I guess it would be, if the hunk hiding out in the castle was anyone other than Vance Reigns.

"I can't believe General Sond is *here*," Annie mutters in disbelief. "Do you think I could get an autograph? A selfie? A letter from him to put on my stan Tumblr?"

"You still keep up with that thing?" Quinn asks, perplexed. "Even *after* he got into all that trouble?"

"Don't police my morals!" Annie playfully elbows them in the side, and adds, "But seriously, can I get an autograph? I know the perfect fanart he can sign."

"Not the one with the—"

"Oh yes, that one."

I massage the bridge of my nose. Now I remember why, last

night as I lay awake in bed, I debated on whether to tell my best friends, and how *much* to tell them. I turn into the school parking lot as Quinn tries to talk Annie out of getting Vance to sign *that* fanart (not like he'd sign anything, but I don't want to ruin their fun yet), until Quinn pops up between the passenger and driver's seat and says, "So, *theoretically*, you could still have that video."

"Video?" I ask as I pull into my assigned parking spot.

"You know, if your phone still works."

"Oh my God—the video! I'd *die* to see it. To see him in all of his bad-boy glory," Annie adds with a heavenly sigh. "I wonder how sexy he is?"

Too sexy, I think, hesitating, before I take my phone out of my pocket and pull up the video. I hit play and hand it to them. The video goes through my adventure through the dark of the house, to the pool, and then—a little garbled since my phone is old, but still clear enough—I hear Vance say, "What are you doing here?" and then I shriek and make a run for it, and then he shouts, "Wait—*stop*!"

Right before I slam my elbow into his nose and take a dive into the pool.

The video ends there.

My best friends stare at my phone for a moment longer. Then Annie takes a sip of her caramel macchiato with soy and says, "Garrett's going to lose his *mind* when he finds out."

I quickly take the phone back. "He's not going to. And you two can't tell anyone!"

"But—" Annie begins.

"Promise? Pinky swear?" I add, lifting my pinky.

Grumbling, Annie hooks her pinky to mine, and then Quinn does. They've never tattled on any of my secrets before—not about

Dad and me losing the house after Mom passed, or having to sell her *Starfield* collection to pay for the funeral costs, so I don't think twice about them blabbing here. They're not the type.

Even when it seems like it physically pains Annie to keep quiet.

"We better get going, Bob's heading for us," Quinn observes, glancing out the back windshield at the man in the golf cart weaving through lines of cars to get to us. His sole job is to write up anyone who tries to sneak out of school in the middle of the day, or students who come in tardy. His silence is easily bought with a breakfast sandwich, but I don't have a peace offering today.

I grab my bookbag from the passenger seat as we hurry out of my car and make our way into the school through the breezeway. Homeroom's already started and the hallways are almost entirely empty.

"Speaking of Garrett Taylor," Quinn says, cocking their head up at one of the TVs in the lobby playing the morning announcement. Garrett Taylor is on-screen, and behind him is the theme for this year's Homecoming dance.

GARDEN OF MEMORIES.

"And I'm announcing, along with these other fine students, I'll be running for Homecoming King! And if I win, I'm taking Rosie Thorne to Homecoming with me! So c'mon, friends, help me make true love happen!"

I nearly drop my books out of my locker. "I *never* said yes to that!"

"Or better yet," he adds, and leans in toward the camera, "write her in as my queen."

I stare at the TV, my mouth agape, as I run through my conversation with him last night. Under no circumstances did I tell him that I'd go to Homecoming with him. There has to be some mistake. He can't honestly think—why would he—why would he think I—

Quinn slides up beside me and says, "You said no, huh."

I did, but I have the sinking feeling it no longer matters.

VANCE

One moment I'm enjoying a blissful nonexistence in a dreamless sleep, and the next a fifty-pound German shepherd somersaults onto my bed. She sticks her cold nose against the back of my neck—and starts nibbling on my hair.

"Oi, oi, not the hair," I mumble, batting her away.

Sansa replies by flopping over on top of me.

"*Gerroff.*"

"Wuff!"

I give up and sigh into my pillow. "I hate you, you know that?"

She whines, knowing that I mean the exact opposite. I roll over and rub her around the ears, because she really is a good doggo—despite almost nailing me in the testicles a moment ago—and I know I don't tell her that enough.

"Okay, you got me. I'm alive," I tell her softly, and Sansa dutifully slides off me. I sit up, but everything hurts since I haven't moved in who knows how long, and my migraine isn't any better. I brush my hair out of my face—and my fingers tangle into it. It's longer than I've ever had it: around my shoulders, and I can't remember the last time I washed it. It hangs in greasy strands, but

I just pull up the hood of my hoodie and hide it.

Sansa slides to the edge of my bed and puddles off it like she's made of slime. I rub my eyes. "Did Elias not let you out?" I ask, and when I realize I'm expecting her to answer me, I grab my gray sweatpants from the floor and slip them on.

"All right," I tell her, rubbing her behind the ears. There are few things I can't say no to, and Sansa is one of them. "Let's go."

She perks up and goes bounding out of the room and down the hall to the stairs, where she takes a flying leap down the steps.

I shuffle after her. By the lighting out in the hall, it's perhaps late afternoon. I open the back door and she tears out into the yard. A murder of crows breaks into flight above us, settling somewhere in the trees.

"Elias, I'm up," I call. No response; he must've gone to the store. I grab a LaCroix from the fridge and glance into the living room. The sofa, and the still-damp spot in the center, reminds me of the events last night.

And of the girl.

Elias said I had to work with her to fix up the library, so I make my way to the library to see just how much work I won't do.

The library door is heavy and made of some sort of dark wood—mahogany or oak—and is carved with flourishes of vines. I hit it with my toe, and to my surprise the hinges give easily, and it creaks open. The library is quiet. A thin layer of dust coats the shelves, and most of the books are faded, their spines broken. *Starfield*, *Star Wars*, *Star Trek*, on top of old Anne McCaffreys and Douglas Adamses and a myriad of other ancient sci-fi authors. They're in no particular order, and there are more books in cardboard boxes stacked against the bookcases. There are at least thirty of them. They're probably also full of yellowed paperbacks.

The book that took a dip with the girl rests on a towel on the desk at the far end of the library. *The Starless Throne* by Sophie Jenkins. I pick it up to read the back summary, surprised to find out that the book is about the character I played in the films—General Ambrose Sond. The villain in *Starfield: Resonance*.

> To atone for the crimes of the Twelfth Order, Ambrose Sond escapes his lifelong imprisonment in the Mines of Mourning and is sent careening into a plot that may destroy not only the Federation but everything he once loathed—until he finds a reason to protect it.

"Sounds terrible," I mutter, tossing the book back onto the towel. It's still mostly damp, and the cover has begun to curl around the edges. To say it's *ruined* would be an understatement. It's pulp. I can hardly imagine that once it was worth as much as my favorite trainers.

I can hardly imagine any book would be worth that much.

If Elias thinks I will help out in any capacity in this library, he's sorely mistaken. I am not here to play housekeeper—that sounds boring, anyway.

As I begin to leave, a magazine on the edge of the desk catches my eye.

PULL THE REIGNS ON VANCE! it says, which is really quite ingenious, I have to admit.

I slowly sneak up to the magazine, as if it'll jump away and disappear, but it's really there. I'm quite surprised, actually, that this magazine is the first bit of the outside world I've seen in weeks, and it's . . . sort of terrifying. But I'm too curious to simply look away.

And the reality of my, well, *reality*, begins to settle in.

"I always thought he was bad news," tweets one of the authors penning the current young-adult book series Starfield: Ignite. "About time his problematic behavior caught up with him."

Vance Reigns has always been somewhat of a hot-button topic. Whether it be the ragers he hosts at his house in Beverly Hills, or the questionable videos on his Instagram in clubs he's not yet old enough to get into, or the revolving door of men and women through his love life, Vance Reigns gave us a little of it all and we drank it in. After all, he's a young guy in Hollywood with too much time on his hands! We've all lived a little vicariously through his exploits.

But his appeal turned sour a few weeks ago when he took a nose dive into a private pond in a Tesla with Elle Wittimer herself, costar Darien Freeman's longtime girlfriend. They claim they were pursued by paparazzi, but the question stands: what were they trying to hide?

Darien Freeman and Elle Wittimer have since broken up—and Vance Reigns's popularity has plummeted. He has become one of the most-hated celebrities on the internet, rivaled only by the polarizing hatred for Kylo Ren from the Star Wars franchise—a fictional character.

And where is Vance Reigns to own up to what he has done? No one knows. While we have our suspicions as to where he might be, Starfield is scrambling to control the narrative of this disaster. There is no doubt Vance Reigns has quite a career ahead of him as a villain of epic proportions.

But the real question is: will the fans let him? Or will his career, like Darien Freeman and Elle's relationship, be canceled?

I feel sick to my stomach and quickly close the magazine. The entire room begins to spin. Somewhere in the distance Sansa barks, but I barely hear her as I sit down in one of the wingback chairs.

Darien and Elle are broken up?

I was supposed to take her back to Darien's place on the west side of LA. It was during the wrap party for *Starfield: Resonance*. We had filmed our last scene that day, and so we were celebrating at Natalia Ford's—our director's—house in the Hills. Which would have been grand, but I had a previous engagement at a club with a few of my other blokes, so I decided to leave the party early.

I was heading back to my car when I intercepted Darien, dark hair messy and shirt crumpled, and Elle in an oversized sweatshirt and jeans. She wanted to leave, he didn't. Classic case, really.

"I'll just call a car," she was telling him.

But he was shaking his head. "No, just hold on—I'll drive you home."

"You want to stay, Dare, and I have an exam tomorrow morning. It'll be fine. Stay and enjoy the evening, okay?" she told him soothingly, and pressed a kiss onto his cheek.

"Get a room," I called as I passed them, spinning the key ring around on my finger, earning a middle finger from Darien. I should've just kept quiet.

"Thanks for the—wait, are you leaving?" Elle called after me, much against Darien's insistence not to.

I shouldn't have stopped, but hindsight is always clearer. I looked back at him. "Does it look like I'm staying, Geekerella?" She hates it when I call her that, most likely because she gets it every time she shows up in the tabloids.

Her face flickered with annoyance, but then she said, "You're heading over toward that club, aren't you? On the far side of the strip?"

"Am I that predictable?"

"Yes," both of them said in unison.

I rolled my eyes. "What do you want?"

Darien began to shake his head, but Elle pushed on and said, "Would you mind dropping me off at Dare's place? It's on the way."

Again, I should have said no. I should have told her to get her boyfriend to take her home, because I shouldn't have dealt with the trouble of her. But I said yes. Not because I wanted to be nice.

I said yes because I knew it would piss Darien off, and I wanted to piss him off as often as I could. He's just so insufferably perfect, like his character in *Starfield*. He does everything right, and he says all the right things in interviews, and he has a beautiful girlfriend, and everyone loves him.

But I think I hated him the most because he loves himself. He loves his life.

It annoyed the hell out of me.

So I agreed to take Elle home just so I could see the look on Darien's face when I led his girl to my car and helped her inside. But once the door was closed and I pulled out of the auto spot, she said, "You really like getting under his skin, don't you?"

"It helps that I have a pretty girl I can use," I replied slyly.

She rolled her eyes. "I'm not helping, and you're not using me. You're taking me home. I have an exam in the morning that I *cannot* fail."

I knew where Darien's apartment was, so I took the quickest route to it. I sighed, "Ah, the life of a college student. A wee bit different from perfect Darien's life, isn't it?"

She gave me a look. "Yes, it's different—but neither is perfect. He has a lot of night shoots. I have exams and studying."

"And professors who already know your name because of who you're dating, and classmates who want to be your friend because secretly they all think *they* should be dating Darien Freeman instead of you."

"Do you always think the world revolves around you?"

"When has it not?"

"Don't you ever get tired of being the spoiled brat?"

"No," I said, but what I honestly meant was—

If I can't be this, what can I be?

But we didn't have time to delve into a therapy session, because a moment later, at a red light, she put a hand on my arm. At first I thought she was getting sweet with me, but when I followed her gaze, she was looking at a black SUV next to us. The window was rolled down. And a bulbous camera lens stared unblinking at us.

This was why I took the shortest possible route. *This* is why I should have told her no, to call a cab, to let her perfect boyfriend take her home.

The news outlets would report that we had tried to get away from paparazzi, and that was when my car took a nose dive into a pond—which was more like a muddy reservoir, but I quickly stopped trying to argue that point, especially when everyone began to narrow in on the part where Elle and I were together in the car.

Elle and Darien set the record straight almost instantly, of course, but by then it didn't matter.

What do you think was more newsworthy, the unfounded rumor that I was trying to get Darien's girl, or that I was—mostly selflessly—taking her home from a wrap party?

It's not bloody rocket science.

My manager thought it would be best if I laid low for a while. If I let everything blow over. My stepfather, at the end of his rope, thought that if I went somewhere without Hollywood influence, I would come out a better man.

But it seems like even without me there, things just got worse. I made everything worse.

I always make everything worse.

ROSIE

THE DISMISSAL BELL SHRILLS and I slam closed my notebook and shove it into my bag. Miss Rayna bookmarks our spot in *Twilight* by Stephenie Meyer and shouts at us to finish the novel. A few students grumble about having to read about sparkly vampires, but the teacher quickly tells them, "As if a ring of invisibility is any more *believable*—there'll be a quiz tomorrow on the differing mythos between *Dracula* and *Twilight*!"

That was met with even more groans. I'd already read both books, so I just needed a refresher course in *Dracula*. Maybe I could rent the 1992 movie tonight. I always did fancy Keanu Reeves . . .

Pulling my bag over my shoulder, I hurry out of the classroom to meet Annie and Quinn.

"I can't believe you get to read *Twilight* in honors class while I had to suffer through Huck Finn," Quinn says as they meticulously file down their beautiful clawlike nails, leaning beside Annie's locker. "It's honestly not fair."

"We also had to read *Dracula*, though," I point out as I jerk open my locker, "which is drier than my love life."

Annie and I have had lockers beside each other since middle school. It's the curse of having T names—Thorne and Trout. Annie says, "Well, there are some one-hander bodice-rippers I can lend you for that."

"Oh, gross." Quinn wrinkles their nose.

Annie shrugs. "Just saying." She takes out her book and closes her locker. "Okay, so I have a crazy idea and I need you both to be super-ultra-supportive of it."

Quinn and I both eye her hesitantly. The last time Annie had an idea we had to be supportive of, she shaved off her brother's arm hair and it never grew back right. Quinn finally says, "Okay, let's hear it."

So Annie flips open her notebook and presents us with a list titled *HOW TO BECOME HOMECOMING ROYALTY*.

"Oh no," Quinn whispers as I look around for somewhere—anywhere—to hide.

"Quinn will become Homecoming royalty instead, preventing one Garrett Taylor from becoming Homecoming King and guilt-tripping you into becoming his date. It's a bulletproof plan," Annie says triumphantly. Then she tears out the list, and I realize she's written it down three times. She hands each of us a sheet and pushes up her glasses, like the nerdy hero of her own rom-com. "Operation Royally Screwed is a go!"

I scan down the list. "This is a terrible idea."

"Who says I even want to be Homecoming King?" Quinn says, closing the locker door. "It's sexist."

"Then who better to be crowned than our favorite nonbinary Overlord?"

Annie has a good point, one that I don't really like, but Quinn seems to have taken the bait. "Overlord, you say?"

"And you get a *crown*."

"I always did like overthrowing the patriarchy," they muse. "Okay, I'm in. This calls for a trip to the library, I believe."

Annie nods gravely. "We need the help of Space Dad."

I grimace and shove *Twilight* and my calculus book into my bookbag. "Why do we need my dad's help? And can you please stop calling him that? It's weird," I add as we melt into the steady stream of students leaving the school.

"Look," Annie says, putting a hand on my shoulder, "he's so beautiful that his beauty is out of this world, so thus—"

"Space Dad," Quinn agrees. "Besides, he loves those trashy sci-fi books so it fits."

I sigh. "I'm never going to win this, am I?"

"Nope," both Quinn and Annie reply in unison.

Of course not. I toss my keys into the air and catch them. "Okay, library it is. Only until four, though. I have a date with a few hundred books after that."

"*And* Vance Reigns," Quinn replies with a wiggle of their eyebrows.

My cheeks warm, but before either of them can notice, I push open the door to the school courtyard. Students slowly trickle out of the breezeway toward their cars in the almost-empty parking lot. I can hear the sound of some sportsball playing in the field behind the school, followed by the out-of-tune howl of the trombones over on the marching band field.

Someone bumps into my shoulder, muttering, "I can't believe Garrett's taking *you*."

I glance back, but whoever it was gets lost in the crowd of students behind us. That was odd. It's not like I want Garrett to take me. I told him no, after all.

But that makes me think of something more concerning—how many people think that? That I'm stealing Garrett Taylor away from them? I mean, Garrett is *popular*, but it's only because he has a few hundred thousand subscribers on his YouTube channel and everyone wants to have their five seconds of fame. Do they think *I'm* looking for five seconds of fame? Suddenly, it feels like everyone is looking at me even though I know—I *know*—they can't all be.

Maybe just most of them.

Some of them.

Enough for me to hurry up my pace. If Annie and Quinn notice, they don't say anything. When we get to my car, they toss their backpacks into the back, and Quinn calls shotgun. I slide into the driver's seat and mutter a prayer to my car.

I turn the key and the engine squeals.

"Not today," I say to it. "*Please* not today—"

Old Betsy sputters to life. Quinn and Annie throw their hands up in a cheer.

"To the library!" Annie cries. "Space Dad calls to us!"

No, no he does not, but I'd rather not fan the flames, so I crank up the stereo—the only part of my car that has never once failed me—and we sing our way to the library where my dad works. It's about a ten-minute ride from the high school, down the main road on the other side of town.

For the record, everything in this town is no more than ten minutes away.

I've lived in this small town for my entire life. It isn't tiny—we have a movie theater and a (slightly dilapidated) shopping mall and a few big-chain grocery stores and a Walmart. It sits on the side of a lake, along with three other towns, so it attracts an array of millionaires to the area looking for a quiet, reserved place to plant their roots. Before I was born, Dad and Mom moved here, and he stayed at home with me while Mom went to work at a nuclear site about an hour away. She was smart in ways I can never be. She could spin numbers as if they were magic, but what she loved most of all were words. She loved reading them, collecting them, coveting them. When she died a year ago, the medical and funeral costs ate up most of our savings. We had to sell the house on the lake, and Dad's favorite Fender guitar, and finally—tragically—the collection of *Starfield* novels she loved so much.

After that, Dad and I hopped from apartment to apartment. He took a job at the county library as the head Youth Services coordinator. He's been there ever since, and Quinn, Annie, and I have spent more time in the library than anywhere else in the world. We know every nook and cranny, and almost all of the patrons—most of whom are older and walk from the retirement facility across the street—know our names.

Dad's sitting on the edge of the Youth Services desk when we come in, flipping through a new picture book for the stacks. He glances up over his Harry Potter–esque glasses and smiles at us.

"There are my troublemakers!" he announces, standing up. "Annie, you won't believe your luck!"

She gasps. "It came in?!"

He rustles around under the counter and then triumphantly holds up a golden tome. "It came in!"

"*Yes!*" she crows, throwing her hands into the air. She's been waiting for the last book in that trashy fantasy series for the better half of two months, and honestly both Quinn and I are happy that she can stop bugging us about "evading spoilers" now. "You are the greatest gift to mankind, Space Dad."

"I try," Dad replies, playing along, because God forbid he puts a stop to this madness. Then he snaps his fingers and points to Quinn. "Speaking of which! I think I found a book for you, too."

"Spare me the agony," they deadpan in reply.

He laughs, pushing his chair over toward the computer, and rustles around under a stack of papers. He pulls out a book. "It's about the Isabella Stewart Gardner Museum heist. I know you like stuff like that."

Quinn's eyes go wide. "You are amazing."

"I try," he replies pleasantly.

Annie opens her golden tome and inhales heavily. "Ah, the sweet, sweet smell of germs and page rot and smut. But I cannot be derailed!" She closes her book and shoves it under her arm. "Space Dad, we have a question."

"A few questions," Quinn agrees.

"Too many questions—you don't have to answer them all," I add, pleading, as Annie presents him with the plan and the now notorious list. He reads through it, scratching at the stubble on his chin.

When he gets to number ten, he hands the list back and says, "I think it's doable."

"Do you think you can help us?" Quinn asks.

I try to give Dad the *please say no* glare. I'm not sure if he just doesn't notice it, or if he knowingly avoids it, but he nods solemnly. "I think I can show you the light, young Padawans. Win Homecoming, you will. Obtain crown, you must."

"Boo-yah!" Annie and Quinn high-five each other.

I lean away from them, glancing up at the clock. It's 3:30 p.m., and it'll only take a few minutes to get over to the castle-house, but I don't see myself being of any more use here. I inch away from my best friends. "I think I'm going to get a head start to my new, um, work."

Dad gives me a somewhat nervous look. "You know, you really don't have to—"

"I know," I interrupt. "It'll be fine, Dad."

"Okay, but if you change your mind . . ."

"I love you over nine thousand." I kiss him on the cheek, grab one of the candies off his desk, and leave my best friends to start planning with my dad. If anyone can help them win Homecoming, it's quite possibly the coolest guy I know.

I'll never admit it to his face, though.

I BITE MY THUMBNAIL, lying sprawled out on my bed, as I consider my choices.

> You are torn between going to the hot tub with Maverick or seeing if Tiffany is okay. Tiffany looked very distraught, but you know this is probably the only alone time you'll get with Maverick . . .
>
> → Tiffany's fine, I need to talk with Maverick about the selection coming up!
>
> → I'll find alone time with Maverick later, I need to be there for Tiffany.

Honestly, Tiffany has been a total asshole to me this entire game, so why should I go see if she's okay? Sure, her father's been in the hospital and she was just called to the producer's room, but it can't be anything *that* bad. And even if it is, do I really want to sacrifice my one chance to be alone with Maverick?

Hell no.

I'm about to select Maverick when my phone vibrates and cancels out of the app. I read the caller ID and quickly silence the call.

Not her.

Not today.

I throw my phone to the other side of my bed. A minute later, the house phone rings.

Don't answer, I pray to Elias, *don't answer—*

"Ah, good afternoon, Elsa. Vance? Oh, no, he's sleeping right now," I hear Elias say from downstairs. "I'll have him call you as soon as he wakes up. Yes, of course. Hope you're doing—oh, right. Goodbye."

Then, as if on cue, my phone rings again.

I silence it and put it in airplane mode, then roll off my bed and slip on my sneakers. The easiest way to avoid *her* is to not be here altogether, because I know she's just going to keep calling until Elias finally wakes me up, or I cave and answer, and I don't want to deal with that right now. I grab my earbuds from the desk and make my way down the stairs to the ground floor. There's a thunderstorm flickering in the distant purple clouds, but they won't stop me.

Elias is stretched out over one of the couches, watching previously recorded episodes of *Days of Our Lives*. He glances over as I hurry down the steps. "Your mother's calling—"

"I'll call her later."

"You said that yesterday."

"I'll say it again tomorrow."

Elias sighs. "She won't stop, you know. And where are you going? Rosie will be here in a few minutes for you both to start on that library."

I bark a laugh. "You really think I'm going to help with that library?"

"Natalia said—"

"Leave me alone," I snap a little sharper than I anticipated, and quickly shove my earbuds into my ears. An apology tinges the edge of my tongue, but I swallow it. It's not as if an apology will do anything, anyway. "C'mon, Sansa," I say instead, clicking my tongue to the roof of my mouth.

My dog looks up from her perch on the edge of the couch and perks up as soon as I call her name. She bounds over to me, and I grab her lead from the kitchen key hook as we leave.

At least Sansa is on my side.

The afternoon is warm, almost sticky, as if to remind me that I'm no longer in dry, balmy California but a nightmarish nowhere town. I abhor it here. Everything about it. Even the dirt road the house sits on. The gravel crunches under my feet as I jog down the lane. The pine trees are tall, and the sky is slowly fading to pinkish red as the storm clouds roll in.

What does it matter if I answer when my mother rings? I can't escape her even if I want to. I am the son of Elsa and Gregory Reigns, heir to Kolossal Pictures. I know where I'm going to end up. I know what my life is going to look like.

And I hate it all.

That's also why I hate Darien Freeman. Because he's good at everything—because he doesn't have to act, but he chooses to, and he loves it. I hate him, but I never wanted to ruin him, or the good things he had.

Like Elle.

But it doesn't matter; I did anyway. I ruin everything that I touch.

As I lead Sansa to the edge of the driveway, a disgusting hatchback pulls up to the curb and that girl gets out. Exactly on time.

She makes a movement to wave at me, but I'm already turning down the road with my dog.

There isn't a single universe where I would willingly arrange a library with anyone, least of all her. It's a waste of time, and I have better things to do.

Actually, I don't have better things to do—I have nothing to do, I'm so bored out of my mind I'm trying to unlock every ending in the dating sim *Dream Daddy*—but she doesn't have to know that. I'm just biding my time, waiting until my birthday, when I can leave this insufferably small town and go back to my life. And there's nothing my stepfather can say or do that could stop me.

I just have to wait it out—somehow.

As I run, the cicadas scream and the purple clouds roll closer, and for the time being the sound drowns out the anxiety pulsing in my head. But it's never for long enough.

ROSIE

"WELL THEN," I MUTTER TO MYSELF as Vance Reigns jogs away, "screw you, too."

I push my hurt feelings down into my gut and fish out my umbrella from the trunk of my car. The thunderclouds on the horizon look angry and heavy, and I don't feel like getting soaked on the way back to my car tonight. I could've warned Vance if he'd stopped long enough, but whatever.

If he gets drenched and catches a cold, that's his own fault.

I highly doubt he'll make it back in time to help me organize that library. I doubted he would to begin with. *You're not here for him*, I remind myself. I take a deep breath and head up the driveway toward the castle-house.

Even in the daytime, this house looks like the kind of place that'll trap me for the rest of my life and steal my soul and have me haunt the second-floor bathroom until the mold is so thick in the tub it grows its own ecosystem. I hesitantly make my way across the drawbridge. It runs over a small stream that snakes between the road and the house, and when I glance down a frog hops into the knee-deep water and submerges. I swallow the lump in my throat and shakily ring the doorbell, expecting some nightmarish gong.

Instead, there's a pleasant ring.

A moment later, Mr. Rodriguez pokes his head out of the door. He's in neatly pressed slacks and his thick peppery hair is smoothed back. He smiles. "Welcome! I'm so glad you could make it."

"Oh, um—was not coming an option?"

"Of course not," he laughs, and flourishes a hand behind him. "Please, come in."

The inside of the castle-house in the daytime is nothing like it felt last night—i.e., a dark and cobweb-infested dungeon. Instead, it's light and spacious, and it smells like fresh laundry. The floor is a warm cedar wood, and the walls are hung with portraits with vibrant splashes of colors. There are a few medieval touches—the chandelier in the foyer is a large iron lantern, and some of the sconces on the walls remind me of torch brackets—but otherwise it looks like almost any other multimillion-dollar house on the lake I've toured with my father while we pretended to be rich enough to afford them.

As I step inside, Mr. Rodriguez asks to take my jean jacket. I hand it off, and the myriad of pins clack together as he hooks it onto the coat rack. "Are you thirsty? Hungry?"

"Water, maybe?"

"Water! Great choice! Lemon?"

". . . Sure?"

"Perfect! I'll bring you a pitcher. I trust you can see yourself to the library." He points like an airplane marshaler down the left hallway toward the library I've already been to before. Then he turns and leaves for what I can only assume is the kitchen.

What a weird, weird guy.

I like him.

The library is just as I remembered it—untouched, bathed in golden afternoon light. Rows and rows of spines, all stretched outward, beckoning me to pluck them off the shelf and dive into the pages. But I realize now that most of the shelves are empty, books hidden in stacks of cardboard boxes, having sat there collecting dust for God knows how long. It's like a bookstore, but all of the books are priceless and treasured and waiting.

For me.

I walk around the circumference of the library. It isn't that big a room, but every wall houses built-in shelves stretched from the floor to the ceiling, waiting for books to fill them. *Star Wars*, *Star Trek*, sci-fi and fantasy and countless editions of A Song of Ice and Fire and *Harry Potter*, and then on the back wall are old and tattered paperbacks, the ones I met last night.

I run my fingers over their bindings.

The Broken Throne.

Starfield Forever.

To Nox and Goodnight.

The entire *collection* of *Starfield* books. All in one place. They remind me of my mother's collection. I blink back the tears coming to my eyes and turn away from them.

This will be more work than I realized. I dump my bookbag down in one of the cushy red leather chairs and pry open the closest box. Inside, Anne McCaffrey spines stare back at me.

"Now, let's discuss what you'll be doing, exactly," Mr. Rodriguez says as he comes back with a tray carrying a pitcher of water and a glass of ice. He sets it down on the expensive-looking mahogany desk and wipes his hands on his jeans. "As you can see, there are a lot of books here. Most of them don't have homes on the shelves, and the ones that do are in no particular order, so that'll be your biggest job, I think. Then, you need to catalog them and note them for damages, if any, and put them all into a spreadsheet"—he points to a nondescript iPad on the desk, bound in the same red leather of the chairs—"so we can know what books are accounted for, and which aren't."

"Right, just like processing books at the library," I reply, running my fingers along another shelf of novels. *Thrawn*, *Black Spire Bloodline*, *Heir to the Empire*, *Aftermath* . . .

"This, of course, will be a lot easier with Vance helping, but . . ."

"But I shouldn't plan on that," I guess, and he makes a wavering motion with his hand.

"He had rough day today. He's really not that terrible, he just needs . . . a little time. To get used to being here."

Right, a little *time*. It just sounds like Mr. Rodriguez is making excuses for him, but it's none of my business so I keep my mouth shut. It'll probably be easier to get this job done without Vance, anyway.

"Either way, all of this needs to be done by October 11. It doesn't give you very much time—a month—but I think it's doable."

"A month?"

"Well, I'm not sure how long we'll be staying after that," he replies with a hesitant smile.

All right, a month. A month to organize the library. A month with my mom's favorite books. Somehow it feels like both too much and not enough time. October 11 is also the Homecoming football game, with October 12—that Saturday—being the actual dance.

Perfect timing, really.

"Yeah, that should work," I reply, because at least it'll keep my mind off Homecoming and Garrett Taylor as my doom approaches.

Mr. Rodriguez claps his hands. "Great! The library and the kitchen are yours to wander through. The bathroom is down the hallway to your left, and you can go out to the backyard if you want on your breaks—don't mind Sansa. She *usually* doesn't escape the backyard."

"If she does, I can go find her again."

"Leave that to Vance, he needs to get out more. Now"—he clasps his hands together—"if that's all, I'll leave you to it?"

"Sounds good," I reply, and he turns to leave. A thought occurs to me. "I do have one question."

He pauses in the doorway. "What is it?"

Why are you and Vance here? Why is he hiding? Why was Elle in the car with him that night? And who the heck owns this house and why do they have the complete extended-universe set of Starfield*?* There are so many questions I want to ask, but I chicken out. "Can I . . . borrow a book to read every now and again?"

At that, Mr. Rodriguez smiles. It's genuine and settles my nerves a little. "I can't say no to a bookworm. Just don't go swimming with another one, yeah?"

"Not unless you ask me to."

He laughs. "I've got a good feeling about you, Rosie Thorne." Then he turns and shuts the library doors after him, leaving me alone with all of these old, whispering novels.

And I can't even.

Like, at all.

Words are—there *aren't* any words, really.

There's only silence, and shelves of plots and possibilities and pages, and looking at them all makes me feel so small. When I make sure I'm finally alone, I go over to the desk, and pick up the waterlogged *Starfield* novel that I almost destroyed. The cover is curled and crinkly, and the pages have drawn into themselves, but I can still read the name of the author, and I trace my fingers across the title.

The Starless Throne.

I know my mom isn't really there. She doesn't exist anymore. Most of the time, I try not to think about it, but sometimes grief comes in waves. It laps against the sandy beach of your soul, again and again, soft and rushing and impossible to escape.

She's gone, but I miss her.

She no longer exists, but the words she loved still do.

I return the book to the shelf and get to work.

VANCE DOESN'T RETURN UNTIL I'M GETTING IN MY CAR, ready to leave for the weekend. My eyes are tired and my contacts are dry from staring at titles for two hours. He's coming down the road with his dog trotting at his heels. The rain seemed to have held off after all. Lucky him. He glances up at me, just for a brief moment, and once again I get that feeling that I've met him before. It bugs me.

A second later, Sansa sees me and her ears perk. She tests her leash, but Vance pulls her back and leads her into the house instead.

"See you Monday!" I call after him, and when he—surprise!—doesn't respond, I get into my car and mutter to the steering wheel, "*Asshole.*"

VANCE

My character gets a laser-bullet to the face.

GAME OVER.

With a groan, I toss my controller onto the couch beside me and lounge back. In my headset, Imogen says, "*Starflame*, Vance, you usually aren't *this* bad."

"I've kinda got other things on my mind."

"Well, get them out of your mind. I've got to get that trophy." She revives me, and my character picks himself back up. We're trying to get our team—who're all lagging behind—to enemy territory and steal their flag. I've always hated this mini-game, but Imogen needs the loot from the win today, and I am bored enough to entertain her.

Her character jumps over the ravine between us and takes out two enemy aliens before she squats to try to claim the flag. I jump over beside her and start to pick off the reinforcements.

"So have you decided what you're going to do about your mom?" she asks. I fail to dodge a bullet, and half of my health gets blasted away.

I quickly take out the sniper on the tower. "I don't know. I haven't thought about it."

"*Seriously?* Vance."

"I'll figure it out eventually."

But the truth is, I'm just hoping that she'll just stop calling if I keep ignoring her. I only have a few short weeks until I turn eighteen, and once I do my stepfather can't keep me here. I can do whatever the hell I want, and the first thing I'm going to do is fly back to LA and pick up where I left off.

"Have any of your friends texted you back yet?" she asks. I can hear the air quotes around "friends." She means the people I go clubbing with on the weekends.

"They're probably busy," I reply.

"Mm-hmm, I'm sure," she replies. Her character ducks behind cover to dodge a hail of bullets. "You know how I feel about those people. Aren't they the only ones who knew where the wrap party was?"

I know what she's insinuating. "They didn't tip off the paparazzi."

"They're *sharks*, Vance." She spins out from behind cover and fires a shot right into the enemy's face, and grabs their flag. She makes a run for the other side of the map to win the game.

"And I'm not?"

"Not in that way—on your left," she adds, passing me in the game.

I hurry to follow her as we make our way back to home base. "Even if they did, it doesn't matter. I shouldn't have taken Elle home, anyway."

She jumps a ledge and catapults herself onto our base. The second her character reaches it, the timer runs out—and the game ends. "You know that's not true. It was shitty of them."

I purse my lips. Maybe it was, but I can't blame them. What do rich kids (at least *these* rich kids) do when they're bored? They make drama. I'm sure they thought it'd be harmless fun, and besides, they're the only kind of people who I know understand me. They're the progeny of tech philanthropists and executive producers and Wall Street wolves and high-profile lawyers. They don't bat an eyelash when I say I've lived in a mansion in the Hollywood Hills beside the likes of Carrie Fisher and Leo DiCaprio. I've always had a bodyguard, a valet, anything and everything I ever wanted at the tip of my fingers.

It's normal to them. They don't want to be my friend because I can give them something—they've got everything already.

The one exception to my group of friends is Imogen, but our friendship is a bit diabolical in and of itself.

"Heck yeah! Got the loot trophy," she cheers from her end as the game deals out our winnings. We're about to queue into the next session when my phone lights up in a silent ring. Speaking of which.

"My mother's calling," I mutter.

"You still haven't talked to her?"

I silence my phone and shrug, even though she can't see it. "What's there to talk about? She sent me here to get me out of her and my stepfather's hair for a while. She picked a great place. Nothing around for miles. I could die and the tabloids wouldn't find out for at least a week. I don't see how anyone stays in this town."

She laughs. "Maybe it'll grow on you. Anyway, I should probably get off. Gotta go help with dinner."

"Same time tomorrow?"

"Oh, not tomorrow—I have a hot date."

"Ugh, with him *still*? What are you two going to do—go Pokémon hunting again?"

"Don't pretend like you aren't jealous, Vance Reigns," she tsks.

I'm not. I don't understand her infatuation with Jess's assistant, Ethan Tanaka. They met at ExcelsiCon last year, and against all odds, they're still going. "Fine, whatever. Have a great date—and don't do anything I wouldn't do."

She laughs. "Well, that's a challenge. What *haven't* you done?"

Then she logs off, and the game kicks me back to the loading screen. What *haven't* I done? The list is longer than she thinks. I haven't done most things normal teens have at my age. I'm seventeen, but I've never flown coach. I've never driven an economy car. I've never worn sneakers that cost less than a Kobe steak. I've never eaten instant ramen. I've never played baseball with my stepdad.

I've never fallen in love.

But I remember the girl on the balcony at ExcelsiCon this past August, and the way she spun the rings on her fingers and laughed at my terrible jokes. I wonder how long I could've gotten away with the lie that I was no one, before the spell had broken.

STARFIELD IS PLAYING AT THE BIG MO DRIVE-IN—back-to-back with the latest *Star Wars*—and I can't imagine a better way to say goodbye to the last vestiges of summer. The evening is cool and the skies are wide and dark and the cherry soda tastes especially good with the fast-food fries from the concession stand.

Everything tastes better when you're watching your favorite movie.

Quinn leans over and dips a fry into a cup of ketchup. "I can't believe you're working at that weird castle-house. What if it's *haunted*?"

"Nah," I reply as I take another swig of cherry cola. "It isn't old enough to be haunted."

"But what if someone got *murdered* in the house?" Annie asks. "It's so creepy."

"It did smell a little like old blood," I agree, earning a slap from Quinn. "Ow! Okay, okay—it's just a normal house. It was kinda clean on the inside. Pretty. Like it's been freshly renovated. And the library . . ." I sit back in the bed of Quinn's truck and sigh.

On the large screen at the front of the drive-in theater, Princess Amara kisses Carmindor goodbye for the last time.

In the next car over, a guy sniffles and wipes his eyes.

I really can't blame him; the scene is beautiful. The way Princess Amara kisses Carmindor, soft and bittersweet, and then traps him on the bridge so he can't stop her. How she boards the escape shuttle with the photon missiles. How she arcs the ship up into the Black Nebula, with swirls of blues and greens and purples curling around the wings of the ship like ribbons. It reminds me of the colors of the library, how the bindings unfurled across the room in muted, faded galactic shades.

"The library was beautiful," I whisper.

Annie *tsk*s playfully. "Don't go falling in love with a library, now. Especially one you can't own."

"Can't I fall in love just a little? At least books won't break my heart."

"Then clearly you haven't read the books I have," Quinn mutters, scooping up the last few fries.

On the screen, Amara's starship explodes and bathes the entire drive-in in a blanket of white. The last scene of the movie is solemn and quiet. It's the funeral of Princess Amara, a menagerie of all the different people she and Carmindor met along their adventure. There are a few nods to the TV series—some Ingarians, two Voltures, a small robot named CL30 bobbing beside a green-skinned rogue named Zorine, all of the characters lost or forgotten in the TV series and the extended universe of the novels.

The last scene fades to black, and the title screen reappears as the triumphant soundtrack plays—*STARFIELD*. People in their cars cheer and beep their horns, and some turn on their headlights to leave before the *Star Wars* film.

We sit back and wait. Even if we *were* going to leave before *The Rise of Skywalker*, we wouldn't do it before the end of the credits. That's a rookie move for any nerd.

Annie props herself up on her elbows as the credits begin to roll. "Okay, so, dish."

I give her a blank look. "About what?"

"Mama needs that sweet, sweet Vance Reigns gossip."

". . . Oh."

"Please don't call yourself *mama*," Quinn says, fishing out a can of red soda that turns their tongue pink. They toss another to Annie, who pops it open and quickly slurps up the fizz bubbling over the tab.

I shrug. "I haven't really seen much of him."

"Isn't he supposed to be helping you?" Quinn asks.

"Yeah, as if." I laugh.

Annie sighs. "Well, that's disheartening. So he really is just like all the rumors say? Hot, spoiled, selfish," she counts, listing off his finer qualities on one hand. "Hot. Did I mention super hunkin' hot?"

"Don't forget infuriating," I add, remembering the way he glared at me Friday evening when he returned from his jog with his dog. Why does he hate me so much? I shouldn't even be on his radar, I'm not in his league. It doesn't make sense.

"So what I'm hearing is that he is Sond. He probably didn't even have to act for the part." Annie fishes for some more bug spray in her beach bag. "Sad, really."

Quinn gives her a look. "You thought he'd be Prince Charming?"

"Well, it'd be nice—for Rosie's sake. Wouldn't it have been the coolest meet-cute? Two lovestruck fools meet for the first time in a sunlight-soaked library. It's the stuff of dreams. Besides, even when you do win Homecoming—and you will, oh you definitely will—she'll need a date for the dance."

I roll my eyes. "Yeah, and it *won't* be Vance Reigns. Not in any universe—oh hey"—I quickly scramble to sit up again—"the bonus scene's on."

On the screen, the bonus scene from the home video release flickers to life, and the crowd quiets. Carmindor steps into a courtroom filled with gnarled old men. I sort of wish that this scene had been included in the theatrical release, but I don't think Sond was announced back then.

It's hard to imagine it's been a year since *Starfield* came out and they announced the sequel. It's hard to imagine that *Starfield* was the last movie I saw with my mom before . . .

Well, just before.

"You've requested me, Father?" Carmindor asks the gray-haired man on the elegant iron-and-rust throne.

"No," another voice interrupts, and a rush of cheers echoes through the nighttime drive-in as on-screen a white coat swishes, and a tall and broad figure steps into frame. White-blond hair, glowing uniform, striking blue eyes—my heart kicks against my rib cage. Because I remember them from a few nights ago, from the first moment I saw him, a shadow with cornflower eyes. And somehow that reminds me of the young man on the balcony, dressed as Sond, but with a smile like a galactic prince. "I requested you, Prince Carmindor."

I let out a hard sigh from between my teeth.

Weird. *So* weird.

Somewhere in the audience, a few girls squeal at his entrance. Annie gives a low whistle. "*Someone*'s ovaries are exploding."

"Ah, music to my ears!"

On-screen, Sond smirks as the scene fades to dark; the last to go are his light blue eyes, bright and sharp.

I shiver a little and quickly look away.

Annie slides off the air mattress in the back of the truck and stretches. "Anyway, I'm gone to pee and stretch my legs a little bit."

"That's not a bad idea. Anyone need concessions?" Quinn stands, too, reaching their hands above their head with a yawn. They brush off their velvet skirt and hop off the flatbed truck. "I want some more popcorn. Do you need a refill?"

"*Please*, you're the best," Annie replies, handing her large ice cup to Quinn. Then she vaults over the side of the truck and makes a beeline for the porta-potties at the back of the drive-in lot.

"Run like the wind!" Quinn calls after her. Then they turn to me and ask, "Need anything?"

"Twizzlers?"

"I think I can do that. Be back in a flash." They set off toward the white building between the two drive-in lots. The other screen is showing the new Marvel and Disney movies, and in the quiet of the evening I can faintly hear some sort of rousing song belting from a pretty animated princess, and I think, if Vance were the spoiled villain of my story, the General Sond I met on the balcony of ExcelsiCon must be the prince.

That's funny, just a little bit.

As I dig for another cola in the cooler, I hear the voice of the last person I wanted to see here. "*Rosie!* I didn't know you liked *Starfield*."

Really? I wear *LOOK TO THE STARS* shirts at least once a week. I fish out a cola from the cooler and turn to greet Garrett with a fake smile. "I do."

"Carmindor's dreamy, right?" he says as he hops up to sit on the tailgate of the truck—*uninvited*. "All the girls love Carmindor."

"I mean, not *all* the girls."

"No yeah, you're right—just the ones with good taste, like you," he replies with a wink.

"Well, that's delightful," I say with that same fixed smile, "because I don't really like Carmindor. He's way too perfect. He does everything right, and he's the hero no matter what. Everyone wants to be Carmindor. What I really like are the villains, like Obscura or Vexel Day or the Nox King or, my favorite, General Ambrose Sond."

His eyebrows furrow because he didn't expect *that*. "Well, I mean, you can't actually like them."

"No, I do. I love them. They're great. I have a poster of Sond on my wall, actually," I reply, and pop open the tab of my cola. Garrett fishes for something to say, because he *absolutely* just dissed me without even knowing it, but I can't stand the slack-jawed look on his face, so I help him out a little. "Garrett, just a little piece of advice: if you're trying to woo someone? Get to know them first."

One of his friends calls his name from a few cars down. It's one of the cheerleaders running for Homecoming Queen, Myrella Johnson, her dark curly hair pulled up into a high ponytail.

The previews for the *Star Wars* film begin to play.

"See you at school," I tell him, and for once he takes the social cue. He slides off the tailgate and returns to his friends.

How come the only people who want to date me are the ones who don't know me at all—don't even want to know me? I'm the girl with the dead mom, I guess that's enough, isn't it? I guess that's what I liked about the guy at ExcelsiCon. He didn't know I had lost a piece of my heart. He didn't look at me with pity, secretly glad it wasn't *his* mom who died. He looked at me. He got to know *me* as we walked in downtown Atlanta and ate scattered and smothered hash browns from Waffle House and played Twenty Questions. It was probably one of the best nights of my life. It was a night, for a moment, when I wasn't boring and dull Rosie Thorne, still waiting for her life to begin.

VANCE

I WAKE UP WITH A PS4 CONTROLLER pressing into my cheek. What time is it even? The blackout curtains make my room dark, but between the middle seam some sort of light finds a way through. Morning, then—or at least early afternoon. I slowly force myself to sit up, wiping the dried drool from my chin. My console must've turned itself off at some point in the night, and I uncurl myself from the edge of my bed.

My mouth feels like sandpaper, and every one of the glasses in my room is empty.

"Elias," I call hoarsely, but when he doesn't answer, I pull up my hood over my greasy week-unwashed hair and crack open the door to my room. "Elias?"

Some indie-pop band blares from the speakers downstairs in the kitchen, so I highly doubt he can hear me. He must be baking—there's a sweet scent in the air. Apple pie?

I shuffle down the hallway and descend the stairs, rubbing at my eyes. I either sleep too much or not enough and I don't know which it is. I fell asleep at some point last night, but I can't remember when, just a lot of shooting and dodging and capturing stupid neon-colored flags with Imogen, until she had to go to bed. She—for some terrible reason—decided to choose morning university classes, something which I will never understand.

"Elias, could you turn that trash down?" I call as I shuffle into the kitchen.

But Elias is not here.

There's a pie in the oven, but I don't see Elias *anywhere*. He must've gone to the loo or something. So I check the pie—definitely apple, one of my favorites—and yank open the refrigerator to grab a cup of yogurt.

And I hear footsteps.

I close the refrigerator door, about to tell him how unsafe it is to leave the kitchen while cooking when—

"Mr. Rodriguez, I've got a question about the organization of volumes fourteen through twenty of the *Starfield* extended—" The girl freezes the second she turns into the kitchen, empty pitcher in one hand, glass in the other, and realizes that it's me. Her face closes off like the snap of a mousetrap.

In the daylight she looks just about as normal as they come—brown hair pulled up away from her heart-shaped face, framed with a fringe that curls every which way in that endearing sort of way I don't quite understand. There is a peppering of freckles across her cheeks. Surprisingly long eyelashes framing hazel eyes. And she can't be more than five-one, so tiny she barely reaches my shoulders.

And in the moment she reminds me of the girl I met at ExcelsiCon. Her hair had been pulled back the same way, exposing a rose-shaped birthmark just behind her left ear—

Bloody hell.

The yogurt cup slips from my hand and clatters onto the ground.

It's her.

She blinks at me.

I know what I must look like—a tall, barely washed guy in a gray hoodie and Naruto boxers (that I am kicking myself for sleeping in). And it's her. The girl from the balcony.

Her.

She doesn't recognize me, does she? No, she can't. I wore a mask that night. She did too, but that birthmark is unmistakable. I asked her about it over hash browns.

"Oh, yeah, I've had it since I was born," she had said sheepishly, picking at her hash browns. "My parents named me after it."

"Rose, then?"

She smiled, and even behind her mask it made something strange flutter in my stomach. "It's a secret, unless you tell me yours."

"I'm no one," I lied.

It seemed innocuous back then. I didn't want to ruin the moment by telling her the truth, but then when morning came, I thought I heard my name so I looked over my shoulder. And the next second, she was gone.

And now here she is, again, reappeared like some reoccurring dream.

Or perhaps a nightmare.

She hesitantly puts the pitcher down on the island counter. "Um—sorry. I thought you were Elias."

"I am not," I reply.

She rubs her hands on her jeans—they must be sweaty; I know mine are—and then holds out her hand as if she wants me to shake it. Her lilac nails are painted with sparkly glitter. "I think we got off on the wrong foot, maybe? I'm Rosie. Rosie Thorne."

A rose-shaped mark.

Rosie.

I look down at her hand.

"Maybe we could—I don't know—be friends?"

Friends.

The only friends I've had, aside from Imogen, have all gossiped behind my back and sold my deepest secrets to the tabloids. And if she finds out—when she finds out—that I was that bloke in the General Sond costume at ExcelsiCon? All of the secrets I told her, all of my fears, and hopes, and dreams . . .

I don't want to risk them getting out.

So it will be best if I don't become her friend at all, because the closer she gets the more likely she will see behind my mask. That night on the balcony was a mistake. Meeting her was a mistake.

I won't make another one.

The tabloids would eat this kind of story up.

So I incline my head instead, pushing the feelings I have toward her down into some deep part of me that will find its way to the top again later, when I'm alone, and tell her in a bored tone, "Sure."

Lies, lies, lies.

Then I grab a can of LaCroix from the refrigerator, leaving her with her hand outstretched.

After she leaves, Elias knocks on my door to check on me. I'm lying on my bed, staring at the ceiling, listening to one of those murder podcasts that seem to always be trending. This one is about a man who killed women and stored their bodies in a refrigerator.

"Well," he begins, "you *could* have helped her a little today—"

"Fire her."

He stares at me. ". . . What?"

"You heard me."

"Vance, she just started—"

"I don't care. I don't like her." My voice cracks at that.

He gives an exasperated sigh. "*Why*?"

Because I'm afraid. And I'm a coward. Because I hated how I liked how she smiled, and how she laughed, and because of that I let myself imagine her, thinking I would never find her again.

And now she's here. And I'm not the prince she thinks I am.

"Because I don't *like* her," I reiterate. "Is that so hard to understand?"

"You don't even know her."

"I don't care!" I bite back, knowing my words are too sharp.

After a moment, Elias sighs and says, "All right." My tense shoulders begin to unwind. Good, now she'll go and live her life and disappear again. But then he says, resoundingly, "No."

I sit up. "*Pardon*?"

"No," he repeats, as simple as telling a child. I am not a child. "No, you don't get to decide this."

"She's a *menace*!" I snap, which is a lie. She's not a menace. Not at all. But I'm not sure how else to get my point across. I am not used to being told no.

I don't like it.

He raises a pointed eyebrow. "What are you so scared of, Vance?"

I scoff.

"She's nice and she's been doing all of the work that you both should be doing together, and she hasn't once complained," he goes on, and my scowl turns pale. "I've known you since you were a kid. I know you. What scares you about her?"

The fact that I opened up more to her than I ever had to anyone in my life. That when she realizes that those secrets belong to Vance Reigns, she'll tell them to the world for enough money to buy that book she ruined a hundred times over.

But I don't say anything.

"Well, whatever it is, get over it. You're not getting out of this so easily—and tomorrow I expect you to help her in that library. That isn't a request, it's an order." Then he grabs the doorknob and slams the door on his way out.

PART TWO

REBEL

The automatic doors slide open, and Amara hears his footsteps before she sees him. General Sond—again. She can sense the strange warped energies that spiral around him like volcanic ash. They're wrong—he's wrong. And yet . . .

"To what do I owe the pleasure?" she asks, resisting the urge to reach for her pistol.

He slowly makes his way around to her seating area. It's a part of the space station that looks out onto her home planet of Plylantha, a beautiful pearl of a world, purple and blue and green. It looked different on the other side of the Black Nebula. No, that's a lie. On the other side of the Nebula, all that remained of her home planet were floating rocks and debris, of a place that once was but was no longer.

"What do I do?" he asks, startling her as he sits down.

"In what capacity, General?"

He lets out a breath. "You think me wicked."

"That's suspect."

"You do," he says, and gently reaches a hand out and turns her head so she must look at him. She could fight against it, but she doesn't. His touch sets her skin on edge, and her nails dig into her palms—but she doesn't pull away. As if she's daring herself to know how far she can go. "I know the look of someone questing for revenge."

"It's not a quest," she replies, leaning closer, testing the inches between them. She doesn't blink as she stares into his eyes, trying to find a soul there. "It's a promise."

ROSIE

I MANAGE TO FIND A PAIR of not-so-dirty jeans on my bedroom floor and shimmy into them as Dad's alarm screeches across the apartment for the fourteenth time.

I poke my head out of my bedroom and shout, "Dad, are you dead?"

From the other side of the apartment, I hear a zombie groan.

Good, not dead.

Since it's a bit chilly this morning—thank God September finally got the memo—I throw on an old sweatshirt and jeans, pull my hair back, and fix myself some coffee. After a few minutes, Dad shuffles out of his room, in a crumpled button-down and orange tie. His silver hair is sticking straight up on the left side. He licks his hand and tries to flatten it down, but it doesn't work.

He yawns as he fixes himself a cup. "So how's Quinn and Annie's Homecoming plan coming along?"

"I think they're making buttons to hand out that say *QUEER HERE TO ROCK and HOMECOMING IS SO GAY*," I say, pouring the rest of my coffee into the sink and grabbing my bookbag. "I can only assume I know which one you came up with."

He snorts. "I'll gladly take half credit for both."

"Like a true hero," I reply, kissing him on the cheek, and hurry out the door.

TUESDAY MORNINGS ARE FOR (MORE) COFFEE and pancakes, so as soon as I pick Quinn and Annie up, we head to the Starlight Diner for some breakfast. Seniors don't have first period Tuesday and Thursday mornings—presumably so we can study for our SATs and apply to colleges—but I highly doubt any of us *actually* use that time as planned.

Why, when you can enjoy a stack of delicious pancakes instead?

We order our usual—three specials with an extra side of bacon—before Annie and Quinn spread out the details of their Homecoming plan across the table. They've already made the buttons, but now they're both working on the posters, which are just as flashy and glittery as I suspected. Today, Quinn has on a fabulous dress—yellow with middle fingers printed all over it. They saw Natalia Ford in a similar print at ExcelsiCon last year and just had to track down the clothing company. They look up to Natalia Ford something fierce.

"She's really everything. I can't *wait* to see *Starfield: Resonance*. It is going to be amazing. Like, not like *Last Jedi* amazing, but like *Star Trek: First Contact* amazing," they're saying as they bedazzle the word *VOTE* onto the poster.

I'm not sure what the difference is (I was never really into *Star Wars* or *Star Trek*), but I nod anyway.

"I just hope Natalia treats Sond like *The Last Jedi* treated Kylo. I'm hashtag no redemption arc," Annie adds, shaking a tube of blue glitter glue.

"But you like the Zuko redemption arc," Quinn points out.

Annie waves her hand dismissively. "But Sond is *terrible*. He was in the TV show and he will be in everything we know about the movie." Our pancakes come, and we clear a spot for them on the table. Annie steals a bite of my blueberry pancake before she continues. "I just don't *understand* how so many people love Sond. How can you root for a villain?"

"Well, he's pretty hot," I comment, thinking about my run-in with Vance in the kitchen. For a moment when we first saw each other, he looked like he . . . was surprised by me. Caught off-guard in a way that caused a little crinkle between his eyebrows. A crinkle that, for an absolutely weird second, I wanted to smooth out.

"Not all that sparkles is gold," Annie replies cryptically as she finishes dabbing the glitter glue onto the rainbow and holds it up for me to see. "What do you think? Glittery enough?"

"It'll definitely catch people's eye."

"That's what we're hoping for."

We inhale the rest of our breakfast, since we only have fifty minutes before our second-period class. Quinn checks their watch and slides out of the booth. "We're gonna be late if we don't run. You done?"

In reply, Annie shows them the poster in all of its incredible rainbow-glitter monstrosity. "Isn't it glorious?"

"It's a beast," Quinn replies, and they fist-bump in affirmation.

I slide out of the booth, taking one last bacon slice as I go, and fish out ten dollars from my wallet. It's my turn to tip, anyway. Annie and Quinn slide out after me, and we wave goodbye to Mrs. Potts at the cash register.

The older woman waves goodbye with a "Study hard!" as we leave the diner and hurry down the block to school.

THE BELL RINGS AS WE ARRIVE AT SCHOOL. I'm a bit late to geometry, but Mr. Rantz isn't in yet either, so it doesn't matter. I hurry across the room to my desk beside the poster of a kitten reaching toward a moon with the inspiring saying, *Reach for the stars!* I sometimes toy with the idea of scratching out *REACH FOR* and replacing it with *LOOK TO*, because honestly it would make the poster one hundred percent better.

But there's someone in my seat when I get there.

Garrett Taylor is leaned back and sprawled out on my chair, legs up on my desk. When he sees me, he quickly rights himself and smiles around a red lollipop in his mouth. "Rosie! Good to see you this morning," he says, and points to the cup of Starbucks at the edge of the desk. "I brought you some coffee. Two sugars and a cream, right?"

"Um—I actually take it black."

"Like your heart, that's so poetic." Then he leans forward, before I can even begin to dissect his negging, and says, "I was just thinking, you know, since Homecoming is coming up in a few weeks, we have to start figuring out what we're going to wear."

I hesitate. Where is the teacher? Usually Mr. Rantz isn't this late to class. And everyone else is staring at me, because of course they haven't forgotten Garrett's proclamation over the morning announcements last week. "I, um, don't think—"

"I was thinking that since you love *Starfield* so much, we could both go in blue. I know just the perfect shade."

"I'd rather not—"

He interrupts me again, as if he didn't even realize I was talking. "What kind of flowers you like? You seem like the sunflower type, or maybe a daisy? I mean, a rose would be too easy, right?"

"I actually like roses—"

"We'll figure it out. We've got some time. I can't wait. Even though you won't be Homecoming Queen, you'll be my queen."

Laughter twitters throughout the classroom. A few classmates glance over to me, a mocking grin on their faces. Embarrassment begins to burn my cheeks.

Mr. Rantz comes blustering into the room, *finally*. Garrett returns to his seat on the other side of the classroom, fist-bumping one of his friends along the way. "Everyone, open your textbooks to chapter three," the teacher says, and I'm only too happily oblige, propping my textbook up so I can hide my embarrassment.

One thing's for sure—Quinn has to win Homecoming. I'll do whatever I can in my power to make that happen.

I refuse to give Garrett the satisfaction.

At least after school I can hide in a library and not talk to anyone.

As I've done every afternoon since I began working at the castle-house, my fingers skim along the bindings of the books until I find the first one—the one I ruined. It's water-damaged beyond repair, every page warped, the binding falling apart. I really did a number on it. Only five hundred were published in 1987, three years before the first episode aired. I put it back, then turn to my task for the day—a set of books located perilously on the top bookshelf.

And there isn't a ladder.

So I push one of the wingback chairs over to the bookshelf and climb onto it. I can *almost* reach them. My fingers brush against the bottom of their spines, where their imprint logo sits. Just a little farther.

Just a bit—

The door creaks open and for a moment there is Sond standing in the doorway, his platinum-blond hair pulled up into a bun. But then I blink and he's Vance, looking about as happy to be here as I am to see him, because here I am stretched halfway up a bookshelf, standing precariously on a rather old and probably very expensive chair. I try to reel myself back, scramble down—

My foot slips and I go down—*hard*. I flip off the chair and land flat on my back.

I groan.

And suddenly Vance is at my side, crouching next to me. "Are you okay?"

I hiss in pain as he gently takes me under the arm and helps me sit up. "I . . . don't think anything's broken?" Though something definitely doesn't feel right.

"Does anything hurt?" he goes on. "Did you hit your head? How many fingers am I—"

I realize exactly why things feel off, and I stare at him and the three fingers he's holding up in front of my face. *That's* what's wrong. "You're being nice to me."

He quickly lets go of me. Reels himself back. And like shutters on a window, the worry on his face closes off into pinched annoyance. He clears his throat. "You—you simply aren't that graceful. And if you got hurt, I *would* have to rearrange this boring library."

"Ah, there it is." I start to stand.

"Here," he mumbles, and outstretches a hand. I hesitate, eyeing it. "I'm not going to bite."

"Could've fooled me."

"*Ha*."

I reach up to take his hand anyway.

He pulls me to my feet, and I straighten out my jumper. Then I turn to the bookshelf I had been trying to reach, and put my hands on my hips, and sigh. Well, my first plan definitely didn't work. Now how am I supposed to get it? I suppose I could climb on the shelves . . .

"You know," he begins, drawing me out of my plotting. I glance back at him, only to find that he's looking at me with this frustrated intensity, like I'm a stain that won't come out of his perfect silk shirt. "I don't understand you. Why are you sticking around?"

I turn to him, baffled. "*Why?* If it wasn't obvious," I say, motioning to the books around me, "I'm not the kind of person to go back on my word. But that does bring to mind a question I wanted to ask you," I add, turning to face him fully, and even though he's a good head taller than I am, I pull my shoulders back to puff myself up. "Why are *you* here?"

His lips thin. "None of your business."

"Don't you have some nightclub to haunt back home? Some private jet to fly off on? Some—some Instagram-worthy vacation to get to?"

"Hey, I live a little," he taunts. "What do you do?"

My fists clench. "I haven't ruined my life, unlike you."

A muscle in his jaw twitches. "Yeah, well, at least I have one."

"*Had*, past tense. You're here same as me, Reigns."

Something unsaid sparks in his eyes. "Not for long."

"Yeah, sure." Then I turn to the bookshelf again and point up to the shelf I can't reach. "Now instead of just standing around gracing me with your tallness, could you please reach those books before you . . ."

But he's already stalking his way out of the library again like an angry shadow.

I let out a growl toward the smooth, crown-molded ceiling. "Fine. I'll do it myself. Like everything else!"

Even if it's almost impossible. Even if, sometimes, I don't like it. I never go back on my word. My mom taught me that. She said you're only as good as your promises, and I intend to pay my debt. And I might never have gotten out of this sleepy little town, but that doesn't mean I never will. Vance is stuck here, same as me, and if he wants to try to get rid of me *that* badly, I'd like to see him try.

He might be stubborn—but so am I.

VANCE

SHE FINALLY LEAVES A FEW HOURS LATER, probably still without having reached those books on the top shelf. I really hope she didn't use the antique table. I don't want to imagine her footprints all over . . . whatever sort of old wood that is. I'm rich, not versed in old stuff. There's a difference. I watch through my bedroom window as she walks down the driveway to the main road, where she always parks her car. She glances at me up in the window and waves goodbye with her middle finger again, then leaves before I can retaliate.

That—she—her—!!

I've never met someone else half as stubborn; it really is breathtaking. I've acted awfully beastly toward her every day she's been here and still she *stays*. Not even my LA friends stayed when I acted like a wanker.

If I'd known she was this infuriating back at ExcelsiCon, I would've—I wouldn't have—

Argh!

I scrub my face with my hands, because she was *right*. I ruined my life, that's why my parents sent me to this place, and now I'm stuck here, same as her.

There is a knock on my door and Elias pokes his head in. "Dinner's about ready. Potato soup tonight—it's the recipe from that show we watched the other night! I found it online and—"

"Not hungry."

He sighs. "Ah, you're still angry."

"Tired, really."

Elias leans on the side of the doorway. "Why do you want me to get rid of her so badly?"

Because she's infuriating, and she's stubborn, and if she knew who I was—

I grab my jacket from the back of the computer chair and shove my arms into it as I squeeze past him into the hallway. "I'm going for a walk."

"But dinner—"

"I'm *not hungry*," I repeat, and leave though the garage door. I didn't bring my car—my Tesla was still waterlogged by the time they sent me here—so I start walking down the road toward town. There's nothing but farms and fields of . . . some sort of crop. I don't know what they grow here. Some leafy green things. There aren't many cars on the road as the sun sinks below the tree line and the sky turns a dark blue, reminding me of the color of Carmindor's uniform.

It might surprise people, but I was actually ecstatic when I was cast as Sond in the *Starfield* sequel. When I was little I didn't have a whole lot of friends. Didn't realize yet that money could sort of buy you them for a while. I played alone a lot. With action figures. Video games. Things of the like.

And I watched *Starfield*.

My nanny put it on, actually. She was a girl from university and going through medical school, so she didn't have much time to entertain me. She'd turn on the telly every day when it came on, and I reckon that was that. My best memories were back then, sitting in that huge living room alone with a bowl of popcorn, and I reckon I should've felt alone, at least—but I never did. I was off in space with Carmindor and Amara and Euci.

Sounds stupid, I know. They weren't real.

But seven-year-old me didn't know the difference.

Ten years later, I'm still alone, but I'm smart enough to know that Carmindor hates salads and complains about high stunts, and Amara has never even seen the television show, and Euci runs an Etsy shop selling his face on T-shirts.

I wrap my jacket tighter around myself, wondering whether I'm heading into town or away from it, when a neon sign comes into view over the hill—a diner. There aren't many cars in the parking lot, and my stomach grumbles because I lied to Elias. So I pull my hood up and walk into the restaurant. The seats are all old and faded red, the tiles checkered, polished silver chrome on the walls. Most of the booths are taken, surprisingly, so I sink down onto a barstool at the counter.

An older woman with blondish-white hair pulled up in a bun comes up to me. She wears garishly pink lipstick and smiles so wide I can see some of it on her teeth. "What can I get you, darlin'?"

I glance at the menu, and then tap my finger on the cheese fries. "And a cup of tea please."

"Lovely choice. I'll order it right up," she says with a smile, and brings back a glass of water.

My phone dings, and at first I think it might be Elias, so I don't answer, but when it dings again, I think better of it.

IMOGEN (6:31 PM)

—Ethan wants to know who you chose to date in that new fast-food dating sim.

—[LINK TO GAME]

—(Also hi there nerd)

I snort, and send a quick reply:

VANCE (6:32 PM)

—I don't play EVERY dating sim.

—. . . But Colonel Sanders was the easiest to romance.

IMOGEN (6:32 PM)

—I KNEW IT.

—It's because he looks like Ron Swanson, isn't it.

I say that I like Ron Swanson's mustache *one time* in an interview and suddenly everyone thinks I have a type. Well, I *do*, but that's beside the point.

By the right order of the universe, I should not be on friendly terms with Imogen Lovelace. I shouldn't even know her—she isn't a model, she isn't an actress, she isn't the son or daughter of Hollywood royalty. Through a series of unfortunate events, I went out on a date with Imogen thinking she was my costar, Jessica Stone. To be fair, they were impersonating each other at the time.

It wasn't until I was on the set of *Starfield: Resonance* that I actually met Imogen—I mean, really met her as herself, and not masquerading as a famous actress. She was visiting the set in

Atlanta, Georgia, to bring lunch to Ethan—her boyfriend—and Jessica Stone.

"Are you always impossibly glum or is your face just stuck that way?" were the first words she said to me.

I glanced up from a dating sim (they're the weirdest sort of guilty pleasure, but this one was . . . odd. It was a Japanese sim about dating a horse guy? I much preferred the one with the pigeons—or *Dream Daddy*), and there she was sitting in Jess's chair beside me.

I had to do a double take at first. "Oh, it's you."

"Alas, it is." Then she glanced down at my phone, and her eyebrows shot up. "Is that . . . the horse dating sim?"

"Don't judge."

"Oh, I'm *super* judging," she replied with a laugh. "Have you played *Hatoful Boyfriend*? That one is crazy."

After that, we just kept talking. She would come on-set to visit Ethan, and then she'd swing by my trailer and we'd talk a bit about the games we were playing, and the new dating sims and *otome* games that were released that week. She's the only one who knows about my deep, dark secret love of these games.

"The I'm-a-Loner Vance Reigns is a romantic at heart," she teased once, and I'd just scoffed.

I'm not a romantic at heart. I just like the stories.

As I wait for my food, I pull out my phone and log into the current game I'm dating through. It's the one with the assistant who gets hired at an agency and falls for the CEO's daughter, but she can also have an illicit romance with the mailroom guy who looks a little like a twentysomething Ron Swanson.

What can I say? I do have a type.

You find yourself torn between going to lunch with Ridley, the CEO's daughter, and taking Oliver up on his offer to have lunch with him in the mailroom . . .

→ I would love to go!

→ Ugh . . . I'm sorry, I have previous plans.

The waitress brings me a cup of hot tea, and I take the string on the end of the bag and absently begin dunking it into the hot water. Of course I'll choose the previous plans—young Ron Swanson is waiting for me, and I never go back on a promise.

Even in a video game.

Though every time I try to get into the world of the game, these blokes in the booth beside me keep distracting me. They're rude, crowding into too small a booth, their plates half-empty, half-strewn across the floor.

When the waitress brings me my plate of cheesy chips—*fries*, whatever—she gives them a disapproving glare before she refills my glass of water and leaves for the other side of the diner again.

I don't much blame her.

"And her friends actually think *they* can beat me," one of the guys says, lounging back in the booth. He picks up a chip and tosses it back down on his plate. "They're not even worth my time."

"Quinn's buttons are pretty cute, though," one of his friends, a stout brown-skinned bloke, says as he licks his fingers. He had previously demolished a bacon cheeseburger with excellent technique. Darien would have been proud.

"Yeah, like anyone'll vote for someone because of buttons." He scoffs and rolls his eyes. "I've got a whole YouTube audience dying to see me dance with Rosie and you know what, I'm going to. Because who better deserves it?"

Rosie? I can't imagine that there are many people named Rosie in this small town, and not many who are around our age. Well, isn't this interesting. I never imagined *her* going to some backwater high-school dance with a bloke like this—

"To be fair," another one of his friends, a girl with short blond hair, points out, "you never actually *asked* her."

. . . I stand corrected.

He scoffs. "Who *else* does she have to go with? I'm doing her a favor."

"She's ungrateful," the first friend agrees. They all seem to do nothing but agree. Do any of them have minds of their own, or are they all just robots?

"And you can do so much better," adds his other friend.

I snort—I can't help it—and eat another chip.

The one in the snap-back cap must've heard me, because he turns to look at me over his shoulder. "You think something's funny?"

She's the one who can do better, I want to reply, and I can't for the life of me figure out why. I don't know this girl, but hearing them talk about her like . . . like . . . like she should be grateful for that sort of attention, really makes me uncharacteristically upset.

If they can't see that she's beautiful, the way her fringe cuts across her brows, the brush of freckles across her nose, the way she sighs in the library, running her fingers along the bindings of the books, when she thinks no one's watching—

Stop it.

"Yo," the guy says, turning around in his booth. "Do I know you? You look familiar."

Shit.

I adopt my best American accent to reply, “I’ve got that face,” before I put a five on the table for the waitress, abandoning half of my plate of chips—*fries*—and slide off my barstool. Better I leave before I say anything I’ll regret, which will perhaps be just everything.

The walk back to the house is short, and when I let myself in Sansa is curled up on the couch with Elias. They’re watching that karaoke show again, and Elias doesn’t notice that I’ve returned yet.

So I creep back into the hall and follow it down into the library. I don’t quite understand why I feel so secretive, as if this place is private. As if I’m not supposed to be here.

Perhaps I’m not.

The library is dark, and more than a little unsettling, before I turn on one of the lamps on the end table. Orange-yellow light floods the room. There are stacks of books everywhere, piled haphazardly in a system I can’t begin to fathom. The wingback chair sits against the bookshelf still, her footprints in the red leather cushions.

She’d only managed to get a few of the books down, it seems.

It really is bad foresight that Elias didn’t even give her a step stool, but then I remember that I’m supposed to be helping her organize the library. I would have been said step stool, apparently.

On the balcony, she had laughed and said she didn’t mind being short. “Besides, it makes reaching upper cabinets a game of parkour.”

“I’d reach them for you, if you’d ask.”

“Would I have to ask?”

“No.”

With a sigh, I push the wingback chair to the side and reach for the books. I take them down, two at a time, and pile them up on the chair where she can see them tomorrow. Then I turn off the lights again and close the door, as if I was never there.

ROSIE

I DUMP MY BOOKBAG DOWN at the threshold of the library and run my fingers along the spines of the books like I do every weekday, saying hello to them. Nothing quite takes my breath away like the library every time I walk in. It's the slant of the sun coming through the two large windows. It's the way the light flickers off the motes of dust that drift through the room. It's the smell of old paperbacks, filling every shelf like hundreds of secret stories from a galaxy far, far away, beckoning me to settle into every page, explore every planet, fall in love over and over again with Carmindor and Amara and Euci and Zorine and, yes, even Ambrose Sond.

Everything is as I left it, like time stops between my visits. There is nothing here but space, and words, and magic. A certain kind of impossible magic, where words people have written years and years ago exist still.

As I round one side of the library, I pause when I notice the books stacked in the wingback chair—the same ones I'd been trying to reach yesterday when Vance walked in and startled me.

I guess things move after all.

I flip open the iPad on the desk and begin my work—I go in order, systematically finding the next book in the series and noting how damaged it is. Some books are rare enough that it doesn't matter how damaged they are—as long as they're legible and still in one piece, they go into the system.

A knock on the door startles me out of my work, and Mr. Rodriguez pokes his head into the library. "I'm heading out for a bit to grab some groceries for dinner. Ravioli good for tonight?"

"You don't have to feed me—"

"I know, but you've been doing such a good job, and I always make too much."

"Well, if you put it that way—I can eat my weight in ravioli. Also, thanks. You know, for the help."

"Don't thank me, I always love feeding people." He gives me a thumbs-up and leaves before I can explain that I was thanking him for getting the books down for me.

I finish my detailed work of volume 12 of the *Starfield* saga—*The Cassius Sun*—and place it on the shelf in order behind volume 11, and search for the dreaded number 13.

But . . . it's not on the shelf, or in any of the cardboard boxes.

At first I think it's just a gap in the books because of their different sizes, but the longer I look for volume 13, the more I begin to wonder if it's even here at all. Most of the books are scattered across the various shelves—volume 1 might be beside the Noxian Guilt series (or volume 73, if you don't section the series out into their respective arcs).

I look through the various shelves and a few of the cardboard boxes one last time just to make sure, but it's not there.

Maybe Mr. Rodriguez has it? I mean, since he took the books off the top shelf last night, and I can't very well ask him right now, since he's not home.

The volume has to be here somewhere. Mr. Rodriguez had said that it was a complete collection, after all, but I can't find it anywhere. Maybe he'll know where it is.

I take out my phone out of my back pocket to call Mr. Rodriguez. It rings twice before he answers.

"Um, hi—I'm sorry to bother you," I say, twisting a lock of my hair nervously.

He laughs into the phone—he sounds somewhere loud and busy. Then I hear the sound of my old manager over the intercom. Ah. The grocery store. My old nemesis. "No worries! What do you need?"

"Um, well—I can't find one of the books? I've looked through all of the boxes and . . ."

"Hmm, maybe Vance borrowed one? I did see him sneaking into the library last night, so maybe he wanted a read."

My heart sinks into my toes. "Oh."

"It's fine. Just pop up there and ask him for the book. He won't bite."

Right. He won't be *him*. Me, on the other hand? He'd probably yeet me straight out the window if he could. "Oh, okay. Thank you."

"I'll be home in a while—good luck!"

Great, I'll need it.

I hang up and shove my phone into my back pocket. Well, there's one mystery solved. I guess I have to confront him in his own territory, which might just be the death of me.

But I will do anything for a book.

"Screw your courage to the sticking place, Rosie," I tell myself as a pep talk, and pour myself a glass of lemonade just to . . . you know, prolong my imminent demise. I know I'm being overly dramatic, but I really don't want to go upstairs to confront Vance, but then again I don't . . . *not* . . . want to go up there. I'm a tiny bit curious. And besides, if he does yeet me out the window, I'll just drag him with me.

I flip through one of the magazines on the counter—*People* and *Star*—as I drink my lemonade. At least one of them has a story about Vance on the cover, and I flip to the page even though I already know what it's about.

WHEN IT REIGNS, IT POURS, the cheesy headline reads, detailing some rumors that have cropped up over the last week. About Vance losing a role in the next James Bond movie, about the (probably fake) talks of CW restructuring *Veten Rule* to write his character out of it. About Natalia Ford's radio silence on whether Sond is returning for the third installment of the franchise—and whether the third installment will be the last thanks to a merger with Disney.

I wonder why Vance keeps them around. I get hives when someone subtweets about me. I can't imagine what it's like to have entire articles printed—mostly untrue, I assume—about me for the entire world to read.

Maybe that's why he doesn't care for me? Because he thinks I also subtweet and buy into all that gossip?

That's silly, especially since he doesn't even know me.

As I finish my lemonade, I realize I can't prolong my appointment with the man upstairs any longer, and embark for the stairs on the other side of the house. I mean, I haven't heard Vance since I got in today, so maybe he isn't here, anyway! He might be out for a walk with his abs. Or running his glutes. Or, I don't know, taking his pecs for a spin.

One can only hope.

I hold my breath and creep up the stairs.

When I reach the top, the entire floor is quiet, and I realize

I don't quite know *which* room is Vance's. Which . . . I guess I should've asked Mr. Rodriguez about before we hung up. There aren't *that* many rooms in the house, so it shouldn't be hard to find. The first room on the left is sparse and neat, with a bed in the far corner, covers turned down and pillows fluffed. This must be Mr. Rodriguez's room, neat and orderly just like him. There is a photograph of him and an older woman who looks like she might be his *abuela*, but otherwise the room is empty, save for the neatly hung clothes in the closet.

They really aren't planning to stay here very long.

The other three rooms are an office, an unused bedroom, and a bathroom. But no book. The last door at the end of the hall is cracked open, and I give a tentative knock before I poke my head inside.

As I thought, it's Vance's bedroom, and it looks like a hurricane went through it. The gray comforter is bunched in the middle of the bed, and the pillows are strewn haphazardly across it, like someone who has a hard time getting to sleep. There are clothes piled on the floor and a fifty-inch TV screen with the television logo softly bouncing from one corner to the other. There's a gaming console hooked up to it, and a Game Boy lying on the floor, screen glowing as a Pikachu wiggles left to right, ready to fight a Hitmonchan. The eight-bit Indigo League music that flooded my childhood sings softly from its mini-speakers.

Huh, I didn't realize he played video games. Or that he was that much of a *nerd*. I bite the inside of my cheek to keep from smiling because I will not smile for Vance Reigns. I will not. I wholeheartedly refuse.

Now where is that book?

I cautiously begin to pick over his things, feeling a bit like Indiana Jones stealing some precious artifact from a remote region he definitely *doesn't* belong in, but it isn't on his nightstand, or his couch, or his bookshelf.

As I turn toward the dresser, a black mask catches my eye. As I creep closer, even in the darkness of the room, I recognize it. Because it hasn't changed in the month since I've seen it. It actually feels like yesterday. But it can't be the same one, can it? Outlined in glimmering gold, speckled with the constellation of Ambrose Sond's home galaxy.

No, it can't be.

But who else would have—

"What are you doing in here?"

A knot forms in my throat.

Slowly, I glance over my shoulder, his mask in my hands.

Vance stands in the doorway in dark gray sweatpants and a cotton T-shirt spread tight over his shoulders. There are spots of sweat on his chest and under his arms, and his platinum hair is pulled up into a bun, stray hairs plastered to his neck. At his heels is Sansa, sitting with her pink tongue lolling out of her mouth, fresh from a run.

He looks like I feel—surprised and betrayed and . . .

It can't be him.

It *can't* be.

As my mind denies, denies, and denies again, his eyes sharpen until they could cut through the space-time continuum and blast me into the netherverse. "What are you doing in my room?"

"I—I came to look for—for . . ."

For a book.

Not you.

And at the same time I think, *I found you.*

I wasn't looking.

But I found you.

"Please leave," he says, stepping out of the doorway. His voice is surprisingly soft, and the edges are shaking. As if I'd stumbled upon a secret he never wanted me to know.

But why?

My mind is reeling as I make my way out of his room.

He clears his throat, and I glance back. "The mask," he says, outstretching his hand.

Oh—I'm still holding it?

I quickly give it back to him. "Why didn't you tell me?"

He holds it tight to his chest. "Because I'm not who you pictured, am I?"

No, definitely not. Not at all. But the guy I did picture—lovely and patient and kind—has evaporated from my imagination, leaving nothing but the raw look of an unwashed Vance Reigns in his wake. "I—I don't know what I pictured," I manage to say.

Which is a lie.

And he knows it. He reads me like an open book.

He scoffs. "Oh, I'm sure I'm exactly who you pictured then, aren't I? Vance Reigns, the guy who can't get one thing right, who ruins everything, who screws up every good thing he gets."

Oh.

"You aren't denying it," he adds to my silence.

I bite the inside of my cheek again and whirl back around on my heel to leave. If I say anything else, I know I'll regret it. I'm angry and confused and wishing I hadn't come up here at all. If I hadn't, then I would've never found out the truth. The spell wouldn't be broken.

And it occurs to me—

He probably thinks the same.

He realized it was me, and wished he hadn't.

I hurry down the stairs. I'll tell Mr. Rodriguez I had to leave early today. I don't want to stay anymore. My eyes are burning and I refuse—*refuse*—to cry in front of this jackass. But I can't seem to shake him, either, because he follows quick on my heels.

"Wait a moment," he says as I leave.

"Fine! You're right! You *aren't* what I pictured—" As I whirl back to him, I don't realize how close my heel is to the edge of the step until I no longer feel the ground, and by then it's far too late. Try as I might, pinwheeling my arms, I can't keep myself from falling backward—so I grab onto the only thing I can:

Vance Reigns.

And I pull him down with me.

VANCE

WITH A PAINFUL GROAN, I roll off my side and onto my back. I had to twist myself to the side so I wouldn't land on top of her, and my shoulder stings from the impact. I suck in a painful breath and push myself to sit up, and once I figure that I'm not broken anywhere, I turn around and snap at her, "Can't you stop falling off things for *two* seconds!"

But she's already trying to get to her feet—and something's wrong. She's leaning too heavily against the wall, favoring her right foot, but she's still trying to walk. Her back is turned to me so I can't see her face. Before I realize what I'm doing, I'm rushing to my feet.

"Oi, you're hurt," I say, reaching for her elbow to steady her.

She wrenches away from my touch, her eyes wide. Tears fleck her long brown eyelashes, and they make me pause. She's crying. I've never been very good with people crying. She quickly rakes her hands over her eyes, smudging her liner.

"I'm leaving, d-don't worry—" She tries to take another step, but her ankle gives.

I catch her, and bend down, pulling my other arm underneath her legs, and swoop her up into my arms. She yelps and wraps her arms tightly around my neck. If she tells me to put her down, I will, but she doesn't, so I carry her over to the couch and set her down on the cushions, before I go find an ice pack. Elias put one in the refrigerator a while ago when he burned his hand in the oven. I hope it's still—ah, there it is, right on top of the peas, where he left it. I grab it, and the first-aid kit underneath the sink, and quickly return to the living room, where she's trying to get up off the couch.

"*Sit*," I command.

"I'm not a dog," she snaps in reply, to which Sansa—being a good girl on her dog bed in the corner of the living room—gives a *haroomp* and flops over.

I try again: "*Please* sit down."

She hesitates, halfway between standing and leaning on the couch for support, but she must weigh her options in favor of sitting, because she slowly sinks back down onto the cushions. I go around the couch and sit opposite her, reaching for her foot, when she knocks my hand away.

"Do you want me to look at your foot or not?"

"*Not* would be preferable."

"I should at least take a look at the swelling," I say.

She hesitates again, and then she squares her shoulders and gives a single nod.

I gently lift her foot to my lap. "Elias taught me," I say before she can ask. "Said if I wanted to do my own stunts, might as well learn how to treat myself, too. He went to school for nursing. Said it wasn't his calling—not enough pain-in-the-ass rich white kids."

"I can't believe he gave up nursing to be your babysit—*ah*!" she gasps as I feel the underside of her foot, and bites her bottom lip hard enough to leave a white bloodless indentation.

"Well, good news," I say after a moment, running my fingers gently along her ankle. "I think it's fatal."

She gives me a withering look. "You're the worst."

"So I'm always reminded. I think it's only sprained, but when Elias comes back we can take you to the emergency room."

She looks away, frowning. "I think it'll be fine."

"It might not be."

To that she huffs, but she doesn't rebuke me again. I gently wrap her ankle with an Ace bandage and prop it up on the coffee table, and go rifling into the first-aid box. "Want some pain relievers? Are you allergic to anything?"

"You."

I offer her a bottle of ibuprofen and the ice pack. "Who isn't?"

She frowns, shifting uncomfortably again, though I can't tell whether it's from her ankle or something else. ". . . Are *you* okay?" she finally asks.

That surprises me. "Oh. Yeah. Of course I am."

The garage door opens, and Elias comes in, laden with two bags of groceries. "Is that Rosie's car still out front?" He rounds into the kitchen when he sees us on the couch in the living room. Then he notices the ice on her ankle, and the first-aid box, and drops the groceries on the ground. He turns an accusing eye to me. "What did you *do*?"

I give him a withering look.

Honestly, not *everything* is my fault.

Except for, maybe, this.

ROSIE

THE POLITE (AND INCREDIBLY HOT) ER NURSE said that my ankle was sprained, so he gave me crutches and told me not to lean on my foot too much over the next few days. Which meant that I would go from uncool to *super* uncool, especially when my dad insisted on taking me to school, which was mortifying enough when your dad is the Super Hot Dad that everyone thirsts over (the last time he graced the halls was for an open house, and the theater kids nearly erected a shrine in his honor), but because I picked Quinn and Annie up every morning, he also offered to take *them* to school, too.

I want to die.

"Space Dad taking us to school is a blessing in disguise," Annie says with a sigh, pressing her hands together in prayer. "My crops are watered and my skin is clear."

I wish I could hobble faster into the school, but alas, crutches only have one speed—painstakingly slow. In the carpool lane, Dad pokes his head out of the window and yells, "Make good choices! Bye, Rosebud!"

I try to ignore him, but Quinn and Annie wave back with, "Bye, Space Dad!"

Traitors.

As Dad pulls away—earning a few looks from some of my classmates in the drop-off area—Quinn and Annie catch up to me. A part of me wonders if I can just toss the crutches and deal with the pain, but as soon as I try to stand on my foot, a sharp jab shoots up my ankle. Nope—no. Bad idea, abort mission.

Quinn holds the breezeway door open for me as I navigate my crutches inside, Annie bringing up the rear. "Hey, maybe Space Dad can do a PSA for me and I can get it aired on the morning announcement," they say.

Annie gasps. "That's an *excellent* idea!"

"No, it's not," I deadpan, but neither of them listens to me as they slowly meander with me to my and Annie's lockers. "Y'all—*aaahh*—" My nose tickles, and I let out a sneeze that almost tips me over my crutches.

"Whoa there," Annie says, steadying me. "You aren't getting sick, are you?"

I sniff and rub my nose. "The ER was crawling with snot-year-olds last night."

Quinn makes a crossing motion with their fingers toward me. "Don't give it to me! I have to go on the announcements tomorrow morning for a Homecoming thing, and the Space Dad PSA was a joke."

"Oh, so I *can't* snot all over you?"

"Negatory, Bob—oh, that reminds me." They fish something out of their backpack and hold it up to me triumphantly. "Here, take this. My mom swears by it. Remember when I got that cold this summer? I took this and—"

"It kicked the demons right out," Annie fills in.

"Something like that," Quinn agrees. "It works."

I flip over to the back of the packet and read the ingredients. "This is basically orange sugar water."

"Don't spill it on a white shirt," they advise. "You can also dye things with it."

"And you want me to *drink* it?"

"Well, if you don't want it, give it back."

"I never said that." I slip it into my back pocket. I'm not opposed to some questionable medicines, honestly, even if it is just glorified Kool-Aid. "Too bad it can't heal my ankle."

Annie closes her locker and asks, "How did you end up spraining it, anyway?"

I took a tumble down the stairs while trying to get away from Vance Reigns, who I found out was the guy I had been dreaming about for the last month, I want to say, but then that'll just birth more questions, like *What dreams?* and *When did you meet him?* and *Is that what you did when we couldn't find you at ExcelsiCon?*

And I would rather not answer any of those questions. Not because I don't love them, and trust them, but because . . .

Because it was mine. The moment, the night. It was *mine*. I know that's selfish, and it's silly, but I was afraid that if I told them about Sond and that night, then it would just . . . disappear. That it would just become a thing that happened, not this magical dream that existed in my memories. I knew I'd never meet him again, and I'd never learn his name, and we'd go about our lives and never cross paths again and . . .

Fool me once, universe. Fool me *once*.

"I fell reaching for a book," I lie.

Quinn scrunches their nose. "Isn't Vance supposed to help you?"

I give a one-shouldered shrug. I don't want to think about Vance. I don't want to think about how long he'd known I was the girl from the ball, because then I'll just think about why he didn't say anything earlier, and isn't the answer obvious? Because he didn't like that it was me. That's the only reason I can think of.

I hike my bookbag onto my shoulder and push my crutches under my arms again. "Let's get to class before we're late—again."

A PART OF ME DOESN'T WANT TO GO into the castle-house today. Not even to see the books. And because I can't drive—well, more like my dad refused to let me—he picks me up, having taken a late lunch, and drops me off at the estate. And I can't tell him that I don't want to go today because then I'd have to admit that I lied to him about how I broke my ankle, and he's already rooting for me to quit—I think he still has his checkbook in his suit pocket to whip out at any moment—and as I keep saying:

I am stubborn as hell. It's part of my charm.

He glances up the driveway as I open the door and toss my crutches out. "You know, Elias will probably let you off today if you want to just go home."

"I'll be fine, Dad."

"But—"

"I'm *fine*," I repeat, pushing myself out of his car. I grab my bookbag and close the door behind me. Dad doesn't linger for very long, because he's on a rather tight lunch break, but he does give me one last look—to make sure that I'm certain—before he drives off.

As I crutch my way up the driveway, I glance up to see if there's any movement in Vance's window, praying that he took Sansa out for a very long walk, and there's nothing. Maybe he's out exploring the town—for *once*.

I head into the kitchen, where Mr. Rodriguez is checking on something in the oven. "Whatever you're cooking smells incredible," I tell him as I dump my bookbag on the island barstool.

"It's a secret tamale recipe passed down from my *abuela*," he replies, wiping his hands on a towel that he then throws over his shoulder. He's wearing a pale pink button-down today and gray chinos. "I made enough, if you want to stay for dinner."

"My dad's expecting me home. We're having Chinese tonight."

Mr. Rodriguez perks. "Oh? He cooks?"

I laugh. "I wish! I'm picking up Chinese from the place down the street, is what I meant. Their egg rolls are to *die* for."

"Ooh, I've been meaning to try that place!"

"Highly recommend." And then—though I don't know why—I add, "Maybe we can all do dinner one night and order out."

The moment those words leave my mouth, I think I should regret them, but I . . . don't? Dad needs some friends, and Mr. Rodriguez *looks* about my dad's age, but I really can't tell with any man over twenty-five. They all look old to me, and it doesn't help that he's always smiling and whistling, and a part of me can't believe that he hasn't quit working for the likes of He-Who-Must-Not-Be-Named yet. He's like a bubbly Hufflepuff.

Then again, I heard Slytherins and Hufflepuffs go together like peas in a pod.

Mr. Rodriguez grins. "I think that's a great idea. We should plan that."

"I'll let him know." My watch beeps. Four o'clock. "I should probably get to work."

"Have fun!—Oh!" he adds as I turn toward the library. "The bathroom downstairs is out for the day. We're having a plumber coming in to fix it but he hasn't shown up yet," Mr. Rodriguez says, wiping his hands on his *KISS ME, I'M NOXIAN* apron. "You can use Vance's upstairs if you don't mind the stairs? I'm sorry for the inconvenience," he adds, eyeing my crutches.

"I'll be fine," I scoff in reply, because I can hold my pee with the best of them, and there's no way I'm ever going back upstairs. My curiosity is sated, after all.

After what happened last night, I half expected Vance to order Mr. Rodriguez to fire me the second I walked in the door, but Mr. Rodriguez doesn't seem to be doing that, so either Vance doesn't hate me, or he has no power over me.

I like the second option even better than the first, really.

Doing anything in the library today ends up being an absolute pain. I end up propping my crutches against one of the chairs and just taking it slow as I unpack a series of fantasy books from one of the boxes. The volume I had been looking for yesterday ended up being at the bottom of a stack of books on the desk, which was fun to discover, but I push that out of my head—along with the thought that maybe it *wasn't* Mr. Rodriguez who took the books off the top shelf for me the other day—and work.

Around 5:30 p.m., however, the bottle of water I chugged after school creeps up on me. I tried it with a little of Quinn's magic medicine, but I only used half of the packet and it tasted so bad I couldn't bring myself to dump the rest in.

And now here I am, ready to pee myself because I don't want to go upstairs to use Vance's bathroom.

But I can't suffer for another thirty minutes, so I make the hard decision: I will take a warp-speed pee break and return long before Vance ever comes home from his walk with Sansa and finds out that I went tinkle on his throne. With my crutches in tow, I quickly hurry my way across the house and up the stairs to the second floor, to the bathroom at the end of the hall.

I close the door behind me and quickly do my business. There's shaving cream on the bathroom counter, and toothpaste, mouthwash, a cheap razor—all the things my dad has on his bathroom counter. With the exception of the orange hair wrap sitting on the sink.

After I wash my hands, I turn to leave when I realize the packet of orange not-Kool-Aid has fallen out of my pocket. I pick it up, about to stick it back into my jeans, when I realize I had forgotten that I had opened it a few hours ago. And . . . it goes *everywhere*.

"*Crap!*" I curse, grabbing the orange hair wrap, and scrub the powder out of the sink and the tiles before it has time to dye anything orange. Thank God it's one of those fast-absorbing towels.

I don't want to ruin anything else in this house.

Least of all the marble countertops.

VANCE

As I jog back toward the house, I don't see the eyesore of a hatchback, so the girl must not have come today. Did Elias *actually* fire her? Or even if she just decided not to show up, it doesn't matter. I would be fine either way, I'm just glad she isn't *here*.

I'm not quite sure how much longer I can stay out in this heat before I get heatstroke. It's almost October and it has barely gotten below thirty-five degrees Celsius—erm, ninety-five degrees Fahrenheit, I guess.

"Tamales tonight," Elias says, stopping me in the kitchen.

"Delicious." I pluck out my earbuds and take the lead off Sansa. She springs into the living room with boundless energy and face-plants into the couch.

"You've been gone for a while."

"Just out running," I reply, opening the refrigerator to get a bottle of water. I unscrew it and toss the cap into the recycling by the island counter. The hair that fell out of my ponytail is sticking to my neck, and all I want to do is go take a shower.

Down the hall, the library door is open and I can hear—humming?

A chill curls down my spine.

"She's still *here*?" I ask before I can rein my surprise in.

Elias blinks. "Well, of course. Her father hasn't picked her up yet. She can't drive *herself*."

Ah. Right.

Stupid me. Of course Elias wouldn't fire her.

I down the rest of my water and toss the bottle into the recycling as I pass. If I didn't know she was here, then she probably hasn't realized I've returned, either. I'd rather keep it that way. I hurry up the stairs as quickly as I can and close the door to the bathroom.

Why am I running away from a girl in my own house? Why was I so terrified when she found that mask yesterday? Why am I *still*?

Because she can go to the tabloids, I tell myself. *Because she can make things worse for you, and you don't need things worse right now.*

The shower, at the very least, is cold enough to shock the thoughts out of me. I sigh and press my forehead against the cool tiles. The cold water and quiet gets my head on straight again as I wash my hair. Can't really recall the last time I properly washed it—when did I arrive here again? Two weeks ago? Time goes so slow in this town, in this house, day after day.

Lately, though, I've been too busy worrying about that girl down in the library.

And what she thinks of me.

I'm scrubbing my hair with the towel to dry it when my reflection catches my eye. Something is off. Slowly, I pull the towel off my head. The same face stares back. Nothing out of the ordinary, except . . .

ROSIE

A SCREAM EXPLODES FROM THE BATHROOM UPSTAIRS.

Uh-oh.

There's a clattering noise, and loud footsteps rush across the ceiling. I hear him storm down the stairs. "WHERE IS SHE?" he yells, his voice cracking with either rage or tears, I'm not sure which one.

Tears, please tears, the barbaric part of me cheers.

Even though I don't know what for.

I hear Mr. Rodriguez start saying, "Why would you—" before something loud crashes in the kitchen, as if he dropped whatever he was holding. "*Dios mío*," he gasps, "what happened to your *hair*?"

Oh—oh no.

Before I can drop the book I'm holding—the seventeenth volume of *Starfield*—and dive under the desk, he storms into the library wearing nothing but a towel wrapped around his waist and fury in his eyes.

Oh.

My God.

His hair . . . his hair is . . .

He jabs a finger at me. *"YOU!"*

His hair is orange. Not like a nice rose-gold sort of orange, brassy with the softest hints of sunrise, but . . . like . . .

Orange.

"YOU DID THIS!"

No I didn't, I think. But then, like a flashback reel in my head, I remember the exact moments leading up to this very scene. Me in the bathroom. Me dropping the vitamin C packet. Me using the orange towelette on the sink to mop it up.

I . . . definitely did it. By accident. Not that he'll believe me. So, as a guilty party would do, I step behind the wingback chair to put some, um, distance between me and someone who definitely totally completely wants to murder me.

"I'm sorry!" I squeak.

Yep, definitely a confession.

"LOOK AT THIS! LOOK AT MY *HAIR*!" he cries, rushing into the library. He pulls at his shoulder-length orange-pop hair. It's like someone spilled an entire highlighter on his head. And I *drank* that? Oh yikes.

You can practically see him from space.

"It's . . . uh . . . not that . . . bad?" I offer.

"It's not that *bad*?" he howls, and covers his hands with his face. He falls into the wingback chair dramatically, and his towel slips a little. I quickly avert my gaze. "I'm *hideous*."

"You're not hideous." Mr. Rodriguez tries to reason with him, following him into the library. He gives me a questioning look to see if yes, I am the perpetrator of this great and terrible sin. Yes, yes I am.

By absolute accident, mind you.

"No one will ever like me," Vance goes on, his voice muffled by his hands.

"I like you," his guardian says patiently.

"What's the point if I can't be beautiful?"

I squint at him. "Are you quoting *Howl's Moving Castle*?"

In reply, he gives another anguished wail and flops half of himself over the side of the armrest. The towel is doing a very terrible job of covering anything up, and I gently pull it over his nether region so he won't have to disgrace himself.

Mr. Rodriguez says, "It'll be fine. Whatever happened, it can't be permanent, and it doesn't look *terrible*. Remember how cute that woman from that pop-punk band you like was with orange hair? Same thing."

"It's not," he mumbles in reply.

A strange smokiness tinges my nose. "Mr. Rodriguez . . . is something burning?"

"My *tamales*!" he cries, then spins on his heel and darts out of the library and back into the kitchen.

After he's gone, I hear Vance groan and lean back in the chair. "I don't know how I'm going to explain this to my publicist."

I don't know, either, but I'm sure he doesn't want my opinion.

The doorbell rings. It's my dad, right on time. So I take my crutches, shove them under my arms, and begin to leave Vance dejected and alone with his orange hair in the library. I pause at the door, though, and glance back.

"If I told you it was an accident, would you believe me?" I ask.

In reply, he pointedly looks away.

No, I guess I wouldn't believe me, either.

PART THREE

FRIEND

Ambrose runs his fingers down the slender length of Amara's neck. They are alone on the observation deck, and he watches as gooseflesh prickles over the princess's soft skin.

"Do you really want to spend the rest of your life on that small little planet, ruling from a throne, watching the stars from a distance?" Ambrose asks softly. "Aren't you going to miss this?"

This being the view from the observation deck. This being the countless stars spread across the sky. This being nights like tonight, when the skies are wide and the universe impossible.

This being alone together.

This being something that will never happen again.

Amara shrugs out of Ambrose's grip. "The view is better on the south side of Metron," she replies almost apologetically, but it's all Ambrose needs to hear.

He looks away, trying to keep himself composed, pursing his lips tightly. He's the Starbright General, after all, the slaughterer of legions, the hero of the Avaril Nebula, and the Noxian King's greatest spy. For a moment he had forgotten that. "Very well, my princess."

Then the princess curtsies, and leaves him on the observation deck with all of the stars in the sky—alone.

He's meant to be alone, anyway.

She is a disaster. That's all there is to it.

At least she doesn't come over on the weekends, and I can burrito myself onto the couch and fester in my cocoon of depression without her nosing through my entire life.

"Stop brooding and sit up," Elias says with an exasperated sigh. Sansa starts sniffing at my face. I push her away, but she just sticks her nose right into my ear—and licks it.

"*Argh*," I moan, pushing her away, and rub my hand against my ear.

Sansa sits down, her tail swishing back and forth like a duster, looking at me as though she had not just invaded my inner ear's privacy. "I hate her," I mumble.

"I know."

"I don't mean the dog."

"You don't mean it."

I melt back into the couch and stare at television. There is a photo of Darien Freeman on *Entertainment Tonight*, walking beside the pop singer who did that unicorn music video. Thalia, or something. They're talking about whether he's dating her. I don't even have to read their lips—I recognize the kind of story it is, a quick news flash of speculation. Only, I'm more accustomed to me being the focal point of those segments.

Elias sighs and turns the channel to *Jeopardy!*, and a black woman chooses Originals in TV Shows—"For six hundred, Alex," she adds.

The tile changes to the question, "This actress was the original Princess Amara in the hit television series *Starfield*."

"Natalia Ford, obviously," Elias mutters. "That's too easy."

I make a wrong-buzzer noise. "Ellen North."

And the woman answers, "Who is Ellen North?"

"Correct!" Alex congratulates her, and the woman earns six hundred glorious dollars.

Elias gives me a sidelong look. "How did you know that?"

"Everyone knows Ellen North was in the pilot episode of *Starfield*, but she was replaced by Natalia for the rest of the seasons," I reply, turning onto my side. My feet hang off the end of the couch because no one makes furniture for tall people anymore, apparently. "I do two things well: I burrito on weekends and I know things."

He frowns. "You *are* going to put pants on at least, aren't you?"

"My hair is orange."

"And you're still in Friday night's pajamas. It's Sunday."

"My *hair* is *orange*."

He throws his hands into the air. "And mine's beginning to fall out! We all have our problems, *mijo*."

"This isn't fair," I go on. "*I* can't leave, since my parents trapped me here, but you can very certainly make *her* leave—so why don't you? Clearly none of us are having any fun here."

"You parents didn't trap you here," he replies patiently.

"Then what's it called when you send your son to some nowhere town with a warden"—I throw my hand out to him—"and no money to get out? No credit cards? No cash? No anything? What do you call that?"

He gives a long sigh and shakes his head. "All right, *mijo*. When she comes in tomorrow, I'll let her know we no longer need her services."

I give a start. "What—really? You're firing her?"

"But you'll have to finish up organizing that library alone."

"A small price to pay!" I reply with a relieved laugh, surprised that he *finally* gave in.

As he leaves I feel just a little bit vindicated. Just for a moment. But the farther Elias gets, the less victorious I feel, until he's gone from the living room and the triumphant smile slides from my face, and I feel just as hollow as before, except with orange hair.

THAT NIGHT, MY ONLY FRIEND also feels the need to turn against me right in the middle of a battle royale. "You need to apologize to her," Imogen's tinny voice says through my headset as I get headshotted for the third time.

DEATH IS ETERNAL! the caption reads as the camera rotates around my lifeless corpse.

I drop my controller and hang my head. "She dyed my *hair*, Imogen. Isn't that retribution enough?"

"You purposefully kept a secret from her," adds another voice—male. Imogen's boyfriend, Ethan. I watch as his character comes over to mine and takes all of my ammo and supplies and runs on to the next objective. "It's really simple. You just go up and tell her 'I'm sorry.'"

"But I'm not in the wrong," I try to argue.

"Oh yeah, you are," Imogen replies.

"Because I didn't want her to know that I was that guy at ExcelsiCon?" I respawn at the next checkpoint and jump off the sandy cliff and into the fray again. "Excuse me if I didn't want to ruin my image."

"*Starflame*. Self-absorbed much?"

That ticks me off. "What's so self-absorbed with letting her have her fantasy? What do you think she thought, Imogen, when she realized it was me?"

"Maybe that she was happy she finally found you?" Ethan challenges.

"Or maybe she thought—oh! Let me go to the tabloids!" When they begin to argue I add, "Whatever—I don't expect you two to understand."

Imogen asks, "Because we don't always see the worst in people?"

"Mo," her boyfriend warns.

"What?" she says. "It's the truth. Maybe you need a friend—like we're friends, obviously—but someone else. Maybe Natalia is making her work there because she agrees."

A *friend*—why is everyone coddling me, thinking that I'm not acutely aware of the choices I make?

I grit my teeth. "Yeah, and do you also think I needed to get away from LA? That it was *good* of me to live in some—some *nowhere* town?"

"I'm not saying that, Vance."

"You don't have to because my stepfather already did," I snap.

"All I'm saying is those stupid friends of yours in LA made you jaded and untrusting and that's not who friends are. People aren't out to find the worst in you, Vance. I thought you would've figured that out by now—"

Someone headshots me for the fourth time, and I give up. Both on this conversation and on the game. I'm too angry to play, anyway. "Forget it. I'm leaving."

"Vance—"

"Good game," I add absently, and sign off before she can say anything else. I wrench off my headset and bury my face in my hands. Because a small part of me thinks—for a moment—Imogen might be right.

And I can't bear to think about that.

ROSIE

I PARK IN FRONT OF THE CASTLE-HOUSE on Monday afternoon, but I don't turn off the car. I've half a mind to just kick my good ole hatchback into gear and drive straight home. Let Dad pay off the rest of the book fee—even though it's probably still more than we can afford. I'll find a different job to pay him back. I'll even resort to Craigslist and risk getting murdered by some Hydra-hailing Ted Bundy with an alarming collection of *The Killing Joke* and the Reddit username FIGHTTHESJWS to find another copy of that waterlogged priceless volume of *Starfield*.

Honestly, that sounds at least a little more exciting than just the *thought* of facing Vance Reigns again. Vance Reigns, who was my mystery prince at ExcelsiCon, the guy I'd been daydreaming about—stupidly daydreaming about.

Because I'm such a fool.

"Pull yourself together, Thorne," I tell myself. "You can do this. He's just a guy. A very hot . . . very tall . . . very good-looking . . . *asshole*." I thump my head against the steering wheel and accidentally honk the horn.

I jerk back in my chair, and quickly turn off the car.

Okay.

Amara up, Rosie. You can do this.

Just march in there, like Amara's gonna march on the Prospero *in the second movie, and take no shit from Vance Reigns. You have one goal, and he isn't it. And you're free of your crutches. You are strong and independent and—*

I take a deep steadying breath, grab my bookbag, and get out of the car.

Breathe in, breathe out.

You'll be okay. Just go in, do your job.

When I get to the door, I let myself in with the key under the mat. I dump my bookbag on the barstool where I always do, but Mr. Rodriguez is nowhere to be found. Usually, if he's gone when I come in, he leaves a note on the counter, but there isn't one today.

I wonder where he is.

"Mr. Rodriguez?" I call, wandering into the living room. I step outside onto the back patio with the pool, but he's not back here either, and neither is Sansa.

Where could they be?

I turn and grab the handle for the sliding glass door—but it won't budge. I try again. The door rattles.

And I realize: I've locked myself out.

A rumble of thunder rolls overhead.

VANCE

"ELIAS?" I CALL THROUGH THE HOUSE, but no one replies. I could have sworn I heard the front door open. But he isn't in the kitchen, and no one is in the library, so perhaps Rosie isn't here either. Did she decide to quit?

"Elias," I call again, stepping out into the backyard. The humid fall air is so thick it feels like walking into a mouth. The day is dark with thunderclouds, purple and heavy with rain. In the distance, the clouds rumble. I don't want to be out here longer than I already am. It looks like it might rain any moment. "Elia—"

From the pool area, Rosie scrambles from one of the chairs, pale and wide-eyed. "No! Don't close the—"

The door slides shut behind me.

"—door . . ." she finishes glumly.

Why would she not want me to . . . *oh*. My stomach drops into my toes as I spin around and try the door. But it's locked. I can't believe this. How stupid can I be? I sigh and turn back to her. "I assume it was you I heard coming in?" I say.

"Probably," she replies, nervously twisting the class ring on her finger.

"And you haven't seen Elias either, have you."

She shakes her head. So that means he hasn't broken the news to her yet, either. Great. I curse under my breath and give one last tug. Still nothing. The glass in the door rattles with the force.

We are officially locked outside.

"Maybe the front door is unlocked by some glorious twist of fate," I mutter, realizing that I don't even have *shoes* on, and start for the side of the house.

"I've already tried it. Can we talk?"

I ignore her.

"Vance."

When she says my name, I can't help but to stop. I glance over my shoulder at her. The clouds above us rumble again. "What could we possibly have to talk about?"

"You—you wish you'd never found out it was me, don't you," she forces out, and fists her hands. She raises her eyes to me defiantly. "Because I'm not who you imagined, am I?"

I roll my eyes. "Right, that's it—"

"I'm being serious!"

"And I'm—"

She grabs my arm roughly and jerks me around to face her, and squares her shoulders so she looks a little taller. Imogen was right—I know she was—I should have told this girl the moment I recognized that birthmark on her neck, but I purse my lips and look away. There are few things I enjoy less than confrontation.

"*Am I?*" she repeats. She steps up to me, and I ease back a little from our closeness. The freckles across her nose look like a constellation, and my eyes follow them down the dip of her nose to her bowlike mouth. She's strangely intimidating, like a squirrel with a butcher knife.

"N-no, that's not it," I find myself replying. "I didn't *tell* you because—"

"Oh, I'm sure it's because—"

"—you'd realize that it was—"

"—you found out that it was—"

"*—me*," we finish at the same time.

My eyebrows furrow. Her hazel eyes widen.

A crack of thunder streaks across the purple clouds, followed by a chest-rattling clap of thunder, and a raindrop lands on my cheek.

ANOTHER CRACK OF LIGHTNING streaks across the sky, and I tense up. I don't think. I grab Vance by the arm and tug him toward the pool house.

There is a brief moment of buzzing—wind rips through the trees. Then a sheet of rain, a gray wall of it, comes rushing across the yard. I throw my hands over my head to try to stop it, but I'm drenched in a matter of seconds. I *just* got my cowlick tamed, too. Vance is just as soaked, his thin white T-shirt stuck to his body like a second skin.

I shove my shoulder against the pool house door, praying it isn't locked. The door gives—thank *God*!—and we stumble inside. It's a small shed with a few pieces of furniture covered in plastic. The light switch on the left doesn't work, and the entire place smells like pollen and timber. The rain pounds against the roof like pebbles.

At least it's dry.

When he clears his throat, I come to my senses and quickly let go of him. Crap, I'm now stuck in a pool house with Vance for

God knows how long, and he's in a very wet shirt that clings to every curve of his broad shoulders and—

Stop it, Rosie, he's a jerk. You don't like jerks.

No, but I can still appreciate the view.

"The storm should pass soon, I think," I say, trying to get my mind off him.

"Mmh," he replies, and wanders over to one of the plastic-wrapped pieces of furniture and finds a barstool. He pulls the plastic off it, drags it up to the window, and sulkily sits down. Water drips from his shirt onto the cement floor, and a shiver runs through his entire body. He rubs his arms to keep out the chill.

Even though it's the end of September, climate change hit us with some late storms—probably the outer bands of Hurricane Diana. There are mounds and mounds of boxes behind the plastic-wrapped couch, so I figure there has to be a blanket (or at least an old towel) in one of them—and hopefully no snakes. Or spiders. God, I hate spiders.

I glance over his way as he sifts through the junk. *Do you actually mean it?* I want to ask. *That* I *wasn't the reason you didn't tell me who you were?*

But I don't know how to begin, so I busy myself looking through the boxes, opening one after the other, finding Christmas ornaments and Valentine decorations and Fourth of July banners from years and years past. I take out the head of a Santa Claus—just the head, not the body—before dropping it back into the box and moving on.

Creeeeeepy.

What is more unsettling, however, is the silence between us. Usually we're bickering—or at least snapping at each other—but this sort of heavy quiet is the *worst.*

Vance must think so too, because he finally says, "I didn't mean for you to get the wrong idea. It's not because of *you* I didn't tell you."

"You don't have to spare my feelings—"

"I'm not," he replies, turning to face me. He's wringing the bottom of his shirt out, like he's nervous. Him—*nervous*? Lightning must've struck me while I was outside. I must be dead. "I recognized the birthmark on your neck. It looks a little like a rose, so that's how I remembered it. It's cute."

Cute. I touch my birthmark beneath my ear, so glad it's dark enough for him not to see me blushing like mad. I dig further into the box and find a blanket.

"And I realized that I had already been terrible to you—well, that I'd just been terrible, period—and I didn't know what else to do. And, I think a part of me was afraid that if you found out it was me, you would go to the tabloids, and I do not need that right now. I'm *here* because of the tabloids. But . . ." He takes a deep breath. "I think the real reason was, though, was that I was afraid that if you found out it was me you would be . . ."

"That I would be . . . ?" I insist, turning to him.

He hesitates and sits down on a pool chair. ". . . Disappointed." His voice is so soft, like the whisper of a secret. I drag the blanket out of the box and crouch in front of him. He hesitates a look at me, cornflower blue eyes framed by blond eyelashes.

"That's funny," I say with a soft laugh, "because I thought you were disappointed that it was *me*."

He shakes his head. "No, never. You're perf—"

I toss the blanket over his head. It's an instinctive reaction. Like flinching away from a punch. Or screaming at a spider. But this is different. It's a compliment I want to hear, but don't, because while he sounds sincere, I don't know how much of him I trust.

At least not yet.

"Your man-nips said you were cold," I say, probably the least romantic thing I can think of, and leave him with the blanket.

He pulls it behind his head. He looks like he wants to say something else, but thank God he drops the romantic act. "Where did you find this?"

"In a box labeled 'Dead Grandma'—kidding. Over there."

"It looks dirty."

"It probably is."

He frowns, but it's too cold *not* to take it. He wraps it around his shoulders even though he clearly doesn't want to.

I shiver, but there was only one blanket in the box and I gave it up for the cause.

"You're cold," he says.

"Nah," I reply. There's a refrigerator into the corner, and though it's not plugged in, it's stocked, and I take out one of the sodas. A Coke. I don't know if sodas expire but why not. I drag up a barstool next to him and look out the window at the pouring rain. He eyes the Coke. "Where did you find that?"

"The fridge. Wanna try it?"

"Definitely not."

I shrug and pop open the tab. There is a little less fizz than usual. I sniff it. It doesn't smell rotten. I take a tentative sip, and it tastes like absolute ass, but I try to rein in my disgust and offer it to him again.

"C'mon, it's pretty good."

"If you poison me . . ." he warns me, and takes a swig of the Coke. "Bloody *hell*," he sputters, and quickly gives the soda back. "That tastes like motor oil!"

"It's terrible," I agree. "I'm pretty sure it expired like ten years ago."

"And you made me *try* it."

"You chose to," I point out.

"I was peer pressured," he replies indignantly, and we fall quiet.

We sit there in front of the window, watching sheets of rain cascade over the backyard, graying almost everything—the way a really heavy rain tends to do. Sansa is jumping across the yard, trying to eat the rain, as if she's never seen water fall from the sky before. The thunder doesn't even faze her.

I close my eyes and listen as another rumble rattles the small pool house. "My mom loved thunderstorms," I say. I don't know why I say it. I don't know why it matters.

After a moment, he replies, "So did my dad."

A flash of light—and then another rolling, long rumble of thunder.

"You, too?" I ask, but really I say, *You have a hole in your heart as well?*

He nods. "My biological father. I didn't know him very well, though. He died when I was pretty small, before I became the patron saint of disappointment."

I tilt my head, looking at him—really looking, for the first time since I met him. It's strange because I've memorized what he looks like from all of the promo posters and the movie trailers, but it doesn't hit me until just then how . . . *human* he looks. It's easy to forget that he isn't even eighteen yet. He's been in the spotlight since he was a kid. I watched him grow up in the newspapers and on television shows. His father—stepfather, I guess—is the CEO of some big Hollywood studio, and his mother is one of those gorgeous philanthropists you see heading charities in Las Vegas and LA. He didn't make it big, though, until his role on *The Swords of Veten Rule*, and by then he was already being treated like the adult actors who work beside him, so I hardly thought of him as someone my age. Someone who needed to make some mistakes to figure out how to make fewer of them.

And that reminded me of a conversation I had with him that night at ExcelsiCon. "Sometimes I feel like I'm trapped," he had said, picking around the onions in our hash browns. "I have these expectations on my shoulders, and I just keep screwing up and disappointing everyone."

"Well, you haven't disappointed me yet," I had replied, propping my head on my hand as I leaned on the table.

He gave a sad sort of smile behind his mask. "It'll just be a matter of time."

Is that why you didn't tell me? I want to ask. *Because you thought that I would be disappointed?* I know he didn't mean to run off the road with Elle Wittimer, and I know he didn't mean to break up her and Darien, and I begin to wonder, when are you able to learn and grow from a mistake—and when does it haunt you for the rest of your life?

As if he can sense what I'm thinking, he says quietly, almost too quiet to hear over the rain, "I didn't want this. Any of this. I make so many mistakes, and I ruin so many things. I guess that's why . . . back at ExcelsiCon, I didn't want us to take off our masks. I didn't want to ruin things because I think I—" But then he stops himself, and shakes his head. "It doesn't matter."

And, for a moment, the mask of Vance Reigns drops, and there's just a boy sitting here beside me, orange hair and too-blue eyes, looking more tired than he should.

I want to reach out and comfort him, but I curl my fingers into fists in my lap and keep them there. He was about to admit to me that I was perfect, but I can't say I feel the same about him. So what right do I have to reach out?

"You know . . ." I find myself saying. The rain is beginning to let up a little, a shaft of sunshine streaking through the sky beyond. "I like you when you aren't being a spoiled, selfish jerk."

He puts half of the blanket over my shoulder as I shiver again, and I quietly grab the edge, resigned to share the smelly, moldy blanket with him. "Maybe because you're not being as stubborn and insufferable as you usually are."

I roll the words over my teeth before I finally voice them. "We could . . . call a truce? I mean, I'll be working here for at least another few weeks, and honestly, I'd rather not hate you. So . . . what do you say?"

"It's not impossible," he replies, and turns his cornflower gaze to me. There's a glimmer of amusement there that makes my heart kick in my rib cage. It's nothing, I tell myself.

It's nothing at all.

VANCE

I CAN'T LET ELIAS FIRE HER.

I realize it as the rain lets up and we abandon the pool shed into the muggy afternoon sun. She's out the door first, stretching her arms wide as the sunlight hits her face. The rays catch in her brown hair, turning it to copper. There is a cowlick in her fringe that curls up at an odd angle, and I find myself fixated on it.

For someone so odd and infuriating, how did things change? And it would feel so awkward to tell her now—that oh, today was supposed to be your last day, pack up your things, you're gone—after I spent the better half of the afternoon with her. It strikes me then—out of the blue, like a bolt of lightning—how much of an insufferable jerk that *actually* makes me.

And while that realization surprises me—the fact that I am a jerk *doesn't*.

A knife twists in my chest.

I'm ashamed, and quickly I pry my eyes down to the wet grass. The humidity clings to me, and the embarrassment crawling up my cheeks just makes me more uncomfortable.

Why am I so *embarrassed*?

She squints at the sky. "That was such an unexpected way to spend the afternoon."

"Bad unexpected or . . . ?"

"Are you fishing for a compliment?"

My shoulders stiffen. "Of course not."

The edges of her lips quirk up into a smile. "I'm not sure what kind of afternoon it was yet."

But it wasn't bad, at least, I think, and as I do it makes my shame run deeper. Because why do I think I can enjoy an afternoon with a girl who I've all but insulted for the last week? I open my mouth to ask her when the sliding glass door opens and Elias pokes his head out. "There you two are! *Dios mío*, I thought you'd killed each other—why are you wet?"

Rosie laughs. "We locked ourselves out."

Elias *tsk*s. "Both of you? That's a surprise. Come on inside and get warm so you don't catch a cold. And Rosie, I need to speak with—"

"No!" I interrupt quickly. She gives me a strange look. So does Elias. I add, quickly, racking my brain for some excuse to my outburst, "No, we . . . won't catch a cold. Because Rosie found a blanket?"

That was terrible. I should feel ashamed.

But I hope Elias understands. He gives me a one-eyebrow-raised look, and then he smirks in that *I told you so* way. "Well, I'm glad you found a blanket. I have to get the groceries out of the car, so let yourselves inside, unless you want share that blanket a little longer," he says, and leaves the sliding door open for us.

I am mortified.

Rosie, for her part, seems oblivious as she runs her hands through her wet hair. "I should probably get going. I told Dad I'd eat some chocolate murder pancakes with him tonight."

"Sounds dangerous," I say.

She nods solemnly. "Double the chocolate, double the murder. I'll see you tomorrow, Vance?"

My skin prickles when she says my name, with a smile that is both secretive and brilliant. *Get a hold of yourself, mate. You aren't a schoolboy.*

"Tomorrow," I reply, but before she disappears into the house I add, "Hey, um . . ."

She pauses in the doorway, and glances back. "Yeah?"

I take a deep breath. Well, if I'm going to feel this way, I might as well do the things she wants. "Since we hit it off so well before, and clearly we don't hate each other, what do you say about . . . going out with me?"

She turns to me slowly, and her eyebrows furrow in this strange, disappointing sort of way. Did I say something wrong?

"We could go out as different people. I can pretend to be a hotshot American again," I add, adopting a midwestern accent—the same one I had the night we met—"and you can be—"

"I don't think so." Her voice is soft, a sigh. "I'm sorry, Vance."

And she disappears into the house, leaving me alone with this weird shiver across my skin, even as I rub my arms to make it disappear.

I don't understand.

I've always gotten everything that I ever wanted. All I've ever had to do was ask. Money. Cars. Dates. Even parts in studio movies.

I—I don't *understand*.

No, I *do*, but I don't want to admit it. And her no feels different from any breakup I instigated, or any friendship I ruined. I've always known what I wanted from someone—their fame, their lips, their companionship. But wanting anything of her feels wrong.

She said no.

And a strange part of me agrees.

I must have stood in the backyard for longer than any normal person, because Elias comes back outside to check on me, a kitchen towel over his shoulder. He leans against the side of the sliding glass door as Sansa squeezes her way in, wet fur and all.

Elias says, "Everything okay? She didn't lobotomize you while I was away?"

"What? Oh, no."

"Then did . . . something happen?" he asks. "I was going to fire her, you know."

"I know. I just—changed my mind."

"Oh?" He crosses his arms and leans against the doorway.

I take a deep breath. "Do you remember that night at the con in Atlanta? When I disappeared and didn't return until morning?"

"Your mother about killed me, of course I remember."

"You know the girl? The one I was with?"

His eyebrow shoot up. "It was *Rosie*?"

I nod, and find myself twisting my fingers nervously. "Um—you know me better than anyone, so I was wondering . . . how do . . . how . . ." I scrub the back of my neck, pursing my lips. *Get it together. You aren't like this.*

"You've dated a lot of people, I'm sure you don't need my expert coaching," Elias fills in with a shrug.

My stomach turns. "She said no."

"Oh?"

"Don't sound so shocked, please."

"Well, I just—I'm not, really," he replies. "I honestly can't blame her."

"Thanks."

He cocks his head. "Well, c'mon, you're going to help me make enchiladas tonight. You said you wanted to learn how, yes?"

I swallow the knot in my throat, and nod. "I'm terrible at cooking."

"And that is why we practice and say to the god of burnt food—not today."

Not today.

As I follow him back into the house to start the enchiladas, I catch my reflection in the sliding glass door. My T-shirt is still damp from the rainstorm, and my sweatpants hang on me heavily, and my orange-*ish* hair is wild and curling out from the sides of my head. I don't look like a prince of Hollywood right now. I am so used to having to entertain people. To use them. To be used. Dates with paparazzi, with scheduled outings and scripted meet-cutes.

But when I was with Rosie in the pool house, for the briefest moment I felt like—

Like she didn't want anything of me at all, not a piece, not a part, broken off to be hoarded and sold to the highest bidder. She was just there, and she was nice when she had absolute no reason to be.

It was a gift I wasn't expecting, and her no was an answer that had been coming for a long, long time.

ROSIE

ANNIE, QUINN, AND I MEET FOR BREAKFAST at the diner as we usually do. Quinn is trying to write out their Homecoming PSA for this afternoon, but they keep on crossing out everything they start. How do you write a thirty-second speech about why the student body should vote for you in a popularity contest? For anyone who isn't self-involved or rolled a twenty on Charisma when they were born, it's pretty tough, I imagine.

I'm still a little distracted by yesterday. The rainstorm, the conversation, me actually turning down the Vance Reigns. I must be absolutely out of my mind. Any girl would die to date him, but in the moment . . .

He ticked me off, honestly.

I wouldn't want to go out pretending to be anyone else, and when he adopted that accent—the accent I met him in—everything sort of just fell into place. He wouldn't mind going out with me as long as he wasn't himself when he did.

Like we couldn't be a match if he was his true self.

I shouldn't be surprised.

I'm not a heroine in a rom-com, and guys like that don't fall for girls like me. Besides, he's so infuriating I sort of want to smother him between my thighs and not in the sexy way. Like literally smother him.

Maybe I can write that as my college essay. Which is what I'm trying to work on right now, staring mindlessly at a blank Word document, but my mind is still stuck in the pool house, my thoughts still damp and my heart beating like a thunderstorm.

". . . Okay, but what if I don't do a speech at all and just do, I don't know, an interpretive dance?" Quinn asks.

Annie gives them a pointed look and spears one of her eggs. "Too avant-garde for the viewership. Ugh, if only there was a way to be really flash and extra."

"They're holding auditions for the mascot again after Bradley broke his leg diving off a bleacher," they muse. "Maybe I should audition . . ."

Annie rolls her eyes. "Ugh, who wants to be a mascot?"

"I mean, I would."

"Don't—Rosie, tell Quinn not to ruin their senior year."

I snap out of my thoughts. "What?"

"Have you *really* not been paying attention?"

"Um . . ."

Annie throws her hands up. "What has been *up* with you today? You're disassociating hard." She leans over the table to glance at my laptop screen. "And you haven't even written a *word* in your essay!"

"It's hard," I mumble in reply, and then I frown, because that's not quite the truth of it, and I need to tell *someone* about what happened yesterday. If I keep it bottled up, I feel like it'll just become this gnarled, tangled mess. "Vance asked me out yesterday."

Both of my friends sit at attention.

"*Excuse* me?" Annie gasps.

"When's the wedding?" Quinn adds.

Oh, good. This is going to go fantastically. I shift uncomfortably in the booth, closing my laptop. "I . . . sort of turned him down."

"YOU DID *WHAT*?" they cry.

The other occupants in the diner whirl around to look at us. I sink lower in my booth. "I know! I know. I just . . ." I frown and look down into my half-eaten breakfast of pancakes and bacon. I guess I should finally tell them. Rip off the Band-Aid. It's not exactly my dream anymore, or a story to keep me company at night. "Remember at ExcelsiCon, when I disappeared for that night?"

"Yeah," Annie fills in.

"Well . . . I met a Sond cosplayer that night, and we went out and . . . had an amazing night. The best night of my life, really. I'm sorry I kept it from you. I just felt like . . . it was mine, for a while."

Quinn gives me a narrow look. "But not anymore?"

"Oh, please don't tell me you're holding out for him," Annie adds.

"No, because I found him." I take a deep breath and say, "It was Vance."

Quinn about chokes on their coffee. "Come again?"

"The cosplayer was Vance," I repeat with a shrug. "I know, it's kind of bonkers and really weird but—we found out a few days ago when I sprained my ankle."

Annie squints at me. "So did you or did you not fall off a bookcase?"

". . . Not."

And I explain to them what actually happened. I tell them

about going to look for a missing book, and being annoyingly curious ("Yeah, that's your MO," Quinn says, and nods in agreement), and finding the mask instead. The same mask that Sond wore that night. I explain the miscommunication between us—how I thought he didn't tell me who he was because he was ashamed it was *me*, and how he didn't want to tell me because he was afraid I would be ashamed that it was *him*, and how I accidentally took a tumble down the last few stairs, and then yesterday how we got locked out of the house and caught in the rain and hid in the pool house.

When I recount it, the entire ordeal sounds like a fanfic in the making, right up until I say, "He asked me out and said we could go on dates as other people, but I met him as someone I wasn't and as someone he wasn't, and I . . . don't want that. I want someone who wants to take me out as himself, you know?"

Quinn and Annie don't respond at first.

". . . Is that weird?"

Quinn puts their napkin over their plate and slides across the booth to me. They wrap their arms around my shoulders and squeeze tightly. "No," they reply quietly, as Annie slips underneath the booth and pops up on the other side and puts her arms around me, too.

"You deserve better," she adds.

I melt into my best friends' hug, and finally for the first time since turning Vance down, I feel okay. "Thank you."

If this morning vindicated my choice to turn down Vance, the special afternoon Homecoming announcement does the exact opposite. It makes me question everything I have every done up to this point in my life. It makes me wonder if I should join a convent and pledge myself to baby Jesus and forget about this whole love thing to begin with.

The Homecoming announcement starts out innocuously enough. I do feel bad about not helping Quinn with their speech, but I can't even write my own college application essay. How the hell could I write a speech that would make the student body vote for them and not, well—

"First up is William Wu," says the *Not Another News Show* news anchor—I forget her name—as the camera pans over to a strikingly stocky guy with a shock of black spiky hair. He's the high school's football captain, so he's popular, which'll give him a few votes at least.

"'Sup, guys," he starts, giving the camera a bro-nod. "You should vote for me, because these babies are illegal in forty-nine states." Then he raises his arms and flexes to an *astounding* degree.

And that's how it begins.

I find myself trying to make a list of worthwhile college essays as some of the other students running for Homecoming King—*Overlord*—make their cases. It's not like running for student body president—they can't enact change, and they can't promise less homework or to bring Pizza Friday back—but they can show off their ridiculous pecs and their popular talents.

And then it's my best friend's turn.

"Hello there, my name is Quinn Holland," they begin in their unmistakable monotonous voice, reading from a small neon-pink note card, "and I think you should vote for me because I am diligent and hardworking, and none of that matters."

Oh, dear.

They drop the card and look deadass at the camera. "Aren't you tired of voting for the same old boring dudes? Sure, I get it, I like a nice snack too, but wouldn't you want someone with a little more substance?"

"Yeah, like *me*," the next participant interrupts.

My heart drops like a lead balloon into my toes. I know that voice. Before Quinn can finish their speech, the camera pans to Garrett Taylor.

He grins and jabs a thumb over to Quinn. "Yeah, you can vote for them," Garrett says with a little too much emphasis, "or you vote for *me* and help me fulfill my dream of taking the most gorgeous girl in school to the Homecoming Dance. I had a good friend tell me the other day that the way to someone's heart is through getting to know them, so what do you say, Rosie Thorne? Would you want to go to Homecoming together and get to know me?"

Oh God.

He took what I said and he twisted it—again. I slide lower in my seat as half of the class turns to look at me. I angle a hand over my face, trying to pretend that no one can see me in my supreme moment of embarrassment. But people are looking at me, anyway.

I want to disappear.

"Vote for me, and let's make our dreams come true!"

Never mind that I wouldn't go with him even if he was the last person on earth, and certainly not now, but try telling that to the entire school.

Soon after the announcements end and the bell rings to dismiss us for the day, a girl from my English class comes up to me as I'm packing up and asks, "Why don't you just go with him?"

I glance over at her, surprised. She's never spoken to me once in our entire high school career. "I don't want to."

"It's messed up that you're playing with him like this," she replies as she leaves.

QUINN AND ANNIE ARE WAITING FOR ME beside my locker. Quinn looks more than a little pissed, and I don't blame them. They're ranting to Annie as I come up and spin the dial on my lock. "And he just butted in! I had an entire thing I wanted to say!" they raged. "I want to win now more than ever. We're not letting you go to Homecoming with him, no matter what."

I put *Twilight* into my locker, beside *Dracula*—poor *Dracula*, discarded after three chapters because I found SparkNotes more helpful—and give them a surprised look. "I'm not actually going to go with that idiot—" From over Quinn's shoulder, I see a flash of a red Spider-Man cap, and I slam my locker closed. "Hold that thought. I have someone to kill."

I push away from my locker and head straight for Garrett Taylor.

"I hope she doesn't actually kill him," I hear Annie say to Quinn.

"I'd be okay if she did," they say. "Thinning the competition."

Garrett's hanging back with a group of friends by one of their lockers near the science wing, high-fiving and relishing in his *pretty sweet* PSA. It was not sweet. It was not even charming.

He doesn't see me before I grab him by the arm. "We need to talk—now," I hiss, and before his posse can stop me from kidnapping their ringleader, I haul him into the open janitor's closet and slam the door behind me. I feel for the light switch and flick it on.

Interrogation time.

He winces at the bright light. "Whoa, Rosie—it's nice to see you, too—"

"Stop trying to ask me out."

He gives a laugh. "Where did this come from?"

"Just stop it!"

"But I thought you said that the best way to like someone is to get to know them! You have no one else to go with. We've known each other for years. C'mon, Rosie, just give me a chance. You never know until you try."

"What part of *no* don't you understand?"

"Then what else do I need to do to prove to you that you deserve me?"

"*What?*"

"What else do I need to do?" he repeats. "Do I need to grovel at your feet? Write a song? Win a Homecoming vote?" That he laughs at, because he thinks he already has it in the bag. "C'mon, Rosie. Give me something here. Let me try."

For a long moment, I stare at him, wide-eyed and wondering how in the hell *anyone* likes this guy. He's getting something out of all this, if not my unwilling participation . . . then what?

I'm not sure, but I definitely do not like it.

I steel myself to say, "The answer is going to be no, Garrett. The answer is *always* going to be no."

Then I reach up for the light switch and turn it off, leaving him in the janitor's closet. He emerges a few moments later, but I duck into the girls' bathroom before he can figure out where I went.

I breathe out a long sigh, locking myself in the farthest stall, and sit up on the toilet. I just have to survive until Homecoming. That's it. Then after that, this entire nightmare will be over.

I just hope I can last until then.

THE DAYS GO BY QUICKLY, and the further Vance and I distance ourselves from that rainstorm and the pool shed, the more I can't forget about it. And neither can he. We tend to orbit around each other like binary stars, trying so hard to avoid each other and yet somehow always finding ourselves in the same vicinity.

He'll be in the kitchen when I get a glass of water, or he'll come down the stairs as I walk in the front door, and every time he'll turn on his heel and leave as quickly and silently as he came in. I never even have the chance to tell him hello.

After a week, it gets irritating trying to avoid each other, and he doesn't turn on his heel every time I come within eyesight again. But he doesn't really pay attention to me, either, even though it feels like I'm hyperaware of wherever he is while I'm in the castle-house—like a flesh-and-blood ghost that just won't go haunt someone else.

Then, on Friday after a particularly bad world history test that I *know* I failed, I come to the castle-house and retreat into my haven—only to find him sitting crossways in one of the wingback chairs in the library. His long legs are stretched over the armrest, his hair tucked up into a dark blue beanie. He's wearing a flannel shirt and frayed jeans and looks much more like the kind of guy I'd find at my local Starbucks than any sort of moody starlet—neither greasy nor sparkling.

Just . . . sort of there.

It surprises me that I find it endearing.

He looks over at where I came to a full stop in the doorway. "I know you're there."

I open my mouth, close it, open it again. *Think of something clever!* "Yeah, I'm here."

Noice.

Giving up trying to look cool or composed or the least bit non-awkward, I pull my bookbag higher on my shoulder and quickly make for my desk, where I boot up the iPad and click into the Excel sheet. There is a counter on the bottom, telling me how far I've come and how many I have to go. Yesterday I just reached the halfway point—half of the shelves are full and orderly—and I thought that if I could survive another few weeks, then I would be done.

Just a few more.

"So, um, what are you doing here?" I ask. I don't see a book anywhere near him.

He slides his long legs off the armchair and sits properly. "I figure I should help you, since that was the deal in the first place."

"I've been doing fine alone, thanks."

"I know, but I got some more books off the top shelf for you," he adds—proudly, I might add—and waves over to the stack of books in the other wingback chair. They are books that I couldn't reach alone, but also . . .

"I don't need those for a while."

He seems to wilt a little. "Oh."

I give him a curious look. "Why are you helping me all of a sudden?"

He gives a one-shouldered shrug. "I guess I got tired of acting petulant."

"Mm-hmm . . . you know this isn't going to make me say yes

to dating you, right?" I venture, and he gives me a surprised look.

"Of course not. That's not why I'm here. I mean, I don't make it a habit of wasting my time—not that you'd ever be a waste of time," he quickly corrects, and rubs the back of his neck, because yeah buddy, you are digging that hole real deep right now. "I just mean that's not the reason I'm here. I don't expect you to change your mind."

As much as I hate to admit it, I believe him.

"Well," I say, "at least I've found *one* guy who takes no for an answer."

"Hmm?"

"Oh, nothing. Just some school drama."

He tilts his head, and the hair tucked behind his ears comes undone and falls into his face. It's back to its normal color now, a washy white-blond, but I sort of miss the orange-ish that it was. "You know, I've never been to school."

I look up from the iPad, surprised. "What, seriously?"

"Seriously. I was homeschooled. Did most of my studying on film sets between takes. I think the only time I've actually set foot in a school was for that indie film I did a few years ago—*An Inevitable Thing*?"

"Do you think you missed out?"

He gives a one-shouldered shrug. "I can't say. I mean, I got to spend 'spring break' in Bali so I don't think I can complain too much."

I let out a low whistle. "The farthest I've been from home is the Harry Potter part of Universal Studios."

"I bet that was a magical time."

"It was for a spell."

He laughs, and I find myself smiling more than I really should.

I like the way he laughs, sort of soft and to himself, like it's a secret that he laughs at all.

I suppose it wouldn't be *too* terrible if I had help for the day. The library does get a little lonely sometimes. But I can pretend like I don't like it. "Well," I say, "I *guess* if you're here and you actually want to help me, get me that box over there."

We work together for the next two hours. I show him what we're supposed to be doing—cataloging the books, and then putting them in order on the shelves—and he helps me by making sure I don't miss one, and reaching the books I usually use a chair to get to. It's a lot quicker work with another person. If he had helped from the beginning, we would've been done by now.

As I'm about ready to wrap up for the day, Mr. Rodriguez calls my name from the kitchen. I exchange a look with Vance, but he just shrugs again—he doesn't know what Mr. Rodriguez wants, either. "Yes?" I reply as I leave the library and enter the kitchen.

Mr. Rodriguez has his cell phone pressed to his shoulder in the way you do when you don't want someone to listen into a conversation. "It's your dad," he says quietly. "He's been trying to reach you for a while."

I tense. My cell phone! It's in my bag. I didn't even hear it. "Is something wrong? Is he okay?"

"Yes, he's fine, but, well . . ."

He offers me the phone, and I hesitantly take it.

On the other end, Dad—sounding frazzled, though trying not to alarm me—tells me, "Thank God I finally got to you! Okay, so, don't panic but—remember the older woman from the circulation desk? Pam?"

I don't understand. "Yeah, isn't it her birthday?"

"Right. I was wanting to make something nice for her, so

I decided to try to bake her a red velvet cake, you know? She loves red velvet and I was going to put a cute little bookish design on the top and—"

My stomach begins to sink. "Oh, you didn't."

"I . . . did. And managed to start a fire?"

"Dad!" I squawk.

"I was heating up some chocolate and I didn't realize you couldn't put tinfoil in the microwave! I walked off for two seconds and, well . . . the good news is we still have an apartment?"

"And the *bad* news?"

"We . . . do not have a kitchen and currently cannot live in our apartment again until our landlord inspects it for safety. Which should be after this weekend! And renter's insurance covers imbeciles like me, apparently. But, um . . . yes. Your father caught the kitchen on fire."

I don't know whether to laugh or cry. Maybe a little of both? Mr. Rodriguez is on the other side of the kitchen, trying not to glance over at me too often, but it's very clear that he wants to know what's happening and I can't *wait* to tell him that my wonderful, smart, and yet exquisitely idiotic father caught our apartment on fire.

"And . . . now for the meat of the problem. Do you have somewhere you can stay for the weekend?" Dad asks hesitantly. "I just got off the phone with the hotels in the area, and because of the college game this weekend, they're all full up. The closest one is about forty-five minutes away."

"*That* far?" I blanch.

"Yeah. I—I guess I'll do it, but it'll be a pain. Do you have any friends you can stay with?"

Quinn is away with their parents this weekend touring Duke,

who early-accepted them, and Annie lives in a two-bedroom row house that can barely fit her family. I can't ask her. But just as I begin to shake my head—I pause.

Mr. Rodriguez cocks his head as I glance at him, an eyebrow raised.

"I think I know someone," I reply, and hope I'm not wrong. "For the both of us."

VANCE

I TRY NOT TO BE NOSY—I truly don't want to be—but they have been talking in the kitchen for the last half hour and I am growing very, very impatient. Another agonizing minute goes by and I hear them laugh. About *what*? I don't care, I tell myself, picking up one of the books I had gotten down for her. She'll come back in at any moment and enlighten me, I'm sure of it.

But when another minute passes, I creep toward the library door. I am not eavesdropping, I tell myself. I am simply wondering if—

Suddenly, there are footsteps.

I try to move back, but the door swings open a moment later. Directly into my face. I curse and double over, holding my nose. Rosie gasps, "*Sorry!* I didn't see you there!"

Mortifying, mortifying, this is all so very mortifying. Before I can sink myself any lower, I quickly turn around, holding my nose, to walk away. She reaches out and takes me by the arm. She stops me.

"You're bleeding," she says.

I look down at my hand that held my nose. It's full of blood.

"You broke my nose!"

She bristles. "I didn't know you were at the door!"

"It's my house!"

"It is *not*."

"Well . . . I'm living here."

Her mouth purses into a thin line. "Then you should've just come into the kitchen instead of loitering like a creeper."

"I was not *loitering*."

"Then you were just standing by the door?"

I pull myself up to my full height, which is a good head taller than she is, but she has her hands on her hips as if I'm the short one. Which is not endearing. Not at all. And no, I am not afraid of her. Not even a little.

. . . Perhaps a little.

"I can stand wherever I please," I finally reply nobly. "What did your father want?"

She takes me by the arm. "C'mon, let's stop the bleeding before you get any on the books," she says, and guides me into the kitchen, where I run my face underneath the faucet in the sink, and hiss as the cold water hits the cut on my nose. She didn't *break* it, apparently, just sliced it open.

I'm not sure which is worse.

Elias finds the first-aid kit and tells me to take a seat on a barstool. Rosie comes into the kitchen, her arms folded over her chest, and watches as Elias applies ointment and a Band-Aid on it. "Will I have a scar?" I ask Elias courageously.

He snorts at my bravado, which deflates me quite a bit. "Not likely."

"That's sad. Chicks dig scars," Rosie adds woefully.

Elias finishes placing the Band-Aid and sighs. "*Dios mío*, this is exhausting."

"I agree," I agree.

"*Both* of you," he replies pointedly, and puts the first-aid kit back underneath the sink. "Please try to get along this weekend."

I give him a strange look. "This weekend?"

Rosie becomes suspiciously fixated on a brown spot on the ceiling.

Elias informs, "Yes, this weekend. Rosie and her father's apartment had a small fire, which is why he called, and since we have so many vacant rooms I figured we could offer them both a little hospitality."

"All weekend," I repeat. My brain is short-circuiting.

"Yes, all weekend. So please try not to kill each other. I need to go out for some groceries—how do you feel about spaghetti tonight, Rosie? Will your father be joining us?"

She hesitates. "I don't think so—he'll be here later tonight, though."

"Perfect! I'll go pick up some supplies and start cooking," he says brightly, and then gives me a meaningful look.

I stiffen. *Me?* I don't want anything to do with that girl. She almost broke my nose! And she had the audacity to try to blame *me*! I answer with a shrug, which suffices for Elias, because he grabs his wallet and keys from the counter and leaves through the garage.

When Elias is gone, Rosie says quietly, "Sorry, I didn't know who else to ask."

"Like Elias said, we have plenty of rooms," I reply, even though I want to ask if her personal things are okay, if anything is ruined.

She breathes out a sigh of relief. "Well, that's something."

I show her to a room upstairs. It's one of the bedrooms that neither Elias nor I have really been into, so the windows need to be opened and the sheets need to be changed because it's so musty, but she doesn't seem to mind, especially when Sansa comes in and curls up right at the foot of the bed. Rosie scratches her behind the ears, and when I leave her alone to go into my room, Sansa doesn't follow.

So much for loyalty.

ROSIE

The doorbell rings. "That must be my dad," I say as I get up to go answer it.

It is, laden with two suitcases full of clothes—our latest laundry load. He rolls them both in and wipes sweat from his forehead. He must've changed out of his work clothes at the apartment, because he's wearing his old band T-shirt and jeans with those God-awful flip-flops I wish I had burned years ago. Mr. Rodriguez rounds out of the kitchen with an outstretched hand to meet him.

"Thank you so much for the hospitality," Dad says, grasping Mr. Rodriguez's hand tightly. "Honestly, it means a lot."

"It's no trouble at all. We've grown really fond of Rosie."

"It's hard not to," Dad agrees, and I notice that their hands linger a little longer than necessary in the handshake. I glance up at the two men, trying to read the air between them, but they're just smiling and I don't understand it at all.

Weird.

Very weird.

"Mr. Rodriguez has food ready," I pipe in, leaving the suitcases by the door and herding Dad toward the dining room. Mr. Rodriguez already has the table set, a large plate of pasta in the middle like in those family-style restaurants. Vance squirms a little in his seat as Dad comes in, but then he forces himself to his feet and outstretches a hand.

"Sir," he says, clasping Dad's hand tightly.

"Nice to see you again," Dad replies.

THAT EVENING, I eat my weight in Mr. Rodriguez's spaghetti and meatballs. Over dinner, we talk about nothing—the weather, the movies coming out, and Darien Freeman's lip-sync battle, which has, by now, been retweeted over half a million times.

Vance doesn't say much of anything throughout the dinner. He just sits and listens and bats his meatballs around the plate, trying not to meet Dad's gaze, and aside from that it sort of feels . . . strange. Not in a bad way, but in a way I'm not very used to. There isn't an empty plate at the dinner table, and there isn't an empty seat where someone once sat.

It feels . . . whole.

"So, what are your plans after high school?" Mr. Rodriguez asks me after a while.

Oh, the dreaded question. I wipe my mouth, hesitating on what to say. *Sorry, I'm a failure and I can't even complete one essay so I'll just live as a hermit in my room for the rest of my life reading* Starfield *novels and eating jerky.*

Ugh, that sounds depressing.

Dad gives me a patient look from across the table, as if to tell me that it's okay if I don't know. He knows I've been struggling with the essay portion for a few weeks now, and time certainly is winding down to turn that in. "Well . . . my mom always wanted me to go to NYU because she went there as an undergrad—that's where she met Dad."

"My wife was an accounting major," Dad fills in.

"So I want to go there, too—except for English, not accounting—but the essay prompt is horrid."

"What's the essay about?" Vance asks.

"Basically, what makes me a good fit for NYU, but what I think they want is why should they pick me over so many other gifted students? And I . . . don't know." I shrug. "And I just don't think they want a sob story about a dead mom." I force out a laugh, because it's just getting too depressing thinking about it. "I'm really not that amazing."

"I'm trying to tell Rosie that she is amazing," Dad says.

"*Dad*," I say. "I'm not."

"Not as amazing as *me*, anyway," Vance agrees ignobly, but I'm beginning to realize that that's his kind of humor. Sort of self-important, but self-deprecating at the same time, because he doesn't believe it himself.

And a part of that's really sad, too.

"Which is not amazing at all," I reply, and he mocks a dagger to the chest.

DAD SITUATES HIS SUITCASE IN THE CORNER of our room and plops down on the end of the bed. Finally, his mask falls away, and he looks about as tired as I would have guessed. I sit next to him and rest my head on his shoulder. He smells like home.

"I keep forgetting how handsome Elias is," he says, and I can hear him smiling. "I should come over more often!"

"*Dad*."

"Is he single?"

I elbow him in the side, and he chuckles. It isn't really rocket science that my dad isn't as hetero as some people may think. He was the first person Quinn came out to as nonbinary—the second being me and Annie. He wears rainbow suspenders all through pride month, and he has a graphic framed on his desk with NSYNC and the words *BI-BI-BI!*— but I never guessed he would like *Vance's guardian*. "Wait until I'm done working for them, at least."

"No promises," he jokes, and tousles my hair and asks me where the shower is. I point him in the direction of the one Mr. Rodriguez showed me earlier and change into my pajamas.

I grab my laptop from his satchel and retreat down into the living room. Mr. Rodriguez has already put the leftovers away, and the lights are out, so I turn on a lamp and curl up in the corner of the couch. I boot up my laptop, figuring I might as well try to write that college essay again, but every time I try to start it, I can't figure out where to go.

Like I had said at dinner earlier—my life hasn't been any sort of spectacular.

It's been me trying as I might to chase after the disappearing shadow of my mother.

I stare at the blank page. The cursor blinks. In, out, in, out, like a heartbeat. I rub my first fingers against the ridges of the *F* and the *J*, trying to will some sort of word, some sentence, some semblance of why I should go to NYU and not anyone else. Why I'm spectacular. Why I'm *me*.

Argh, it's no use.

I give up and close my laptop, and find my way into the library again. I don't turn on any of the lights, and in the darkness the room reminds me of the first time I snuck into this house. I run my fingers along the spines of the books, closing my eyes, remembering the way Mom used to sit in her reading chair in those golden afternoons she loved so much, reading page after page after page, as if she was running out of time.

I wonder if she knew that she was.

I try to hang on to those memories, where she's sitting at her sun-drenched chair with her round glasses pushed up the bridge of her nose, her brown hair pulled high into a bun, chewing on her fingernails as General Sond or Carmindor or Amara spiraled through the galaxy. But whenever I think of her at her chair, I remember that we no longer have that room filled with all of those books she loved. I remember that we had to sell the house to pay for the medical costs. I remember that we had to sell those books to close her casket.

Some days I still wake up and forget that she's buried in Haven Memorial Gardens at the edge of town.

I don't talk about my mom often. Whenever I do, my heart hurts in a way that nothing can really help. Like there's this hole drilled into the center of my soul, an unending pit that keeps going and going, tempting me to fall in and get lost in the echo of who she was. Because she's gone now.

She no longer exists.

But here, in this library, I can feel her, even though I know she's gone. I can sense her sitting in one of the wingback chairs. I can hear her flipping the pages of a novel, slowly, and humming to herself as she reads.

It's been a year, but it feels like longer.

I miss her so much.

My fingers stop on the one binding that is a little warped, the pages crinkled, and I pull it out of the shelf. *The Starless Throne* by Sophie Jenkins. I smile to myself a little and take the book out of the library, like I did that first night. But this time I don't leave for the patio. I return to the couch, and I curl up with my mom's favorite book, and I get lost in a universe where perhaps, on some distant star, she's still alive.

I'm not sure how long I sit here reading, but after a while some movement near the stairs catches my eye and I glance over, expecting to see Dad coming to look for me—

Blond hair. Plaid pajama bottoms.

No shirt.

I quickly avert my gaze, but my brain is already short-circuiting. I was fine when he was in a wet T-shirt. I was super okay when he had on a loose tank top.

I am . . . extremely not okay now.

He must see me at the exact same moment my brain starts to melt, because he quickly about-faces and flees back up the stairs. My tense muscles begin to unwind, and I melt down into the cushions. That was too close. I let out a sigh of relief, and return to the page I was on, when I hear footsteps down the stairs again.

Vance returns, this time pulling a T-shirt over his head.

A T-shirt that reads *GENERAL SOND IS A PUNK*.

I snort even though I try not to. At least he's self-aware. I watch him, apprehensive, as he gets a LaCroix out of the refrigerator and comes to sit down on the couch beside me. He glances over at my book. "Read me something," he says.

I give him a baffled look. "What, like that scene in *Fangirl* by Rainbow Rowell?"

"I have no idea what that is, but if it has something to do with reading a book aloud, I'd much rather think of this as that scene from *Titanic*."

"There isn't a reading scene in *Titanic* . . ." I trail off as he stretches out across the couch and strikes a rather ludicrous pose, like one of those '60s pinup girls.

"Read to me like one of your nerd friends," he says valiantly.

I snort despite myself and shake my head. "I'm sure you don't want me to."

"Try me."

"It's about General Sond." I show him the cover. "He gets sent on a mission from the Nox King to infiltrate a Federation outpost, but unbeknownst to him, Princess Amara is also undercover at this outpost, trying to solve a murder."

He scrunches his nose. "Is this a kissing book?"

"I suppose I'll have to read it so you can find out."

In reply, he takes a pillow from the edge of the couch and tucks it behind his head. He settles down and waits. "I suppose you do."

For the rest of the evening, I read to him from my mother's favorite novel—and for a little while I can forget that my apartment went up in a (very) small fire, and that some toxic guy wants to take me to Homecoming, and my college essay is still woefully unwritten.

For a few hours, nothing matters and I think, *This is the best it's going to get.*

Until the next morning when I wake up to the smell of chocolate murder pancakes.

VANCE

I WAKE UP TO THE SMELL OF SOMETHING BURNING. It twinges my nose, and even when I burrow my head under the covers, the smell doesn't go away. It's not like an electrical fire sort of burning, or a woodfire, or any of that sort. It *smells*, honestly, like—

Breakfast.

Oh, that's right. We have guests.

I spring up and tear the duvet off, scrambling out of bed. Sansa isn't curled up at the foot of my bed, so Elias must've let her out already. How long have they been up? Laughter bubbles up from the kitchen downstairs. A man, and then—Elias. And Rosie. I remember now. She and her father are staying with us for the weekend.

I slide on my sweatpants and make my way to the stairs. From the top I can see Elias at the stove in his cooking apron, holding the frying pan, and Rosie's father trying to explain to him how to flip an American pancake.

"It's all in the wrist," he's saying. "You gotta feel it."

"I've always been bad at flipping things in a skillet," Elias replies, troubled.

"I believe in you!" Rosie cheers on from the barstool at the counter.

"One . . . two . . ." Then Elias flips the brown pancake. It spins through the air—misses the pan completely—and lands smack on the ground.

Everyone stares at the downed pancake.

I clap slowly.

Startled, everyone whirls around to me.

"Vance!" Elias says. Rosie's father scoops up the sacrificed pancake from the ground and tosses it into the garbage bin. "Did we wake you?"

I put my hands in my pockets and give a half shrug. "Not really."

"Come and eat with us," Rosie's father says. "We've got two left with your name on them! I bet you've never had anything like it before."

That's an understatement.

"I . . . probably have not," I reply cautiously, sliding up to sit at the counter next to Rosie. She excitedly wiggles back and forth on the barstool, grinning, still in her pajamas, too. They have little duck prints all over them, and I'm hard-pressed to say they're cute. But.

They're not . . . *not* cute.

"Chocolate murder's the only thing my dad can cook," she whispers to me. I recall her saying something about *chocolate murder pancakes* earlier in the month, but nothing prepared me for the sight of what Rosie's father placed in front of me: two cocoa-flavored chocolate chip American pancakes drizzled with syrup and powdered sugar, and topped with a maraschino cherry. He slides it to me with a smile. I stare at it like—how in the bloody hell am I supposed to eat this monstrosity?

I glance at Rosie, who apparently has already eaten, and so has everyone else.

He gives me a fork and a butter knife and says, "Try it!"

"It looks like a sugar coma," I reply.

"That's why it's called chocolate *murder*," Rosie chides.

The plate definitely looks like some sort of murder. The syrup runs off the side of the chocolate pancakes and pools at the edges. I lift one with the fork, inspecting the butter sandwiched between. I haven't eaten something so unhealthy for breakfast since my mother fired my first nanny, who fed me ice cream some mornings.

I gently cut off an edge of the pancake, already drowned in syrup, and with everyone watching, I eat it, wondering how much I should act like I love it—

Until the taste explodes in my mouth. Chocolate, but more pancake-y than I realized. Fluffy, and yes the syrup is sweet, but it offsets the bitterness of the chocolate. I wouldn't eat it every morning, but the surprise on my face is genuine.

Rosie's father grins and leans against the counter. "So, what do you think?"

"It's . . . good," I reply, surprising myself.

Elias seems just as surprised as I am. "That's a glowing recommendation from Vance."

"So I passed the test?" he asked, speaking more to Elias than me.

"He's not complaining."

"Hey, I never complain," I complain, and everyone laughs.

As I eat, Rosie's father teaches Elias how to flip a pancake on the griddle, so by the time I'm done they've made at least five more with the leftover batter, and Rosie's father looks rather pleased with himself. I watch him and Elias with interest as

I set down my fork. I can't eat the last few bites—it's too sweet for me.

Rosie's father checks his watch. "I'm heading to the apartment later to talk to the landlord and the insurance company about the damages. They have to rip up the carpet and see if the hardwood is ruined or not."

"I'll come with you," Rosie says. "Just let me get dressed first."

"You don't have to."

"I know, but I want to help—and besides, it's silly to have two cars here. We can ride back here together this evening."

Elias agrees. "And since you treated us to breakfast, I can treat you to dinner."

Rosie's father hesitates, but he's won over when Elias gives him a smile. My eyebrows jerk up, and I glance over at Rosie, who is smiling from behind her fingers. Oh. *Oh*. "Well, all right—but just tell us when we start to impose."

"You aren't," I say before Elias has a chance to, and the words surprise even me. I shove a piece of chocolate syrup–drowned pancake around on my plate. "I mean, the house is so large I didn't notice either of you here last night."

Rosie finger-guns her father. "And it helps we don't snore."

"Right you are, Rosebud," he replies, finger-gunning her right back, and then he nods toward the stairs. "Okay, go get ready."

She jumps off the barstool and races up to her and her father's room. She's down in five minutes, in jeans and a large T-shirt, pulling her hair back with a black scrunchie. Rosie's father tries to clean up the kitchen, but Elias decides to have none of it and shoos him out.

"You cooked, I clean," he points out.

"Fine, fine—ready to go?" he asks Rosie, putting a hand on her shoulder, and they leave through the garage.

When they're gone, Elias gives me a sidelong look. "Not *imposing*, hmm?"

I spear the pancake, trying to quell the blush blooming on my cheeks. Because the Vance of a month ago would've not said anything. He would've asked them to leave as soon as possible. He would've hated this sweet disaster of a breakfast. He wouldn't have admitted that, in the darkest part of his heart, it really wasn't that bad. Instead I clear my throat and tell him, "You have a crush."

He scoffs. "I do *not*."

"Do *too*."

"That's ridiculous," he replies, but he's so flustered his ears are beginning to turn red. He grabs my plate from the counter even though I'm still pushing the last bite around in the syrup and dumps it into the sink to start washing it.

"Whatever you say," I reply, and slide off the barstool. I grab Sansa's lead and whistle at her between my teeth to take her out on a walk while he's sorting through his feelings.

I might never have been in love, but I know what it looks like, and Elias is head over heels.

ROSIE

THAT EVENING, AFTER DAD AND I RETURN from the apartment, where the electrician tore out the oven and the wall that had been damaged, we ate dinner with Mr. Rodriguez and Vance again—we order Chinese this time, from the great little takeout place down the street. I didn't realize Vance could put down so much food; it's really quite monstrous, because I thought I was the eggroll-eating champion. Alas, it seems I was dethroned. I didn't mind it that much.

After we watch a few hours of TV and Mr. Rodriguez retires to bed, I do the dishes with my dad and talk a little about the new oven and microwave being installed tomorrow, and the plasterwork, and having to repaint half of the kitchen again—but I really don't mind. I hated the old appliances anyway.

"And what have we learned?" I ask, handing him the last plate.

He replies gallantly, "Never put tinfoil in the microwave."

"Good."

He kisses me good night and leaves for his room. I change into my pajamas and slink down to the couch again, thinking everyone has gone to bed—but I freeze on the bottom step.

I was wrong.

Vance is lying down, legs flipped up over the back of the couch, head lolling off the other side. With his eyes closed, he doesn't look as worried or brooding as he usually does, which surprises me. I thought he probably frowns in his sleep, but he actually looks . . . well, *not terrible to look at* is the only concession I'm giving.

I turn to creep back up the stairs when he says, a little blearily, "Can't sleep either?"

. . . Guess he's not asleep after all.

I turn back around to him. He pushes himself up on the couch and motions for me to come sit. I do, mostly because I *can't* sleep. This house is too big and too quiet.

As I get closer, he holds up a book. "I want to know what happens."

The Starless Throne.

I bite the inside of my cheek to hide a smile. "Do you, now?"

"I've been thinking about it all afternoon."

I climb over the couch to sink down beside him. "Probably not *all* afternoon."

"Does Sond get out of prison? Does Amara save the planet? Who's the murderer? Are they ever going to kiss?" He asks the last one a little impatiently. "I want to know."

In the dim light of the living room, his golden hair shines in a platinum halo around his head, and his cornflower eyes are bright with curiosity. He really *does* want to know what happens. I've read it a thousand times, I can recite most of the chapters by heart. I know what the words sound like in my head, but I don't know what they sound like in his.

I push the book back to him. "Read it to me."

"You can't be serious."

I yawn. “I’m tired. I worked all day. You’ve lounged around playing video games.” Which he doesn’t dispute, because I know him well enough by now. I’m not sure *what* kind of video games he plays, though. I close my eyes, curling up in the corner of the couch, and rest my head on the cushions. “Please?”

For a long moment, he doesn’t say anything, but then I hear him flip open the book, the pages buzzing between his fingers, until he settles on the page where we last left off, and he begins to read in a soft, steady cadence. The adventure of Amara and General Sond spills softly from his mouth, and I’m not sure when I drift off to sleep, but when I do my head is filled with stars.

A GUST OF WIND SHAKES THE TREES, and I watch as yellowing leaves scatter across the yard. It's early afternoon, and Rosie's father's already gone back to the apartment again. Rosie slept in this morning—her father told us not to wake her, since she hasn't slept in for a long time. "Not since my wife . . . well, you know," he had said with a shrug. "She always makes me coffee in the morning, like Holly used to. I think she thinks she has to take care of her old man now." I remembered that her mother passed away, but I didn't realize how recent it was. Only a year.

I tap out "I Like Big Butts" on the grand piano in the living room, because I can't think of a more ridiculous song to play on a five-thousand-dollar instrument, putting my ten years of music lessons to excellent use.

I'm working out the notes to *round thing in your face you get*—when my phone, sitting on the bench beside me, pings with a text.

DARIEN (3:47 PM)

—Hey man, it's been a while.

Yeah, no kidding. It feels like an eternity. I keep tapping away at the notes, adding a bass chord as I get more acquainted with the song.

. . . with an itty-bitty waist and a round thing in your—

My phone pings again.

DARIEN (3:48 PM)

—You okay?

Just two words. But they're enough to thoroughly ruin my fun. I should text him back the truth, that I'm having about as much fun as anyone else in the lowest circle of hell, but when I pick up my phone I can't do it. We made our choices, and this is how the dominoes fell. He made the right ones, I made the not-so-right ones.

Instead, I turn off my phone, and as I close the cover on the piano keys, the *Star Wars* theme echoes through house. Elias's ringtone, but he's out running errands. His phone is vibrating on the edge of kitchen.

He forgot it—again.

I stare at it, because the first thing I think is that it's my mother. Or my manager. Or a reporter. Or my mother.

And none of them I want to talk to.

The call goes to voice mail, and my anxiety begins to ebb. I shove the bench underneath the piano and start for the stairs when—

His phone goes off again.

What if it's important? a voice inside me whispers.

My stomach flips into a knot and I make for the counter and swipe up on Elias's phone. It's not my publicist, or my manager, or a journalist. It's . . .

My mother.

I haven't talked with her since our fight, and I have strategically avoided her every single time she's tried to call me, and despite everything, I do miss talking to her, even as I try to remember why I'm so bitter about it all to begin with.

Because she sided with my stepfather. She sent me here, to nowhere. To hide me away because she, like my stepfather, is ashamed of me.

That's the part of all of this I don't like thinking about.

"Um, Vance?" I glance behind me. Rosie stands in the doorway to the living room with her suitcase and her bookbag. Her hair is pulled behind her head in two short pigtails, and she tugs on one of them nervously. "Dad just called. He said the apartment's back in tip-top shape! I hate to ask, but Elias has gone to the farmer's market, so . . . do you think you could take me home?"

I turn around and send my mother—again—to voice mail. "Your chariot awaits, Princess."

ROSIE

He leads me out into the garage, where a simple economy car sits. I buckle myself into the passenger seat. It surprises me—I didn't think he'd be caught dead in anything less than an Aston Martin, but I suppose that would stick out too much in this town.

Out on the main street, trees unfurl around us, curling up toward the sky in a tunnel. He flicks on the brights, the radio murmuring soft pop songs.

He shifts in his seat. "So, if I liked that book . . . which one would you suggest next?"

I give him the strangest look. "Seriously?" I chew on the inside of my cheek to keep myself from smiling.

". . . What?"

"I'm sorry—this is just so weird. I never would've thought that I'd ever be in a car with you, asking me for book recs."

"Well, I will admit this is a first for me as well. But . . ." As he coasts to a stop at the stoplight, he tilts his head, frowning, "it's not a *bad* thing, yeah?"

"No, it's really not. Well, what kind of books do you like?"

"Ones that aren't boring."

"Well, that's all of them."

He gives me a sideways glance, and I smile and pull out my notebook from my school bag. "Fine—how about court intrigue? Assassins? Starship battles? *The Star Brigade* is a good one to start with." I scrawl the name out onto the top of a spare piece of paper, tear it off, and hand it to him.

"Thank you kindly," he replies, and tucks it into the fold in his beanie.

I shove my notebook into my backpack. "You know," I say, and hesitate for a moment, before I continue, "I like this."

"This?"

"We aren't sniping at each other for once."

"I know, it's ghastly," he replies with a laugh. A moment later, the light turns green, and we drive on. "We should at least be *arguing*."

"I know, you're a terrible villain."

"I like to think of myself as an anti-hero."

"Byronic? Take a left here," I add as we come to the next stop-light, and he turns onto my street. I tap on the window, indicating my apartment building on the right.

"I am not nearly that broody, thank *you*," he says as he slows down in front of the entrance to the building. It's nothing like his castle-house. It's a three-story walkup apartment complex with a smaller-than-normal kitchen and a leaky toilet, but it's home.

"Not *broody*? Now I know you're lying."

He mocks a gasp. "And I thought we were *friends*!"

Friends. I like the sound of that, strange enough, even after I turned him down for a date. But a friendship—one between him and me, Vance Reigns and Rosie Thorne—doesn't sound too terrible. I lean across the middle console toward him and when he looks back at me my breath catches in my throat, because his eyes are so blue and he smells so warm, and for a brief moment—I can see him.

The boy I fell for on the balcony of ExcelsiCon.

"There you are," I whisper. The words slip out of my mouth before I can reel myself in. His eyebrows furrow, and I quickly pull myself back and push open the car door. "Good night, Vance."

"See you tomorrow?" he calls.

"Tomorrow," I promise.

He waits until I'm inside my apartment before he drives away, out of the gates, and onto the main street again, but my heart never stops racing.

VANCE

I CAN'T REMEMBER THE LAST TIME I woke up before noon, but I didn't actually sleep very well. My stupid brain kept replaying last night over and over—like the theater previews before a film. I saw her every time I closed my eyes, illuminated by the soft light of the dashboard, fiddling with the radio even though she never picked a channel, just so I wouldn't notice the blush across her cheeks.

But I definitely did.

It could have nothing to do with you, I think as I fish for a shirt in my dresser drawer, my hair damp against my neck from a shower.

But still.

I wish I'd said something—something remotely flirty, I guess—but instead I made up *cat puns*. And the way she laughed, and smiled, and leaned over the console in the middle—

There you are, she had said, as if she'd been looking for me underneath Vance Reigns this whole time.

I scrub my head, abandoning any hope of finding a clean shirt, and pace my bedroom. Oh, I'm in so much trouble. I have half a mind to ask Imogen what to do, until I remember that we haven't talked since our fight, and I haven't seen her online since.

I really did bungle that up, didn't I?

Elias knocks on the door before he pokes his head in. "Hey, sleepyhead—oh, you're awake."

Sansa squeezes through the crack in the door and jumps at me, tail wagging. "Oof! Easy, girl."

I scrub Sansa behind the ears, and she thwaps down on the carpet and rolls over for me to pet her belly.

"So, did anything . . . happen last night?"

"What? No, we didn't fight or anything, if that's what you mean." I grab a button-down shirt from the clean-laundry basket and put it on. It's wrinkled, but it isn't like I am going to impress anyone today.

Rosie doesn't care about wrinkled shirts.

. . . Does she?

"That is not what I mean," Elias replies as he comes into my room and sits down on the edge of the bed. "Now, tell me all about it. I can see it on your face. You've got something on your mind."

I give a one-shouldered shrug. Sansa nudges my hand when I stop petting her, and I resume with the scratches. "I just . . . I don't know, honestly. I like her, but do I deserve to?"

Words aren't usually this hard, are they? *I like you. I want to date you. Okay, let's bone.* That's the extent of my relationship vocabulary, which now, come to think of it, is wholly lacking in . . . literally everything.

"I want so badly to be part of something again," I say slowly, trying to figure out exactly how I feel. "To care about something. And we both know that I don't. Back in LA, I rarely cared about anything. I didn't need to, or maybe I was just afraid to, I don't know. And once I return to the real world, to being *me*, there's no way that someone like her and someone like me . . ."

I frown.

Because that's the root of it, isn't it? She deserves so much better than anyone I could ever be.

"*¡Ay mijo!*" he says, shaking his head. "You're falling hard."

I put my face in my hands. "Oh God, I am, aren't I? What do I do?"

He puts a hand on my shoulder.

"I just want her to be happy," I mutter, realizing it's true the moment I say it. Because every time I close my eyes, I see the way she looks at that library full of stories, and I've never seen anyone look so hopeful and alive and . . . *home*, somewhere before.

There's a warmth in my chest—it's been there for a while now—that is soft and sure, and I realized last night, as I watched her walk into her apartment, what the feeling was.

Happiness.

The kind I've never felt before.

And that's when I get the idea.

"Elias, do you have Natalia's number? Can I have it?"

He gives me a peculiar look, but he doesn't ask why.

ROSIE

I will *never* tell Vance Reigns this, but I wake up to him every morning.

Literally.

Because on my wall is a fanart poster of Ambrose Sond, shirtless and more than a little disheveled, one hand behind his head, the other snaking underneath the sheets that artfully cover up the bits of him that probably are *also* unclothed. It's such a trash poster. I got it from ExcelsiCon last year on the down-low and smuggled it out of the convention so strangers wouldn't know my shame.

And now I see the real-life version of him almost every. Single. Day.

Every morning, his sharp cerulean eyes remind me how much smut I've read online and how much smut I probably should *not* have read online. I have so much PWP bookmarked on my secret fanfic account that if anyone ever found it they would try to exorcise the demons that are most definitely in me.

And now I can't even read *any* of them because instead of Sond? I see Vance. Instead of my sweet, wonderful Ambrose, all

I hear is Vance's soft, subtle English accent as he reads to me my mother's favorite novel.

My phone goes off a moment later—a text. I reach over to my nightstand. It's the group chat with Quinn and Annie.

QUINN (6:45 AM)

—RISE AND SHIIINNNNEEE~

—IT'S COFFEE TIME!

ANNIE (6:45 AM)

—ugh

ROSIE (6:46 AM)

—morning lovers!

— LOSERS*

*—** I MEANT LOSERS*

ANNIE (6:46 AM)

—also lovers.

—I will take no alternative.

QUINN (6:47 AM)

—That's McLovin to you.

Sunlight creeps in through the lace curtains, and I groan and roll onto my back. And Sond stares at me from my wall, smirking at me like he knows my secret.

"*Starflame*." I groan, shoving my pillow into my face so I don't have to look at that smug, beautiful face. "I am so, *so* boned."

QUINN AND ANNIE ARE WAITING at the edge of the cul-de-sac when I swerve around to pick them up. They hop in, greeting me with, "Hey, lover."

"Hi, McLovin," I sigh in reply. We have ten minutes to get to school and said school is, oh, fifteen minutes away, so we say our morning pleasantries on the road.

Annie begins to rage about the Homecoming game coming up as I pick up her coffee from the middle console and hand it to her. "Thank you—I mean can you believe my brother? He's so stupid. Like, he knows he's no match for the quarterback of this Friday's Homecoming game, and yet he just bet *fifty bucks* on himself! That he'll win!"

Quinn nods regally. "I hear the quarterback for this week's team is massive," they say.

"He's only a *junior*! He's the youngest first-string quarterback in that school's history. His name is Milo something-or-another. Ugh, if only Redfair High didn't have that doping scandal last year, we could actually play a *local* rival team. Instead, we're paired with some team from Asheville and we're gonna get pulverized." Annie sighs and sips her iced latte. "No, correction: my brother is going to get pulverized."

I frown. "Aren't we supposed to play easy teams so we can *win* Homecoming games?"

"You'd think," Quinn replies with a shrug. "I can't spare the brainpower to worry about that. Garrett is *still* in the lead for Homecoming Overlord, and I've run out of ideas . . ."

And if Garrett wins Homecoming, then it'll just make my life even worse, because I am not going to the dance with him with or without the title. But if I don't, everyone will think I'm some kind of stuck-up snob. Is it too much to ask to go back to the days of when I was absolutely invisible?

In all honesty, I wouldn't mind going to the Homecoming dance if I had someone—besides Garrett—to go with. Vance flashes in my head, and I wonder for a moment what he would look like in the Federation's perfect shade of blue—

"Red light!" Quinn cries, and I slam on the brakes as the light changes.

"Sorry," I mutter.

Annie, in the passenger seat, slowly releases her death hold on the oh-shit handle. "Are you okay?"

"Yeah, I just have a lot on my mind."

"Oh?" my friends ask.

The light turns green and I turn left onto the main drag that leads to the high school. "Well, Dad caught the apartment on fire and . . . I spent the weekend with Vance." I try to make it sound nonchalant, because it's not like anything happened. I just stayed in a house with a lot of rooms with my father and one of the most-hated guys on the internet. No biggie.

Just a normal weekend, right?

"*WHAT?*" they both cry.

"Dish," Annie orders.

"You can't hold out on us," Quinn adds.

So as I turn in to the school, I tell them what happened. All of it. All of the boring bits—staying at his house, him asking me to read to him, the Saturday morning my dad and I taught Mr. Rodriguez how to make chocolate murder pancakes, the quiet afternoons when Vance would find me in the library while Dad was at the apartment overseeing the maintenance work and ask if he could join, the silence that settled between us that was warm and comforting, the night he took me home and I saw him—the real him, the him I remembered since the night of the ExcelsiCon Ball.

There you are, I had said.

I don't tell them that part. Partly because it's private, and partly because I don't know what I meant. Did I mean that he finally had that curious look in his eyes that he had the night we first met, that half-cocked smile resting on the edge of his lips, the comfort between us where there may have been masks, but there were no secrets.

There you are, I had said, but what I meant was, *I found you, finally*.

When I finish the story, we're way late to class, but Quinn and Annie haven't budged from my car, and the parking lot attendant is making a beeline for us in his off-white golf cart.

My friends exchange a look—the same look—as if they're in agreement.

"You've got it bad." Annie breaks the news to me.

A blush creeps across my face. "What? No, of course not. Why would I?—"

Quinn puts a hand on my shoulder. "You've got it *really* bad."

My shoulders droop. "Oh balls. I do, don't I?"

They nod severely. "And we need to get to class before we get written up again. I can't go to Homecoming if I have after-school detention. Do you have the emergency bagel?"

"It's a day old." Annie nervously takes it out of her bookbag, but I grab it anyway.

A moment later, the parking lot attendant parks his golf cart beside my car, gets out, and knocks on the window. He's stone-faced and regal, his graying hair gelled back and his shirt pressed beneath his too-loose football jacket.

"Miss Thorne," he greets me as I slowly roll down the window.

"You're a little late."

I give him an innocent smile and present him with the day-old breakfast bagel. "Umm, hungry?"

He shakes his head.

Ruh-roh.

"Break for it!" Annie roars, shoving open the passenger-side door. I quickly grab my bookbag, phone, and science notebook, which were strewn on the floorboard, and go scurrying over the middle console and out of the passenger door with her. Quinn vaults out of the back seat, and we haul ass across the parking lot before the attendant can get back into his golf cart and come after us. We don't slow down until we're through the breezeway and into the school.

I lead the charge, and turn the corner into C Hall when—

I collide with a brick wall.

Quinn and Annie catch me before I bite the dust, but the contents of my arms go everywhere. My science notebook, with all of its loose pages, poofs into the air.

"Watch where you're—*Rosie*!" Garrett calls my name, surprised to see me.

The worst person I could run into right now.

"Sorry, Garrett, can't stay and chat," I reply, gathering up my science notes with the help of Annie and Quinn, and I hurry by him before he can stop me. I'm not all that worried about the parking lot attendant writing me up for being late, but Mrs. Angora in homeroom?

She has a penchant for making tardy students suffer.

Luckily, she's lenient today and lets Annie and me sneak in about five minutes late, before the morning news begins. Quinn's homeroom is one class down, but their teacher doesn't care how late they are, which is lucky. We can't afford to have Quinn ejected from the running this late in the game. The morning announcements ramble off the student festivities for Homecoming week—spirit days, the colors we're supposed to wear to the game on Friday, the ticket price for the dance on Saturday, and worst of all, the people leading Homecoming King and Queen.

"For Homecoming Queen, it's a tight race between Myrella Johnson and Ava Singh, but as for Homecoming King, Garrett Taylor is winning by at least thirty votes. You can vote every day during lunch in the cafeteria, and don't forget to dress in school colors this week. Go Wildcats!" the news anchor says, signing off.

Great. Of *course* Garrett is officially winning.

It isn't until halfway through second period that I realize I don't have my phone. I must've left it in the car, though I could swear I grabbed it. I was in a hurry, though. Ugh, great. Today is already shaping up to be one hell of a terrible Monday, because after second period I find out why Garrett was out of class this morning, too.

He was hanging up a poster for Homecoming in the common room of the high school. A ten-foot-tall poster that says *VOTE GARRETT TAYLOR AS YOUR KING!* It towers over the entire student body every time class changes. You can't miss it, and I certainly don't.

My doom now looms over me as the bell rings every hour.

As lunch wraps up, I steel my courage and walk up to the table selling Homecoming dance tickets. They're beginning to pack up, locking the money box, when they see me standing at the other side of the table.

"Oh, sorry," Savannah, the school president, replies. "Rosie, right? Did you want one?"

"Two, actually."

"I think Garrett already got yours," says the other student.

"Probably not," I reply, and repeat, handing them a twenty-dollar bill out of my back pocket, "Two, please."

They exchange a look, but then the president shrugs and accepts my cash, and hands me two golden tickets. They have roses on them. Of course they do. The theme for this year's Homecoming is "Garden of Memories."

Then why do I feel like I already want to forget the whole thing?

So, I TAKE IT BACK—there is at least one thing more embarrassing than a ten-foot-tall poster of Garrett Taylor and realizing that you wake up to the smoldering looks of one Vance Reigns every morning combined: it's going to a boy's house after realizing that you might have a very small, unsubstantial, *incredibly* overcomable, crush on him.

The boy in question is sitting at the counter, eating an apple, when I let myself in and dump my bookbag in the corner of the kitchen. He looks up from another *Starfield* novel I recommended to him this past weekend, since he didn't want to read any more in *The Starless Throne* without me.

"So I see you decided to read it," I say, trying not to think about how incredibly hot he looks reading. He really should do it more often.

"Mmh, yeah, but I can't really get into this one," he replies, and takes another bite of apple.

"Really? Don't like the political intrigue of the Noxian Court?" I slide up onto the stool beside him. "And the ball. I love the ball. Magic spells. Daring sword fights. A prince in disguise."

"I definitely figured *him* out in chapter three," he replies, amused, and puts a bookmark in before he closes the book. "Everything okay, Thorne?"

I sigh, sort of hating how he can see right through me. "Have you seen my phone? I thought I left it in my car, but apparently not."

"You lost your phone?"

"Don't act so surprised. It's old! It's better as a paperweight, so I just don't really use it unless I have to."

He cocks his head. "Huh, so that's why you never asked for my number."

"What?"

Instead he says, "Maybe someone at school will turn it in."

"Maybe," I mutter, stealing a slice of apple as I make my way to the library. He grabs the plate with apple slices and follows me. "At least it's password protected." That I say more to myself than to him, because I still have that video on my phone—from when I first broke into the house and found Vance. I don't want to think about how he'll react. I'll find my phone. I probably just lost it at school.

There's no need to worry.

It was probably fate telling me to *not* text him, anyway.

I was hoping the library would ease my mind, but I still feel anxious. My heart hammers every time I catch a glance of Vance on the other side of the room, reaching for a book or flipping through another.

It's driving me crazy.

I shouldn't feel this weird in a place that has become my sanctuary. Am I standing properly? Is my hair doing that weird cowlick thing? Do I have anything on my face? Why does it *matter*?

Because, in the golden afternoon, he looks so perfect, illuminating his hair in a halo of platinum. He walks through the folds of sunlight and comes to a stop in the shadows, his cornflower eyes brilliantly bright, almost glowing. He puts his hands into his pockets and tilts his head just enough.

Just enough for a piece of hair to come undone behind his ear.

Just enough for his perfectly symmetrical countenance to shift to something quite different, almost endearing.

Just enough for my heart to thump wildly in my chest, like a jackrabbit.

I don't understand.

"Is that all?" he asks.

"Yes," I lie, turning away from him to boot up the iPad. There aren't many books left to shelve. The boxes have all but disappeared, stacked empty in corners, the library filling slowly to full, like a soul waking up from a long sleep. I try to busy myself with the next set of books, the last of the cardboard boxes. When it's done, so will be my job.

I won't have to come here any longer after that.

Why does it make my chest hurt?

"I mean, why would you think otherwise?" I ask, my back turned to him. "Everything's fine. I'm fine. Why wouldn't I be? We're almost done with cataloging and all of these books have taken *forever* to file, you know? But I loved seeing all of the original covers for the *Starfield* collection and—" I turn around and find him right *there*, so close I have to stop myself from running into him.

He gently presses the spine of the book he's reading against my lips. "You're babbling, Thorne."

We're so close I can feel the heat from his skin, and smell the soap from his hair, and laundry detergent—the latter of which I'm *extremely* happy about. At least he isn't wearing the same clothes for a week straight anymore.

And I can't remember when he stopped. Or when he began washing his hair again. Or when he started coming in to keep me company while I worked. Was it just in the last week? Or longer?

It seemed so natural at the time, I hadn't thought anything of it.

But now, with him so close, reminding me that I babble when I'm nervous, I start to wonder—at what point did he realize I babble when I'm nervous? When did I tell him? Did I ever? Sometime in the last few weeks, he started paying attention.

I've already read about romance. About what it feels like to fall in love. I had always thought I would linger on his eyelashes or his soft cornflower eyes or his smooth pale skin, his halo of golden hair, but—

All of the books are wrong.

It misses the space between. The strange, thick air that fills with electricity as Vance leans closer. My skin tingles as he swipes a piece of hair behind my ear, his fingertips brushing against my cheek, and my breath catches in my throat. In all the books I've read, the author always described the physicality—the heat of their skin and the freckle on the left side of their lip and the way their eyebrows bunch together as they lean in, slowly, questioningly—but never the soft feeling of . . . just *being*.

Where I feel safe.

Where I don't have to be anyone amazing, where I don't have to fit into some stupid mold, where I'm not the girl with the dead mom, or the girl with the hot dad, or the girl who was asked to Homecoming by the most popular boy in school.

It's just a space, small and warm, that fits for Rosie Thorne.

This is unimaginable.

My heart jumps like the *Prospero* into hyperspace because I want to—because I need to—

"Amara up," I whisper.

"Wha—" he begins to ask, but the moment he opens his mouth I take his face in my hands and pull his lips down to mine and kiss him. He makes a surprised noise against my mouth, tense and rigid. I quickly realize I have no idea what I'm doing, and let go of him.

My face turns ten shades of red. He stares at me, eyes wide, still bent toward me like a tree in a hurricane.

"I—I—I am so sorry." I fumble, beginning to pull away, but his fingers snag into my jeans pocket to stop me. My stomach flips. I don't know if it's from butterflies, or if I'm about to be sick. "I—I've never kissed anyone before. It was bad, wasn't it? It was so bad, and you've kissed so many people, and God I am so *mortified* and—"

"Gentler, Thorne," he says tenderly, a smile tugging at the edge of his lips, and he presses his soft mouth against mine.

My heart kicks against my rib cage like a wild horse. My back presses against the bookcase, the spines of *Starfield* novels flat against me, stories of Sond and Carmindor and Amara, and I forget about all of them. His teeth graze my lips, nibbling, toying. I don't know what to do with my hands—they migrate from his chest to his neck to the sides of his face, and then curling deep into his platinum hair. His one hand stays in the pocket of my jeans, the other curling around the back of my waist, anchoring me, his thumb slipping between the hem of my shirt and the edge of my jeans, brushing against my skin so lightly that goose bumps ripple up my body.

His mouth migrates down my neck, and he plants a kiss where I know my birthmark is, lovingly, tenderly, and I shiver.

"You need to ask Vance to go with you to Homecoming. I mean, imagine! You! Homecoming with *the* Vance Reigns! With General Sond! *And* your father's going to be there as a chaperone!" Annie presses her hands together in a prayer and sighs. "Blessed be to the gods of hot people everywhere, we will have truly been graced with an abundance of hotness this Homecoming season if it comes to pass."

"You need an intervention." I shake my head, searching through the racks of Goodwill dresses for something that isn't stained or thirty years old. I don't have the money to buy a new Homecoming dress—since I stopped working at the grocery store, I've barely had any money to spare. I take out a sparkly green dress and hold it up to me. Green really isn't my color. I frown, putting it back.

"And besides," I add, "I don't know if he'll even say *yes*, yet."

"If he says no, he's stupid—also, we'll be your date," Annie replies, and fist-bumps Quinn.

"If I knew anyone with a sewing machine, I would say you could repurpose one of my old dresses," Quinn says, taking a bedazzled '90s monstrosity off the rack, and quickly putting it back. "I think my back's too wide for you to fit into any of my clothes without some alteration."

"I'm sure I can find something," I reply. "Thank you, though."

Annie pulls out a pink dress with puffy sleeves. "You can reenact *Sixteen Candles*."

"How about let's not—oh." I spot a dress at the very end of the row and pull it out. I fit it against me and turn to my friends. "What do you think?"

Quinn and Annie glance over and pause. But then Annie smiles. Quinn says, "Oh yeah, I think that's the one."

"Bingo," Annie agrees.

FOR THE NEXT FEW DAYS AFTER SCHOOL, in between cataloging each last book in its proper place, he teaches me how to explore. I become lost in the ebb and flow of his lips, and mine, and then his again, his tongue playing against mine, dancing. He tastes like the chocolate chip cookies Mr. Rodriguez had on the counter when I walked in, sweet and satisfying, and oh my stars I am *lost*.

Is this what Amara felt when she kissed Carmindor for the first time? Or is this more like the times she kissed Sond in Mom's favorite books? Like a newfound star burning so bright, ripping through the darkness like a lightsaber?

He kisses so meticulously, with the certain sort of patience only strategy can provide, the kisses tender, but the edges sharp. Vance is not Sond, but I daresay he kisses like him, and every place his lips touch—my mouth, my nose, my cheek, my neck—lights up like a star in a constellation of us.

And suddenly, we're at the final book, and it's just irony that it's the last *Starfield* novel ever written, before they discontinued the series. *The Last Carmindor*.

I turn to Vance. "Want to do the honors?"

He pushes the book back to me. “All yours.”

So I reach up and slide the last book into place at the end of the shelf. Like the puzzle piece clicking into place, the library is complete. “Well, that was an adventure,” I whisper, my voice cracking a little at the edges. Because now it’s over, my job is done, and just like that—

Vance took my hand and squeezed it tightly. “It’s not over yet.”

THE LIBRARY IS COMPLETE.

Yesterday, when I took Rosie's hand and told her the adventure wasn't over yet, I meant every word. I would never have dreamed of saying something so corny a year ago—even a month ago—but maybe people can change.

Maybe I can change.

I want to.

Today is October 11.

My birthday. It was also supposed to be the last day in this nowhere town, but now I . . . think I can last another week, you know? Or two. I mean—it really isn't that terrible. Perhaps it never was.

After a week of playing phone tag with Natalia, I finally catch her between meetings. "Vance, it's a pleasant surprise," she greets me in her sharp, gravelly voice. "How's the house doing?"

"You undersell it every time you call it a house—it's a castle."

She laughs. "Ah, my ex-husband loved building weird shit. Isn't the library gorgeous?"

I pace in the kitchen. "That's actually what I'm calling about. That *Starfield* collection you have—how much do you want for it?"

That seems to surprise her. "How much?"

"Yeah."

"Oh, I'm not sure. Truthfully, I bought the *Starfield* collection from a local last year," Natalia says. "They were selling it for much less than it was worth. Most of the books were in mint condition, too! There was only one that wasn't. It was personalized."

Personalized?

I run my fingers along the spines of the books, slowly circling the room. "Which one?"

"Oh, one of the first ones, I think—one about Sond's imprisonment, perhaps? I think he falls for Amara, but I can't remember. I'm sorry, Vance," she says, and there's a beep on the other end. "Christ, can't anyone just leave me *alone*?" Grumbling, she says something else under her breath, silencing the incoming call, and adds, "So, why do you want to buy the collection? You aren't a very big reader."

Absently, I pick through the books, trying to remember if there were any that fit that description. "I guess people can change."

"They certainly can."

My fingers come to rest on the waterlogged copy that began this entire ridiculous scenario, and for some reason—I pull it out.

"Well, I have to go, but if you like those books so much, they're yours. Happy birthday, Vance. Thinking of heading back?"

I let out a breath. "I don't really know, honestly."

And that means I . . . can *leave*. I can go back home. I can go back to my old life. My stepfather and my mother can't keep me here anymore. All my life I have been trying to be what my parents have wanted me to be, and I often rebelled—oftentimes to ruination.

But today, I'm in charge of my own life for the first time, though it doesn't feel anything like I thought it would. It feels like I've been offered the pilot seat and a vast galaxy and no coordinates. It's overwhelming.

"Oh!" Natalia adds as she begins to hang up. "I do remember that the inscription wasn't where it normally is, which was why we bought the collection in the first place, thinking they were all unmarked. It's at the very end. Last page. God, I almost missed it! Have a great birthday, Vance."

"Thanks, you too," I say absently as I hear the call end, and I drop my phone onto one of the chairs and break open the waterlogged book. The spine crinkles as I leaf toward the first page. Not the title page but the end—*where* at the end?

I start prying every page unstuck one at a time until—

My breath catches in my throat.

A moment later, I see movement out of the corner of my eye and I glance up, and there is Rosie standing in the doorway. Her hair is pulled up in a bun, and she's wearing garish school pride colors—a blue-and-yellow sweater with a yowling wildcat—so it's almost impossible to miss her. She smiles at me and comes inside. In the sunlight that slants through the windows, her brown hair shimmers with strands of auburn, and her hazel eyes look almost green in the sun. My chest feels tight, as tight as my grip on *The Starless Throne*.

"I don't think I'll ever get over this sight," she says in awe, spinning around looking at the books and her hard work, floor to ceiling. "It's beautiful."

"It is," I reply, unable to take my eyes off her.

The library was already completed before she walked into it, but now it feels whole.

She walks up and plants a kiss on my lips. It still feels so strange when she does, like each one is the first. "Okay, so this might be a weird question . . . but I remember you said something about never going to school before," she begins, twisting a lock of hair that had come undone from her bun.

"Well, aside from that one indie film—"

"That doesn't count," she admonishes me, and then reaches into her back pocket. She takes out two golden tickets. "Would you . . . want to go with me? To Homecoming?"

I stare down at the tickets, the answer on the tip of my tongue.

"I mean, I'm really bad at dancing, and I'm probably going to be the absolute worst on the dance floor, and if Garrett wins Homecoming King tonight I don't even want to begin to think what sort of problems that'll give me, but—"

She's nervous. *That I'll say no*, I realize.

I tap the edge of the book against her mouth, and she quiets and blushes. "I'm babbling again, aren't I?" she says.

"This is for you," I reply, outstretching the book to her.

She accepts it with a strange look. "*The Starless Throne*?"

"Open it up."

I CRACK OPEN THE BOOK, CONFUSED. There's nothing on the title page, but then he tells me to keep going, and—

On the last page of the novel, my mother's handwriting loops over the top in an inky blue script. Somehow it didn't bleed all that much when it took the dip in the pool, and I can still make out the words—her words.

To my Rosebud,
This is only the beginning of
your story, not the end.
With all my love,
Mom

My breath catches in my throat. I never opened her books after she died. I never thought to see if she left anything in them for me. I couldn't bear to, because I was afraid I would see her in every word, and the hole in my chest would open up larger and larger and swallow me whole.

But here it is—here *she* is—so easy to miss unless I read to the very last page. I never flipped to the end first. It's a rule. But she probably thought I would get to the end of my favorite book someday, again, and there I would find it.

Her words.

I press the open book to my chest, tears coming to my eyes. I wipe them away with the back of my hand. "H-how did you find this?"

"I found out the books were purchased locally, so I used my one brain cell to figure out that it must've been your mother's collection." And then he takes a deep breath and adds, "It's yours now."

My eyes widen. I stare at him, wondering if I'd heard properly. "This book?"

"The entire collection."

I gawk at him. "All of them?"

He outstretches his arms. "It was yours to begin with. I'm just giving it back to you—you can take them, or you can keep them here."

Take them—or keep them? This . . . this is too much to comprehend. I shake my head. "No, I—I know how much those books sold for. This must've cost . . ." I trail off, because I can't even begin to think how much money it would take to buy something like this, or how much money Vance needed to give for its owner to relinquish their hold.

He rubs the back of his head, a little sheepish. "Do . . . you want the rest of them? I mean, I'm sure they can be sold for—"

"What? No! Please!"

His eyes widen in genuine surprise. "Then . . ."

I hug *The Starless Throne* to my chest. Why does this feel like goodbye? It feels like it's permanent, as if he's going away.

"Why?"

"Because you seem happy with these books."

Oh. I am. But he only has half of the equation. Because I've felt happiest not just with these books, but with someone to share them with, and I don't know how to say that. "And . . . you? If I keep these books here—will you be here, too?"

He smiles, but there is something bitter hidden behind it. Something I'm not sure I trust. "Of course I will. I've still got loads more boring books to read."

"They're not *boring*," I chastise him, but his words make me feel better. I step closer to him, and I take him gently by his chin, and move his face down toward me. I kiss him. "Thank you," I whisper against his lips. "I could stay here forever."

"Mmh," he mumbles against my mouth, "but don't you have a football game to get to?"

I gasp, pulling away from him. "Oh, shit! I told Annie I'd pick her up!" I try to hand the book off to him again, but he pushes it back toward me.

"Take it. You might get bored," he says, the edge of his lips twisting into a grin.

"I'll come back later? And we can finish *The Starless Throne*," I add. "I love the ending. It's one of my favorites." As he agrees, I kiss him one last time and rush out of the library—our library—and out of the castle-house to my car waiting on the side of the road.

The Homecoming game can't be over quickly enough. But first: we have to make sure Garrett does *not* win Homecoming King.

I ENVY THE PEOPLE WHO LOVE FOOTBALL GAMES, because I don't understand the sport at all. Even as I make my way up the aluminum bleachers with Annie, picking our way between popcorn on the seats and gum on the ground to an empty section next to the band, I don't understand the appeal. It's October and the air is sticky and humid still, and there's a weird smell that I can only assume is coming from the marching band, but otherwise it's a beautiful night. It's almost game time, and the band is beginning to file out of the bleachers and onto the sides of the field, near the end zones, to start the pregame show.

During halftime, those running for Homecoming will parade onto the field one last time, and the principal—Mrs. Rogers, an ex-Marine whom I am thankful I have never crossed paths with on the disciplinary scale—will announce them one last time. Garrett and a few of his buddies are already down by the sidelines, along with most of the other contestants.

I frown, squinting down the sideline. "Where's Quinn?"

Annie, with a tray of nachos, shrugs. "Dunno. They said they didn't need a ride to the game."

"Really? They're your best friend!"

"Yours too, don't forget. And there are things neither of you know about me, so it ends up being fair," she replies mysteriously.

I roll my eyes. "Your AO3 username isn't as hidden as you think, you know."

She mock-gasps. "How dare you! It's very hidden."

"I guarantee I can search '*Starfield* Carmindor/Sond hurt-comfort fantasy AU amnesia' and your fic will be at the very top."

She blinks, frowns, and then shoves a chip into her mouth and says around it, "I have no idea what you're talking about."

"Mmm-hm."

We laugh, because she knows that I am one hundred percent right, and I've definitely read her fic and it's smutty as hell. I know her deep dark kinks and will take them to my grave.

"Excuse me—pardon me—*starflame,* is it really so hard to get through the bleachers?" a girl with pink hair mutters, her popcorn raised high. Behind her, a tall and lanky boy with dark hair follows.

"Mo, you know we sit on the *other* side of the field, right?" the lanky boy says, irritated. "With our team?"

"There aren't any good seats over there. And this side is better—go, Milo!" the pink-haired girl cries, and points to a spot beside me. "Is anyone sitting here?"

"Nope," I reply, and scoot over a little toward Annie to give them more room. "All yours."

"Excellent!"

Her companion gives a tired sigh. "Well if we'd gotten here sooner, maybe all of the good seats on the other side wouldn't be taken."

"Stop grumbling like a grumpy old man and sit down," she says, patting the bleacher beside her, and he thumps down. She snuggles up next to him, to the point that I think his grumpiness is mostly an act, and cheers again, "Go, Milo, go!" which earns her quite a few looks on this side of the bleachers. "My brother's going to kick everyone's ass."

She doesn't seem to care at all who glares.

Annie leans in quietly and says under her breath to me, "I think that pink-haired nuisance is now my mortal enemy."

"Um, why?"

"Her brother's Milo Lovelace. The other team's quarterback." Fire ignites in her eyes, and she jumps to her feet and shouts, "Go,

Keith! You can do it! Knock the Goliath out!"

In return, the pink-haired girl narrows a look at her, then shouts, "You got this, Milo!"

"Keith! I believe in you!"

I sink down between the two of them and pull *The Starless Throne* from my backpack. Vance was right, it turns out. This book is coming in handy, and I tune out Annie and the pink-haired girl shouting over each other for the next ten minutes until the clock runs down and halftime begins. Our mascot, a Wildcat, grabs a lightsaber from the sidelines and runs toward the other side, where they have a short mock battle with the Blue Devils while the football teams leave the field, which ends in the Blue Devils force-choking the Wildcat to the ground. The score is tied, but I don't know what any of it means, really. Annie tries to explain to me that the teams are tied because we can't run the ball—whatever that means—and so we've had to take two field goals, and they missed an extra point.

. . . Whatever *that* means.

"I still don't see Quinn, do you?" I ask, to which Annie frowns.

"No, I don't," she says, but then she pulls out her phone and selects Quinn's name in an app, and a pin pops up on a map of the area—exactly where we are. "But they have to be here. Their phone's here."

My eyes widen. "Hold up, can you pinpoint my phone, too?"

"You *still* haven't found it?"

". . . No."

She rolls her eyes and selects my name, and the exact same coordinates come up. Annie frowns. "Huh . . . are you *sure* you don't have it in a pocket or something?"

I give her a deadpan look. "I'm not that forgetful."

She just shrugs. "Oh, they're starting."

Principal Rogers makes her way out onto the field with a wireless microphone, and the band marches out with her, making a (sort of) cornucopia shape on the field. They play the school fight song, and when they finish the principal looks like she might need new eardrums.

"Well, that was riveting! Everyone give a round of applause to the Marching Wildcats!" she cries, and we all sort of clap halfheartedly in that *at least you tried* sort of way. "Now what we've all been waiting for—one last look at your Homecoming contestants!" Behind her, starting from the left end zone, Bob, our security guard, in his golf cart, pulls a trailer with a *HOMECOMING* banner. Behind him, a line of students in their formal best walk out onto the field.

The principal introduces all of them, but Quinn still isn't in the lineup.

I eat a nacho nervously.

"And now, here are the top two students in the running for tomorrow's Homecoming royalty . . ." the principal announces, taking out an envelope from her suit pocket. "For our Queens—Myrella Johnson and . . . Ava Singh!"

The two girls screech and clasp each other's hands, happily bouncing up and down with each other. Annie snorts. "Well, *that's* a surprise."

"And for Homecoming King," the principal goes on, "Garrett Taylor and . . . Quinn Holland!"

Ohmygod.

Ohmy*god*. Quinn is in the top two—Quinn is in the top two! Annie and I grasp each other's hands and jump to our feet, cheering, "YES! GO QUINNIE!"

On the field, however, Garrett Taylor doesn't feel the same way, and grabs the microphone from the principal. "Rosie, I'm pretty sure you'll go with me tomorrow," he says.

I sit ramrod straight.

"Rosie?" the pink-haired girl mutters, exchanging a look with her boyfriend.

I can feel Garrett glaring at me, and a chill curls down my spine. I curl my fingers tightly around the book in my hands. The people around me begin to stare. "I didn't get it at first," Garrett goes on, "I didn't understand why you'd turn me down. But now I know. I should've seen the signs. You'd rather be with an asshole. You like the villain type, not the nice guys. You *never* liked nice guys—"

Suddenly, the mascot breaks out across the field, Wildcat-head bobbing in the wind, and takes a flying leap toward Garrett and tackles him to the ground. The mascot wrenches the microphone from him as its head goes rolling, revealing—

Quinn pushes themself to stand over Garrett and says into the microphone, "Sorry, I'mma let you finish but Rosie isn't like that. And just because she doesn't want to go out with you doesn't mean it's because she's being pressured or brainwashed or whatever. I doubt anyone could pressure Rosie into doing anything she doesn't want to do. Maybe—just *maybe*—she doesn't want to go out with you because you're a spineless nerf-herding Noxian scumbag and she just doesn't like you. Oh, and those thirty votes to tie you? They came from the football team, because they all know I'm a bigger person than you'll ever be."

Then Quinn, my friend, my confidant, my Patronus, outstretches the microphone and drops it onto his chest.

The bleachers are quiet for a moment.

Then they erupt with applause.

I would, too, but my mind is reeling, because what did Garrett mean by *I'm pretty sure you'll go with me tomorrow*? I don't have to wonder long, because Annie puts a gentle hand on my knee and leans into me.

"Rosie, we've got a problem," she mutters, and shows me the TMZ headline on her phone—

VANCE REIGNS IN ANOTHER UNSUSPECTING VICTIM!

Along with released video footage of the night I met Vance and fell into the pool, complete with the town and home address.

"Oh, no," I mutter.

I'm growing cold all over. Garrett. When I bumped into him on Monday, I must have dropped my phone. "How long has that been live?" I ask her.

"Thirty minutes."

Half an hour.

I think I might be sick to my stomach.

The pink-haired girl beside us gives me a wide-eyed look. "Wait—*you're* Rosie? *Vance*'s Rosie?"

Has word gotten around that fast that even a stranger knows my name? I can't think about it. I need to get back to Vance before this becomes a narrative I can't control. I don't have my phone, so I can't call him. And I don't want to imagine what sort of lies are spreading across the internet, festering like poison.

I just know I need to get to Vance.

Now. Before it's too late.

THE DOORBELL RINGS.

I turn the page in *The Trials of the Marked*. "Elias, can you get that?" I call, but when the doorbell rings again I shout, a little louder, "Elias!"

He doesn't answer—and the bloody doorbell rings again. I sigh and shove the bookmark into my book. There better be a good reason why someone's at the door, it was finally getting good. Sond was on trial for his transgressions, and I want to see if Amara will come to his rescue like the *previous* book, or if Carmindor will finally send his best friend to prison—again.

I bet Amara'll come and save the day. That's usually how these sorts of stories go.

The doorbell rings again.

"Okay, okay," I call, rubbing the back of my neck. What a pain. Where is Elias anyway? As I step into the foyer, he comes down the stairs drying his wet hair with a towel.

"Is someone at the door?" he asks.

"I guess," I reply with a shrug, but I doubt it's Rosie, since she usually just lets herself in with the key under the mat, and neither of us ordered any food to be delivered.

So, my curiosity is piqued when I look through the peephole in the door. I realize the moment I do, I've forgotten one important rule over the course of the weeks:

I am Vance Reigns.

Black SUVs and news vans have pulled up in front of the house, people piling out of them with cameras with long lenses and camcorders on their shoulders and microphones in their hands. News anchors and paparazzi and journalists and people streaming video on their phones. There aren't very many—at least not as many as I would usually attract if I was in my natural habitat of LA, but enough for me to remember who I am.

I jerk away from the peephole and press my back against the door to bar it from the vampires outside. Elias stands just behind me, the color slowly draining from his face. His phone begins to ring. "It's your stepfather," he says numbly, before it goes to voice mail.

Mine follows a moment after, and I read the caller ID. *GREGORY.*

My stepfather.

So, here we are.

Elias gets another call—my mother this time—and sends it to voice mail, too. He stares at his screen for a long moment. The doorbell rings again.

I tighten my grip on the doorknob. "How do they know about Rosie?" I ask, my voice shaking.

"Well . . . because of this," he replies, and shows me an article on TMZ. An article with a video attached. It plays automatically, a shaky phone video of a dark house, but as soon as it turns the corner into a dark room, I recognize the bare bones of the library. Rosie's hand slowly reaching for *The Starless Throne*, not yet water damaged. The rest I don't have to see. I know what happens.

She goes onto the back patio. I ask, "What are you doing here?"

And she screams and falls backward into the pool.

I close my eyes, gritting my teeth so hard my jaw begins to ache—

"Vance, you can't honestly think that she'd do this," Elias says patiently.

"*Didn't* she?" I force out, because the truth is right there on the internet. And then, quieter, "I guess I deserve this."

For a moment I didn't hate being *Vance*, being me, because for once I was a person to someone, and not Vance Reigns. He isn't a person. He's a character. He's a vehicle other people can live vicariously through. For other people to pretend to be close to. To pretend to know. Pretend to love.

I should have known better.

The paparazzi on the front lawn remind me. That even in this house, far away from the life that I knew, I'm still Vance Reigns, and I'm still fodder for everyone else's lives. A moment, and then discarded. It's either use or be used, and I was used so bloody badly.

I was a fool.

"Vance, what are you doing?" Elias asks.

What I should've done at the beginning. I wrap my fingers around the doorknob and wrench it open, and the bright flashes of camera lights are blinding. They remind me of the flash of paparazzi the night outside the wrap party for *Starfield: Resonance*. Of the night that my mask slipped for a moment, and I actually decided to care about any of this. If only I'd never agreed to take Elle home, then none of this would've happened.

I always knew how to disappoint people.

Why would disappointing myself be any different?

When people assumed that my actions broke Darien and Elle

up, I didn't bat an eye. If the world needed a villain, I'd play it. I was already good at it. I would get even more attention, more press.

I wonder how much TMZ paid her. I wonder how much other tabloids are clamoring for our text messages, our call histories, our stories. I told her so much—too much. I should've kept my mouth shut.

I should've played my part.

The moment I open the front door, the vultures rush toward me like hungry vampires, waiting for me to welcome them inside.

"Vance! Is it true that—"

"Did you really coerce—"

"Is it true that you *made* a girl—"

"Is this *Rosie Thorne* working for you?"

And then another voice cuts through the cacophony of questions. "*Vance!*"

I raise my gaze toward the crowd, the flashing cameras and bulbous lenses, to the girl pushing her way through the crowd. She gets elbowed by a paparazzo and shoves them back with equal vigor.

"Vance!"

She catches my gaze, and her face breaks open with relief. But only for a moment—a breath—before it fills with dread. Because she must see it now, the mask. The one I've worn for so long it's become the face everyone sees.

I'm no one I recognize, and for a few weeks, that was nice.

Her lips move in a question. "Vance?" I can't hear her anymore over the other questions, the people vying for my attention, and when I blink she's just another face in the crowd.

That's all she should've been to begin with.

I take one look at them, the briefest glance, before I say, "Piss off," and slam the door in their faces.

PART FOUR

HERO

Her name is Amara Avanrose, and she is the princess of the Noxian Empire. She has lived through the Starless Wars, the coups to overthrow her father from his throne, the brief tête-à-têtes with Prince Carmindor. She has survived ship scrimmages, assassination plots, imploding stars.

But she isn't sure she is going to survive this.

He wraps his arms around her legs and presses his face into her middle. "I must not lose you. I cannot. It will tear me asunder, *ah'blena*."

"It will not," she replies, cupping Ambrose's face in her hands. He turns his gaze up to her, and she memorizes the cut of his cheekbones, the glow of his white-blond hair, the way he looks at her with those eyes, so sky-blue they make her want to fly.

"I have made so many mistakes," he whispers, closing his eyes. "Oh, Sol curse me, conscript me, make me forget."

"Then you'll forget me, too." She runs her thumb across his cheek. "Sometimes the universe deals us fates that make us happy, but sometimes it simply deals us fates that make us. I love you, Ambrose, but you need to love yourself first."

Then she lets go of his face and steps out of his embrace, and even though she knows he wants to hold on, he lets her slide out of his arms, and then she turns away from him, and leaves him kneeling in the empty room of the Starless Throne.

ROSIE

I DIDN'T DO IT.

I keep mouthing those words as I stare up at the poster of General Sond on my bedroom ceiling. I didn't do it. I *didn't*. But it doesn't matter, because he thinks I did leak the video. He thinks I'm that kind of person—the *nerve* of him! It's almost enough for me to hate him. Him, and this stupid sleepy town, and Homecoming—I hate all of it. I don't see why it even matters. Why any of it matters.

I don't know what I'm hoping for—that Vance appears at my door? That he smiles at me with that kind of smile he keeps tucked away so no one can see, and tells me what the *hell* happened? That yesterday was just a terrible fever dream and that he knows I didn't do it, that we'll figure it out? Or did he close the door because it was the other way around—that now that someone shined a light on his little vacation here in nowhere, he wants nothing to do with me?

Was that all I was—just a *vacation*? That's depressing. And sad. And it makes me feel so terribly small.

I roll over in bed when I hear my phone buzz, and I check it even though I know who it's going to be. Today is the day of the Homecoming Dance, after all.

ANNIE (2:13 PM)

—hey, talk to us?

QUINN (2:15 PM)

—Please?

I don't want to talk to anyone. I don't want to admit that I was a fool, and that I screwed up. That when he looked at me in the sea of paparazzi, the Vance I had come to know—the one who kissed me in the library, who drove me home and let me read to him all my favorite passages and called me weird with that secret sort of smile—*that* Vance disappeared in the blink of an eye, and the one I had met at the beginning comes back, his lips set into a thin line, his blue eyes distant, his face impassive—like a curse returning.

He looked at me like he didn't even know me.

And that hurt the most.

I know I'm fooling myself, but for a moment it felt like I was living some unimaginable story, some impossible fairy tale. It was kind of impossible, wasn't it? A girl from the middle of nowhere meeting the guy she fell in love with at a comic-con, only to find out that he was a jerk of an actor, and yet . . .

And yet.

Forget it. It doesn't matter. Though even as I tell myself that, it feels like a part of me has broken.

I can never sit on the barstool in the kitchen again as Elias cooks dinner. I can never walk into the library again. I can never run my fingers along the aged spines of hundreds of books. I can never look up the expanse of stairs to the second floor. I can never see Vance at the top of them again. I can never pet Sansa again. I can never read *The Starless Throne* while lounging on a pool chair in the backyard, or read it to him, or have him read Sond's lines in that distinctly silky voice.

I can never, never, never again.

One moment it was all there, at the tip of my fingertips, part of my life in a way nothing has ever been before, and the next—gone.

All of it, gone.

I hug my pillow to my chest and try to keep the well of sadness inside me, but I can't. This doesn't hurt as much as losing Mom. Nothing will ever hurt that much, but it hurts all the same. Tears spill down my cheeks, and I bury my head into my pillow.

You knew it wouldn't last, I think. *It should've never happened to begin with*.

A part of me wishes I could go back to who I was before the library, before the rainstorm, before the kiss, before all of it. I wish I could dig up the starstruck love I had for that boy in that midnight mask, when the world was simple and straightforward. I was happier with the stranger in my head, instead of Vance. Because knowing the real one stings too much. Knowing that he could have been someone different, that for a moment he seemed like he wanted to be someone better.

I would much rather have been in love with the phantom in my head.

Afternoon light spills into the room, and it reminds me of all the afternoons I spent in that library, sunlight falling through the windows, shining off the dust particles in the air like flecks of stars. Dad won't be home for another few hours, and I don't have leftover food to heat up that Elias gave me, and I don't have a book I snuck out of the library to read underneath my covers.

I just have me.

As I roll over in my bed again, I hear a strange sound. It's music, blasting from—from the parking lot? No, not just music . . .

"LOOK TO THE STARS! LOOK TO THE STARS AND SEE! FIND OUT WHERE YOU BELONG! AND FIGHT FOR IT, FIGHT FOR IT, FIGHT FOR LOVE IN A STARFIELD, A STARFIELD, A STARFIELD OF LIGHT."

. . . The theme song to *Starfield*?

I sit up and hesitantly approach my window. Other people are coming out onto their balconies and peeking out of their apartments toward the blaring music in the lot beneath us. And there Quinn and Annie stand with a boom box pointed at my apartment.

I quickly abandon my window and head for the door, stumbling into my shoes as I leave the apartment, and come up to the railing on the side. I try to push away the tears flooding my eyes, but I can't seem to, and the next I know they've abandoned the boom box and both of them are wrapping their arms around me.

So tightly, I'm not scared of rattling apart anymore. I come undone in their arms, and I know they'll be there to keep me in one piece.

VANCE

THE LIBRARY IS EMPTY WITHOUT HER.

I should feel angry, but I don't. I just feel . . . hollow.

Our bags are packed. We're just waiting for the car now. Everything else in this house—the smaller things, the TV, the gaming console, Elias's cooking supplies—will be boxed up by a moving company and shipped back to LA within the next few days.

My fingers find the part of the bookshelf where *The Starless Throne* should be, but I know Rosie still has it with her.

We all occupy space for such a short period of time, even though sometimes it feels like eternity. We're here, and then gone, and our stuff stays behind. The things that we used, the things that we loved, the things that we treasured, and adored, and despised. Those trinkets exist far longer than we do, and I've always imagined them as that—just *things*. To be bought, sold, gathered.

But things, it seems, can persevere. Small things. Treasured things. A favorite book, an old battered album, a DVD of an old sci-fi TV series passed from father to daughter. They can cast a spell to ensure that people you've never met will miss you when you're gone.

I've never met Rosie's mother, but when I run my fingers along the spines of her collection, I miss her.

And . . . and I still have *my* mother around.

I'm just too afraid to talk to her, because I know she's disappointed in me, and I know she knows I can be better than I am. I just never was, and never cared to be, so I got scared. And when my stepfather sent me here, I thought that since she didn't stop him—she didn't like me anymore.

That, perhaps, she's done with trying to see the good in me.

Whatever little good she saw to begin with.

There's a knock on the library door, and Elias pokes his head in. "The car'll be here in about an hour. Is everything you're taking in the hallway, *mijo*?"

"Yeah," I reply softly. "First day of freedom, doesn't it taste great?"

"Well, of course, but we don't have to leave, you know."

It seems like an innocent proposition, but I can't stay here, either. I don't belong here; I figured out that much yesterday with those cockroaches at my doorstep. Isn't that the worst kind of twist? Your parents cast you off to some no-name town to get you out of the way for a while, and you end up liking it. Or, at least, not *hating* it.

I doubt they expected *that* twist.

"I can't stay here forever," I reply, and flash him a grin. "Besides, when my stepfather steps down, who'll be there to inherit Kolossal Pictures? *Sansa*?"

At the mention of her name, my dog perks up on the floor and sticks out her tongue. She wags her tail gently, and it thumps on the rug.

Elias sighs and scrubs her behind the head. "Right. Okay. Just so you're sure."

"I'm sure."

I have to be.

When he leaves, I sit down in one of the wingback chairs and take out my phone. My mother dominates the missed calls—almost all of them—so it isn't very hard to find her phone number.

With a deep breath, I call her.

The phone rings once—twice—before she answers, honey and light and sweet. *"Darling!"*

I don't realize how good it is to hear her voice until I do, and my throat tightens.

"Hi, Mum," I reply softly.

"Oh, darling, I'm *so* glad you gave me a ring," she says. "You know, after I saw what the gossip was about, I was going to ring you again but I figured—well, I'm glad you called. Are you okay? Is Elias feeding you well? How was your birthday yesterday?—"

"I'm sorry," I interrupt, my voice breaking.

"Oh, darling, you've nothing to apologize for," she replies, and her voice is understanding and soft, and that's it. Those are the words I didn't know I needed to hear, but when I finally do my eyes sting, and I press the palm of my hand into my eye. My breath hitches, and I can't remember the last time I cried, but it feels like a string inside me has finally come undone, the tension gone. "I love you, darling, and I can't wait to see you home," she adds, and I can imagine her sitting at the dining room table at home, twirling a lock of her graying blond hair, a thousand-piece puzzle stretched out in front of her. "Gregory stepped out for a moment, but he would love to talk to you, too—I can ask him to give you a ring after Shabbos?"

I hesitate, tightening my grip on my phone. "I would like that."

"And about this gossip that's been going around—"

Before I can gently guide her away from the topic, a familiar voice calls my name—"Vance!"

At first, I think it's my imagination, but then when the voice calls—again—

"Vance!"

I push myself to my feet. The voice is coming from outside, when normally it's screaming at me through the headset, telling me to revive her.

This is new.

"Can I ring you back?" I asked my mother.

"Oh, of course! Kisses!"

"Kisses," I repeat, and put my phone into my back pocket. Then I go to the window, still hesitant that there might be paparazzi around. At first, I don't see her—but then I'm not sure how I could miss her. She stands in the middle of the driveway, her hands planted on her hips, pink hair almost neon in the sunlight. She sees me peeking out the window and smiles at me with this sort of eat-shit smile that really itches under my skin, and waves one finger at a time. She's wearing a purple *LOOK TO THE STARS* sweatshirt and holey black jeans, and she's gotten a few new additions in her ears, earrings all sparkling different colors.

I am baffled at her being here.

"I-Imogen . . .?" I ask as I push the window open, thinking this must be some mistake.

"Vance!" she calls, throwing up her arms. "Get your sorry ass out here right now!"

I stare at her. "How in bloody hell did you even get here? And why?"

"Long story involving a football game where the mascot turned out to be running for Homecoming Overlord?

Anyway—that's beside the point. The point is, I'm here to punch some sense into you!"

". . . What?"

She pushes up her sweatshirt's sleeve to show her bicep and flexes. "You heard me! Get out here right now! You *know* she didn't leak that video and you just—just *blame* her anyway!" she rages, her voice grating into a higher octave. I'd only heard that tone once before when an enemy teammate in a battle royale match had been cheating with a two-second glitch. It's not the kind of voice you want to hear out of her.

My confusion becomes a pinpoint of fear. "She . . . didn't do it?"

"No, you big dumb nerf herder, she didn't," Imogen replies. "Elle called me and said that one of her contacts at TMZ told her the video came from some guy."

Some . . . guy? Not Rosie? My chest begins to constrict. Because I realize what I've done, how massive a mistake I made. And it feels like an anvil pressing against my chest. I can barely breathe. "Oh, shite."

"Yeah, so, what are you gonna do about it?"

What am I going to do about it? What am I going to *do*—?

Anything—everything—to get her back. Because I messed this up. I backslid and I thought the worst of her when I should have known better. When I *did* know better. And because I miss her. I miss the way she brightens a room like sunshine. I miss how she smiles at every book she touches, like they're close friends, and I miss the papery smell of her hands, like warm wood and old stories, and—

Oh.

This feels like one of those dating sims that I play often, where the game prompts you to make a decision you can't come back from.

What will you do?

I . . .

The words slip out of my mouth. "I'm going to go find her, and I'm going to grovel an apology."

"Wow, I didn't expect you to *admit* that—"

"Thank *God*!" Another—male—voice says from the side of the house before the owner of said voice crawls his way out of the bushes with a suit in a black bag. Ethan. Imogen's boyfriend. He picks the twigs out of his hair and shakes them off the bag.

I stare at him, not quite believing my eyes. "You too?"

"Listen, we're going to make sure you're doing this the right way," he replies, and holds up the suit bag. "We didn't get a hotel for the night just to watch you go up in smoke."

ROSIE

It is a truth universally acknowledged that if you are the daughter of a librarian who was also the president of your kindergarten's PTA, your father will volunteer to be a chaperone to the Homecoming Dance just to destroy any prospects you might have for a good time.

"Get! Pumped! Get! Pumped!" Dad cheers as he sashays out of his room in a silver sequined jacket that catches the living room lights and throws stars against the walls. "Are you ready to—Rosebud, why aren't you dressed?"

Oh, I guess I never gave him the memo.

I sit on the couch with my two best friends on either side of me and slowly sink into the cushions. I don't meet his gaze.

"She won't come," Quinn fills in for me.

Dad gives a start. "But it's your last Homecoming! You can't all be sitting it out! You're going to be crowned, aren't you, Quinn?"

Annie throws up her arms. "That's what *I'm* saying!"

"It's just a crown," Quinn replies, "and it might not go to me."

Dad pouts. "But Vance! You asked him to the—"

"He's not going," I say. If I could melt into the cushions and live among the dropped food crumbs and lost pennies, I would. "Sometimes things just don't work out."

Because sometimes you're fooled not once, not twice, but three times by a selfish asshole who thinks that *you* leaked that footage. I wouldn't even know how to leak it—who would I send the video to? How would I do it? With a sassy subject line reading *I REIGNED VANCE IN*? It's ridiculous.

I thought he knew me—or at least trusted me.

But apparently not.

"Oh, Rosebud, I'm so sorry. I would stay home with you, but . . . I can't. They're expecting me to chaperone."

"It's okay, Dad. You can go and tell me how it is," I reply.

He finishes tying his bow tie and comes to sit on the coffee table in front of me. "Okay, but I just want to give you a little piece of advice first."

"I really don't need any."

"I know, but humor me?"

"Ooh, Space Dad has advice!" Annie says, clapping her hands. "This has to be good!"

"Speak wisdom to us," Quinn agrees.

Why are my friends like this?

Dad leans forward, his elbows on his knees, and says, "Amara up, Rosebud." Then he stands, grabs his keys from the bowl on the end table, and leaves. When he's gone, the apartment is quiet, until he starts up his beat-up Ford and it chugs out of the complex.

Quinn and Annie exchange a confused look. "Amara up?"

"Princess Amara, maybe?"

Amara up, Rosebud.

Mom used to say that to me all the time when I was afraid to do something. She would kneel down to me, tap me on the nose, and say in that gravelly voice of hers, "Amara up," every time I tried to let my what-ifs and anxieties get in the way.

Amara wouldn't sit at home, dateless and alone, instead of going to a dance. She's the princess of the Noxian Empire, the purveyor of justice, the hope of a dying star. She wouldn't cower, and she wouldn't hide. She would go—alone, if she had to.

What am I doing, letting Vance Reigns dictate how I live my life? So he pissed me off, so he blames me, so he's making me go to this dance alone—this is my Homecoming Dance. And my *best friend* is going to be crowned Homecoming Overlord and they're thinking of staying home with my sorry ass and—

I push myself to my feet and turn back to my two friends on the couch. "We're going." I force the words out.

Annie and Quinn blink up at me.

"Wait, what?" Annie asks. "But I thought—"

"We were going to stay here and watch *Starfield* reruns," Quinn finishes.

"Sure, we can do that—*after* I see Garrett's face when you take the crown from him," I reply, and march off toward my room to squeeze into my dress and sharpen my eyeliner to kill—because I'm going out.

I TIE MY TIE—THE PERFECT SHADE OF BLUE, reminding me too much of Darien's Carmindor uniform—at my throat in the car mirror. My hands are shaking. The night is cool but I am sweating so badly I keep tugging at my collar to make sure it's not sticking. "I don't even know if she's going to be there. What if she doesn't come?"

"She'll be there," Imogen replies, and resituates herself in the car. "It's *us* who might not get there," she adds under her breath, and slams on the horn again. We're stuck in traffic a mile from the gymnasium, at least per Google, and it doesn't seem to be moving at all. We're sitting, at a standstill, in the middle of town, to the point where people are beginning to park and walk to Homecoming from here. In the back seat, her boyfriend, Ethan, is lying down over the seats, tapping his phone mercilessly because the gas station beside us is a Pokémon gym and he is relentless, if not predictable.

I give her a sidelong look. "But how do you *know*?"

"That we won't get there? Well, the traffic—"

"No, Rosie."

"I have it on good faith."

"Good faith?" I frown. "Is this the same good faith that told you where I lived?"

"No, *that* was TMZ," she replies, and mutters something heated under her breath. She lays on the horn again. "C'mon! What's the holdup?"

I would rather wait in this traffic for eternity, but I know that's only an option for cowards and Vance-of-a-month-ago, which in a Venn diagram is a circle. I smooth out the front of my tuxedo, trying to keep my patience.

Rosie won't stay at the dance the whole night. She hates dances.

This feels like another choice in my dating sim app—

> You are stuck on the main road in and out of town, and time is of the essence. The girl who has made you feel more human than anyone else you've ever met is waiting there, but she may be gone by the time you arrive. What do you do?
>
> → See what the traffic jam is.
>
> → Wait. Because if you miss her at Homecoming, then it was fate that you didn't deserve her to begin with.
>
> → Get out of the car and run to her, you bloody prat!

"Maybe if I—Vance, where are you going?" Imogen asks as I open the door and get out. The autos aren't moving, and I doubt they will for a while. I don't have time to sit here in this traffic, on the only road in and out of town.

I loosen my tie. "I'll get there from here," I say, and lean back into the car to add, "Thanks—for everything."

Ethan sits up in the back seat. "Did Vance just *thank* us?"

"Write that down, Ethan, it's a *miracle*—"

I close the door before I can hear the rest of Imogen's smart comment and begin to jog down the middle lane between the autos. But what if Rosie's already there? What if she's leaving? She asked me to Homecoming, and I never gave her an answer. I should have—

I shouldn't have doubted her.

My feet begin to move faster.

I shouldn't have thought the worst.

I trip, but I right myself. I start taking longer strides.

She deserves better than that.

She deserves better.

I don't realize that I'm running until my lungs begin to burn and sweat prickles my forehead, but I don't stop. I've run for the last month around this minuscule town. I always ran while she was there, I ran to get away, I ran so I wouldn't have to deal with her.

I know the irony now that I'm running toward her.

I don't want to miss her—I *can't*. There are so many things I have done wrong in my life so far, and so many things I never bothered to apologize for, or fix. But I want to start.

At the next cross street, I find her school. When I think of American high schools, I imagine something along the lines of *Riverdale* or *Gossip Girl* or—I hate to admit it—*Seaside Cove*.

Rosie's high school is nothing of the sort. It is a sprawling brick building with trailers out back for more classrooms, I suspect, and a breezeway that links to the local technology center. The gymnasium is near the back of the campus, towering like some blocky colossal god, the mural of a pouncing wildcat painted on its front, but tonight there is a banner blocking most of the mural, fluttering above the entrance to the gym, that reads *GARDEN OF MEMORIES*, which, I suppose, is this year's theme.

How bloody kitschy.

The parking lot is packed with autos. Students make their way to the front of the gymnasium in everything from chinos to boat shorts to tuxes, and I feel as though I have been slightly punked, since I am wearing none of those. All of these people should make my skin itch, but I barely notice them.

I barely care that they stare at me as I race up the steps to the front of the gymnasium, my hair sticking to my sweaty neck. After I catch my breath, I right myself and adjust my jacket. It's the first time I've worn anything other than shorts and a hoodie in a month and a half, and I feel weirdly exposed in a form-fitting tux.

This feels like a scene from one of Rosie's books, except—despite Imogen's insistence—I'm not sure if Amara is waiting inside.

ROSIE

"TICKET?" THE BORED PARENT at the table in front of the gym asks, and I hand her one. Mine. She tears off the admittance side and hands it back to me, and Quinn and Annie hand her their tickets. A soft pop-rock beat thuds through the doors into the gymnasium, and I hesitate at the threshold.

Garrett's going to be in there. I know he is, and I'm going to have to face him alone—

Annie and Quinn loop their arms through mine.

"Ready?" Annie asks.

I nod. "As ready as I'll ever be."

And with my two best friends on my arms, I step into Homecoming. The three of us, together. Which, come to think of it, is probably how I should've gone to Homecoming to begin with. The theme for this year is Garden of Memories, and the best memories I've ever had are with my best friends. Like a good bra, they lift me up to stand tall.

The gym is dark and there are cutouts of hedges circling the bleachers, where a few other people who also came alone sit. I don't see Garrett anywhere, and for the moment I'm so glad my chest burns. The lights pulse with the beat of the DJ on the stage, and parents line the edges of the dance floor.

Dad's talking with another chaperone, and I wave at him. He smiles, happy, and mouths, *You look killer*.

I smile back, even though all of these people are beginning to make my skin prickle.

I'm not really the dancing sort of person. This isn't my scene at all. There's a reason why I escaped the ExcelsiCon Ball when I could. There are too many people, and too-loud music. My friends must notice my discomfort, because Quinn squeezes my hand.

"Do you need to go?" they mouth.

I shake my head. No, not until I see Quinn crowned. I can last that long. So Annie and Quinn lead me out onto the dance floor, even though I can feel that some people are staring—how many of them went online last night to look up the lies on TMZ? The video? The hot takes about how I was coerced into working for Vance Reigns? I want to tell them all that he isn't like that; that yes, he sometimes makes some very stupid mistakes, but he wants to get better—and why can't people let him?

If you aren't allowed to grow, then what's the point of changing at all?

Even after all of this, I believe that. Not that he has a chance in hell with me now, but you know, it's the thought that counts. If I ever see him again I'm going to punch him right in the—

"Ooh, I love this song!" Annie shouts at us, and shimmies in her purple dress. I'm terrible at dancing, and I mostly just weave back and forth, but my best friends take me by my hands and spin me around, and I find myself laughing at it all. Because the last few months have been so incredibly confusing. I fell in love with a boy in a mask whose name I didn't know. I was asked to

Homecoming by one of the most popular guys in school because he felt sorry for me. I fought my way into a *Starfield* library. I destroyed a nearly priceless book. My best friend decided to run for Homecoming Overlord. I became friends with the most notorious bad boy of the internet.

And he gave me back a piece of my mother I thought was lost forever.

If this is where this chapter ends, I wouldn't really mind, because now I know I have plenty more chapters to write. I thought my story ended when my mom died—because I didn't think there was a book without her.

Because I know it was just the ending of a chapter. It was the close of part one. Even though Mom is gone, she's still in every word of my story, because hers lives on in me. It lives on in the books that she read, and the ones she shared, and the people she met. Like mine will. There is a whole universe out there waiting to tell our stories. And for the first time since she left, life doesn't feel like the end of a sentence. It feels like a prologue, and I have my two best friends beside me to follow wherever that adventure takes me.

And that, I decide, is what my college application essay will be about.

After the next song, the music quiets, and the principal climbs onto the stage with a bunch of note cards. She clears her throat and leans into the microphone. "Hello, students, I'm glad to see you all here tonight. Go, Wildcats!"

The student body cheers.

"Now's the announcement you've all been waiting for—it's time to announce our Homecoming King and Queen!"

Everyone cheers. I take Quinn by their hand and squeeze it tightly. They squeeze back. "Just so you know," I whisper, "even if Garrett wins, you're still Homecoming Overlord to me."

The principal opens the letter. "And our Homecoming King and Queen are . . ."

Annie and I lean close to Quinn, hoping, praying—

"Garrett Taylor and Myrella Johnson!" she reads, and she sounds a little disappointed. My stomach feels like a lead rock in my toes. Somewhere in the crowd, I hear Garrett crow and make his way up to the stage.

Annie and I press our cheeks onto Quinn's shoulders. They sigh. "Well, we tried."

"I just want to thank you for voting for me," Garrett says, before the Homecoming Queen takes the microphone out of his hands.

"This is a dream come true, thank you so much," Myrella cries into the microphone, and honestly I'm relieved she won. "My mother took this crown, and I'm so happy that I get to have it, too. I can't wait to tell her." There is a commotion near the back of the gym, and I glance over my shoulder to see what's wrong, but I'm cursed with shortness and I can't see beyond the sea of heads. "And I just want to thank our King tonight, Garrett Taylor—"

"Congrats, you deserve it." Garrett takes the microphone from her again, ignoring her professed love, which is a little awkward, honestly. He hops down off the stage and makes his way toward me. "Rosie, may I have this dance?" he asks, and outstretches his hand.

My skin prickles as all eyes turn to me.

No one else knows that he leaked that video of Vance from my phone, but I don't think pointing that out will do anything. He just won't *quit*, will he? I open my mouth to tell him just where he can shove that date of his—

"Thorne!"

The voice cuts through the crowd. I know it. Deep, crackly at the edges, with the softest hint of a British accent. No, it can't be.

My heart slams against the side of my rib cage.

I turn around, and there he is in the sea of people, dressed in a blue tux that's a little bit too small for him, but he makes it work in a way that makes my stomach twist. I swallow the knot in my throat. His hair is wild, pushed back out of his face, his tie loose and suit disheveled. His chest heaves, as if he ran to get here. I always thought he was beautiful, but it just now hits me—like a ton of bricks. It hits me after I resigned myself to never seeing him again in person, to him leaving on a jet plane back to his life, leaving me here in the middle of nowhere.

But here he is.

In nowhere.

For me.

"Vance *Reigns*?" Garrett laughs into the microphone.

"Vance Reigns?" someone else whispers.

". . . the Vance Reigns?"

"Who the hell is he?"

"Isn't that Sond?"

Garrett grins, and it's the kind of shit-eating grin I want to punch off his smug face. "What are you doing here, buddy? Here to ruin our night, too?"

A dangerous look flickers across Vance's cornflower eyes. He begins to roll up his sleeves. "I assume you're Garrett?"

"Yeah, and you aren't supposed to be here—*aah*!" He dodges the first swing and scurries away. "What the hell are you doing?"

"What I should've done back in the diner when I first met you," he grinds out, trying to grapple for him again. Wait—at the diner? So they've met before? I stare, gape-mouthed, at them as they, well—I guess you would call it fighting? But this is less like a fight and more like . . . well. They're *trying* to kick and punch each other but they don't want to get hit so they're definitely not landing any blows and it just looks very anticlimactic.

And kind of pathetic.

Two guys are fighting over me, and I'm not even impressed.

"All right, all right, just gimme a moment," Garrett says, pushing Vance off him. Vance eases back a little, smoothing back his hair. "You know, you surprised me. I didn't think you'd be here."

"I surprised myself, too."

"Then maybe you should *leave*!" Garrett leaps at him, again catching him off-guard, and grabs Vance by the hair. They go spiraling toward the refreshment table, slam into the side of it, and flip over it, taking the catering with them. The chaperones are clawing their way through the students watching, but none of them will get here in time.

"Should we stop it?" Annie asks.

"I don't know. I'm sort of rooting for Vance," Quinn replies thoughtfully. "He likes Rosie the way she is and he gave her a freaking *library*."

"Yes, but he apparently doesn't trust her."

"But Garrett thinks negging is flirting," Quinn replies.

"Oof, this is a hard one to call."

I look to the rafters. "This is *ridiculous*," I mutter, and pry Annie and Quinn's arms from around me. Then I step up and grab Garrett by the shoulder as he rises to stand again. "Hey, asshole."

He spins around, his face crumbling into anger. There is a mini-donut stuck to the front of his tux. He says, "I can't believe he has the *nerve* to show up here and—"

My dad taught me a lot of things. He taught me how to ride

my first bike. He taught me how to rhyme in iambic pentameter. He taught me how to put books back where they belong on the library shelves.

But my mother taught me how to punch. Thumb out, fingers curled in, reel back with your body weight and—

To be fair, I probably should've warned him before I postmarked his nose to the North Pole, but I don't like him enough to bat an eye at his future in modeling. I just send my fist flying into his face. He stumbles back as his nose starts gushing blood all down the front of his stark white tuxedo.

I shake my hand out, hissing in pain. Mom never told me how much punching actually *hurts*.

He holds his nose, cursing. He glares at me, then at Vance, disheveled, beside me. "What does he have that I don't?" he asks.

"The ability to take no for an answer," I reply, and then I steel myself, and I turn around and I face the boy who broke my heart. "But he better have a good reason to interrupt my Homecoming."

VANCE

Panic claws up my throat. She's absolutely *frightening* when she's angry. The way her eyebrows furrow, crinkling the skin between them, her bowlike lips turned down into the most disdainful frown. I should leave, I think, but as I turn around to escape out the side exit I came in from—preferably *not* running—Rosie turns to me, in that golden dress as beautiful as a sun—the same color, I imagine, Amara would have worn on page three hundred forty-seven of *The Starless Throne*.

My throat tightens, but I force out, "I'm sorry. I'm so sorry—"

"You keep saying that. You know I didn't release that video. I wouldn't."

I wince. "I know. That's why I'm here. To apologize. I shouldn't have pushed you away. I should've trusted you."

"Yeah," she replies, "you should have."

I stare down at the ground, because I can feel all her classmates looking at me, I can hear them whispering, judging, though that shouldn't bother me as much as it does. It's par for the course for my life in LA. But this isn't LA.

"I'm sorry," I tell her, "and I know that isn't going to be enough, but before I leave I just wanted to tell you the truth." And I take a deep breath. My fingers are shaking. Everything is shaking. "I like to read now because I imagine your voice in every word, and I like how happy you look in that library, and I like how you're so stubborn, and I like how you make me want to be better, and I like how you don't give me an inch when I mess up and—"

"Get to the point," a redhead interrupts impatiently, and the teal-haired person beside them ribs them in the side with a look.

"The point is," and I swallow the knot in my throat. Why is this so much harder than anything I've ever done before? "The point is—I'm here because I want to dance with you. Once. As myself. No masks, no fake accents, no pretenses, but now that I'm here I realize how absolutely entitled that sounds and so I just—I'm an idiot, Rosie. I'm an idiot and I love you, and I'll understand if you tell me no, and I'll go away, and I'll never bother you aga—"

She presses a finger to my lips. Everyone around us begins to whisper. I see her father out of the corner of my eye, watching us carefully. I want to tell her that she is the kind of story I have been looking for, and I want to be a part of it.

So, so badly.

And I'm here, standing in the middle of this dark gymnasium, hoping that she wants me still in hers, too.

She slowly drops her fingers from my mouth, cups my face, and smiles.

"There you are," I say.

He tilts his head into my hand. "Here I am," he echoes back, and squeezes his eyes shut. I rub a tear off his cheek with my thumb. His chest shudders, like he's trying to keep himself from crying.

Oh, you stupid boy.

I want to tell him that he should have talked to me. I want to tell him that it will be okay. I want to tell him that I forgive him, and that in an infuriating way it was sweet that he wanted to protect me, and also kick him in the shins for thinking that I couldn't protect myself.

But none of those words seem right in this moment.

"Sir! Excuse me, you don't have a ticket, you can't be here," one of the flustered parents says, finally clawing his way through the students to get to us. "I'll have to politely ask you to leave."

I give Vance a wide-eyed look. "You *broke* in?"

"I didn't have a ticket," he replies sheepishly.

"Sir," the parent tries again.

"He's my date," I reply, and when the parent again repeats

that he doesn't have a ticket, I pull the extra one out from the hidden pocket of my dress, which is probably the second-best part of my dress. The first being the neckline. Because I have definitely, *totally* caught Vance sneaking a look at it. "He just forgot his ticket."

"*Date*?" someone mutters.

"Vance Reigns?"

"But didn't he coerce her?"

"Who's going to tell her this is Stockholm syndrome?"

The parent takes the ticket and tears off the admittance side, and balefully hands it back to us. I don't know if Vance takes the ticket, because I can't quite believe he's here.

"I'm sorry," he says, soft and uncertain, "for yesterday. I know I'll have to win back your trust, and I know it's not going to be easy, but . . . can you let me try? Or start to try? Or—"

"Vance," I interrupt, and he gives me a hesitant look, before I grab his cravat and pull him down toward me. "Amara up."

And I kiss him under the starry lights of Homecoming.

SIX MONTHS LATER.

It's the perfect night for a double feature. The skies are clear and the stars are bright, and it's just cold enough to still need a blanket and snuggle up with your friends and eat nachos with plastic cheese and warm pretzels. The back of Quinn's truck is parked in the dead center of the drive-in, in the perfect spot to watch the double feature of *Starfield* and *Starfield: Resonance*.

"I really hope this is gonna be good," Annie says as she reaches over to steal a nacho from Quinn.

"No pressure or anything," Vance mumbles, pulling the blanket tighter around us. He shivers. "It's so bloody cold—*why* are drive-ins charming, again?"

"Your spoiled is showing," I remind him, and he mutters something to himself and puts his cheek on my shoulder. "And I'm sure the movie will be fantastic."

I'm not just saying that because we're sharing a flatbed truck with Darien Freeman and Elle Wittimer, either, though we most definitely are. I'm trying not to stare at them too much, but honestly how can I not stare? It's Darien Freeman! With *Elle*! And they're holding hands! There hasn't been any official news in the media about them getting back together, and I've had to stop Annie from asking more than a few times tonight, but honestly I want to know.

"Why couldn't Jess come?" Elle asks.

Imogen rolls her eyes. "You know her," she says. "She's supporting her girlfriend's art exhibit in Chicago this weekend." She takes a pack of Twizzlers out of her purse, breaks open the package, and sticks one in Ethan's mouth. "There's no Pokémon out here, babe."

"I know." He sighs. "I guess I'll just have to converse with all of you instead."

"What a *travesty*," she agrees sarcastically.

The large screen at the front of the drive-in flickers, and an animated popcorn scene jumps to life.

"Ooh, it's starting!" Annie taps Quinn on the leg and tells Darien, "Turn on the radio!"

He reaches up behind him and fiddles with the dial. As he does, I take out a letter from my back pocket and I show it to Vance. In surprise, he also shows me a folded-up piece of paper.

"Oh, you too?" I ask, and we trade papers.

He opens mine, first. His breath catches. "You got in?"

"Full ride," I reply, smiling. "Your girlfriend's about to be an English major at NYU."

"I'm so proud of you." He laughs and kisses my forehead. "I knew that nerdy head of yours was good for something."

"Hey! I expect you to come visit."

"Visit? My stepfather owns an apartment in SoHo. I might just move in. Always fancied New York City."

I roll my eyes. "*Ugh*, I forgot how lucky you rich kids are."

He laughs as I elbow him in the side, and motions to the

folded-up paper in my hand. "Your turn."

My fingers are tingling with anticipation. I'm not quite sure what it is, but I have a guess . . . If the rumor boards are right, then he might not be able to come visit me for a while. I unfold the piece of paper. First, I see the screenwriter, and then the logo. It looks like the first page of a script. But what script could it be?

Then I see the title.

THE STARLESS—

I gasp.

"Ugh, quiet down back there!" Annie complains as I hide the title page from view. "You're making us miss the previews."

Vance puts a finger to his grinning mouth, and I settle into the nook between his head and shoulder. "I hear the villain's quite good in this one," he mumbles into my ear, and I feel my mouth spreading into a grin.

"Worthy of a sequel?" I ask.

"Worthy of a redemption arc, at the very least."

The speakers hiss with white noise before Darien finds the station, and the triumphant *Starfield* theme trumpets from the boom box. The projector flings stars across the weathered screen, swirling into cosmoses, taking us into another impossible world, and I think—

Mom, you were right.

This isn't the end of my story. It's the beginning.

To my Rosebud,

This is only the beginning
of your story, not the end.

With all my love,
Mom

"What now, *ah'blena*?"

Amara looks out over the impossible expanse of stars and sky, and there are so many places to see, worlds to explore. Carmindor's *Prospero* streaks across the sky, on its way to some other destination in the far-off regions of the Federation. With him, a little of her heart leaves, but it leaves room, too.

For new people.

For new loves.

For new impossibilities.

"The universe is wide," she replies as she turns on her heel, and even in the darkness of the observation deck, Ambrose's white-gold hair glows like a crown of starlight. "And I have a kingdom to rule."

Then she snakes her fingers into the buttons between his uniform and pulls him close to her. He quirks a singular golden eyebrow. She reaches up on her tiptoes and plants a kiss against his strong jawline.

He asks, "Where to, Princess?"

"The stars."

THE END

Acknowledgments

Okay so, confession: I love *Beauty and the Beast*. I love it more than peanut butter, more than coffee shop AUs, more than the G note in *Welcome to the Black Parade*, more than *Yuri!!! On Ice*. I've consumed so many versions of *Beauty and the Beast* over the years—sort of like in fanfic, when you really like one particular trope (the angry bad boy ends up being soft Hufflepuff trope), you go hunting for them all. You become well-versed in what you really love (famous actor meets small-town nobody trope), and what you want to recreate (that one scene in *Howl's Moving Castle*), and what you can't live without (the getting caught in the rain trope). And you just . . . run with them.

And this book? It's all of the pieces of my favorite things. It's the soft parts of *Beauty and the Beast* that I love, and the hijinks of a small-town romance.

I wrote this book for me.

So, if you didn't really enjoy this book, that's okay! You'll find one that you love. Like hunting through AO3, sometimes it takes a little time before you find that story that feels like your favorite song. And if you can't find it? Then write it! Never let anyone tell you different.

Stories—fiction, extended universe tie-in novels, drabbles on Tumblr, AO3 one-shots, a dusty library bookshelf—they bring us together. We might not all like the same things. Some of us like heroes, some villains, some the Byronic brooding idiots in-between, and that's the kind of magic that makes a bookshelf full of impossibility.

And there is always room for more.

My stories would have never been possible without my agent, Holly Root, and my editor Alex Arnold, who sharpened and honed my wild ideas into book-form, and all of the wonderful people at Quirk, past and present, who have given me the opportunity to tell a few impossible stories and fill them with all of my favorite fanfiction tropes: Blair Thornburgh, Nicole De Jackmo, and Kelsey Hoffman. Thank you to copy editor extraordinaire Amy J. Schneider, project editor Jane Morley, and designers Elissa Flanigan and Molly Rose Murphy. Thanks to Shae McDaniel who came up with the fantastic title for this book. And to Nicole Brinkley, who told me this story needed a dog.

And lastly, thank *you*, dear reader, for helping me make impossible stories.

Look to the stars. Aim. Ignite!

6:32 PM
Ethan wants to know who you chose to date in that new fast-food dating sim.
(Also hi there nerd)
I KNEW IT.
it's because he looks like Ron Swanson, isn't it.